A KINGDOM WITHOUT A KING

A KINGDOM WITHOUT A KING

A novel by Frank J. Marquez

A KINGDOM WITHOUT A KING
1.0 Edition

BRAVOBAY BOOKS
Los Angeles, California
bravobaybooks@gmail.com

ISBN: 9798-3960-6732-5 (AMAZON)
9798-9888-2931-7 (GENERAL)

Cover Design by S. David Acuff

Dedication

Special thank you to my Lady Nubia, for all
of your love and support.

To my children, Frank, Alyssa & Rebecca,
You are my joy and pride.

To my uncle, Albert Ramirez Marquez, it is an
honor to walk in your footsteps.

To David Acuff of BravoBay Books for all your help,
mentorship, and guidance. Keep up the dream.

Finally, I'd like to thank all those people who helped me during
the development of this book, by general feedback
or by other assistance.

TABLE OF CONTENTS

Prologue

In the mid-14th century, in the northern region of Spain, King Celestino Garcia died and left a significant legacy to his two children Gerardo and Camila. Each received a territory of the kingdom, and both made the best of their kingdoms, according to their virtues and capacities. Both became well respected in their own right; however, they were very much opposites to each other in the way they ruled over their lands.

Gerardo flexed his military muscle to carry out his bold plans for expanding his territory. Camila, on the other hand, showed a quiet courage and strength by caring for all of her citizens while smartly maintaining peace and security throughout her lands. One thing they both had in common was their desire to honor the memory of their father and their ancestors in their own way.

Now the kingdom was a prosperous and desirable land where the monarchy and its loyal subjects were under constant siege from internal and external forces; yet the land remained proudly defended under the House of Garcia from generation to generation.

Chapter 1
A Kingdom Under Siege

Once upon a time, in the middle of the 14th century, there was a castle in the northern region of Spain. It was in the Christian Kingdom of Asturias. The castle was known as el Castillo del Eliseo, and it was enormous—visible from a great distance—and one that would rival Windsor Castle, as we know it. The castle displayed the king's impressive lineage and wealth.

Inside of it there were large rooms to accommodate massive gatherings and substantial living quarters to host a good number of noble guests and their entourages whenever the need arose. Which was often. The grand monarchy room displayed the king's ancestral portraiture and coat of arms, which could be traced back to the 10th century. The coat of arms, displayed in various locations throughout the castle's great halls, was azure-colored and depicted a warring eagle in profile; its wings open and lowered in flight, the chest wounded and bloody on the edge. Underneath some of the coats of arms were the words "Valiente en la Batalla" or "Brave in Battle," one of the many definitions of the prestigious Garcia name.

The grand entryway to the castle had two rows of pillars that stood as tall and handsome as the armored battalion of knights beneath it. The load-bearing columns gave the castle its strong foundation and provided stability to the upper levels of its structure, which included a ballroom for large events, as well as a church.

These areas were open for the king's guests to gather. The castle also had its high council room, where the king and his royal knights gathered to discuss current events and the status of the kingdom's needs, resources and strategies. The castle had its own lower levels, too, where the knights were quartered, the horses were kept, the food supplies were held, and the underground tunnels were located. The secret passages led from the belly of the castle to a safely hidden exit beyond the walls. These served as escape routes in case of a castle breach. They also provided the ability to send an army out to ambush an attacking force and surprise them from behind.

The castle overlooked the kingdom from a high mountain hillside, which allowed for an exquisitely beautiful view of the surrounding lands. From here, one could appreciate the ocean view to the north, and peaks and valleys to the south, where a waterfall dropped from one of the mountains. This location gave it the best defensive position, as it afforded an unhindered view of the land across the kingdom. Each year the land cycled robustly through all four seasons, which gave it its beautiful shades of lush green and brown or snowy white undertones according to the different times of the year.

Presently, the landscape was green with patches of trees that would soon shed their leaves during the fall with a vibrant burst of autumnal splendor, leaving fallen dead leaves littered across the roadways. The land had a calm and peaceful feel to it. It had open, fertile fields, and these elements made it prime real estate and a very desirable prize.

The poorer civilians—the servants and the clansmen of the kingdom—had their own housing areas near the castle. Each noble had his own land with its villages scattered throughout. That evening, the king and his royal court, known as the Green Dragoons, were gathered in the castle's high council room, where Duke Pablo Cervantes—Commander of their elite brigade and the regular army—was presenting the current activities of the kingdom, its daily administration, and the people's well-being to King Celestino Garcia.

"Your Majesty," the kingdom's marshal Diego Skaggs barged into King Celestino's meeting. "Sire, the land is under attack. We have received word that the attack is coming from the south and will be approaching the castle by nightfall, my lord."

"Prepare for battle," shouted King Celestino, jumping to his feet. "Ready my Green Dragoons," he instructed Duke Pablo. "I will personally lead the defense. Send word to all the clansmen to be ready and meet me at the break point."

"Yes, Your Majesty. Knights, squires, archers, prepare to defend the land," Marshal Diego bellowed down the chain of command.

The king's troops mobilized themselves within the hour to meet the attacking forces making their advancement. The king's army was composed of the following divisions:

King Celestino led the way, escorted by Duke Pablo Cervantes commanding the Green Dragoons alongside Marshal Diego Skaggs. The king's son Prince Gerardo was escorted by Count Daniel Lemus, division captain assigned to the cavalry, along with Marshal Miguel Valente. Baron Edward Preston was the division captain assigned to archers. Baron Christopher Varney was the division captain assigned to foot soldiers, along with Marshal Saul Torres. The clansmen were led by Commander Juan Carlos Herrera and Captain Ivan Escobar. There was an additional division held behind to protect the castle. Princess Camila oversaw that division from within the safety of the castle's walls together with Baron Gregorio Gutierrez.

Upon their arrival, the evening had become night. The Dragoons were the first to arrive at the break point, a mountainous cliff that gave the occupiers of it the tactical upper hand with the high ground's overwatch capabilities; from here it was very easy to spot an oncoming attack. The enemy would have to ride up the narrow hill off the shore after arriving onto the land and would be completely exposed.

The king began to delegate commands to his divisions, and together they coordinated the defensive strategy. "Edward, bring your archers to the front line; Christopher, have your men set up at the trench area and bring the poles to the second defensive point," commanded the king.

"Yes, sire," Christopher said as he drove his spurs into his horse to hasten his exit.

"Knights, archers, get a move on. Gerardo, take your division and position yourselves behind the trench unit."

"Como mandes, Papá," Prince Gerardo said and then spun around to his captain, "Count Daniel, you heard my father, set up behind the trenches."

"Juan Carlos, we need your men to assist the first division," the king continued.

"As you wish, Su Majestad. Ivan, send your men to help with the trenches," Juan Carlos ordered.

"Yes, Commander," Ivan replied.

"Pablo, we will stay ready by the first division, to command from there."

"Yes, my lord."

King Celestino was now able to hear the enemy's approach down below. These attacks were nothing new to him. They were common and consistent, often coming from different regional clans like the Bragas, the Brangancas, the Coimbras, or the Barbarians from the south, to name a few, usually led by some unscrupulous and enterprising lords that wanted to expand to their territory.

The knights of the land were experienced and proficient in combat. Many had made names for themselves representing their clans in battle. Nevertheless, this night was different. Not only was it cloudy and cold, but the entire valley was covered with patches of ground fog. That diminished any strategic advantage of the high ground, as visibility was spotty at best.

The full moon sliced through breaks in the clouds and pockmarked the area in natural light shafts. Constant thunder and lightning lit up the sky and announced the threat of an approaching storm. With these atmospheric assists, King Garcia and his knights could better discern troop movements with occasional glimpses of the enemy's approach.

The troops were nervous and waiting with anticipation. King Celestino's powerful voice echoed with each command. In addition to his own instructions, his ranking knights seconded each call to their divisions.

"Form a line," commanded Celestino.

"Form a line," the Green Dragoons echoed.

"Archers, be ready to light up the night upon my command. Knights, position the long poles with spikes under the trenches to stop the oncoming cavalry attacks. Everyone else, stay alert and yell out any sign of incoming attacks that you may see at any given moment."

"Yes, my lord," the knights responded.

The enemy's cavalry attack was heard before it was seen. The mountain echoed the sound of the galloping horses of the approaching enemy at fast speed. Still there was no visibility of the attackers obscured by the night and the fog. The sound of the armor and fast galloping of the enemy horses was getting louder and louder as they got closer to the top.

The enemy was being led by an experienced lord whose identity was unknown. He carried the curved cutlass of the Arabians. Almost like a pirate's sword. And this faris warrior knew exactly where and how to attack this night. He commanded his marauders from a safe vantage point by the mountain cliffs, however, as the lightening continued, his position was easily monitored by King Celestino.

The faris lord was not big of stature, but he had a commanding presence that was intimidating. He wore an armor resembling more of an Arabic style than the traditional European one. He displayed a copper tone medal and had a cape overlaying his back, which was secured on his top chest plate. His helmet was open faced but had a nose guard shaped like an arrow which matched the helmet's pointy top.

Overall, his presence exuded an air of royalty and wealth. His army however did not seem to have a single common trait and no matching look between them, as if they were a ragtag band from all different ethnic backgrounds; yet they were all armored and well-trained.

The threatening lord stood at the top of the hill and waited for his warriors to continue the charge while he calmly observed from his safe vantage point away from the danger zone. By his side stood another knight dressed in similar armor as his. He looked to be his head protector, a leader of some sort. This guardian held a longbow, and he had a shield that was placed behind his back while a Damascus sword protruded from the sheath on his waistband. A fine specimen he was.

Suddenly an opportunity opened for King Celestino to catch a glimpse of the oncoming marauders, and he immediately commanded, "Archers, light up the road *now*."

The archers released their arrows, which illuminated the sky with fire. However, the hard-charging enemy was already upon them. Their cavalry was too fast and had a strong momentum. Even though the enemy's first line of attack was taken down by the striking arrows, there were still rows upon rows of knights that continued to charge forward, undaunted.

When the two opposing lines crashed into each other, King Celestino's front line took on a lot of casualties. The force of the oncoming charge was devastating. His knights and archers were getting their limbs and heads cut off with the enemy's strong attack.

Soon a layer of blood began to form on the ground from all the king's fallen men, making the ground slippery

"Retreat to the safe point! Retreat to the safe point!" the king yelled to his knights. Some of them were able to get out of the way and survive while others were not so fortunate. Things were getting out of hand; King Celestino's troops were dying by the dozens.

The next defensive fallback area was at the trenches. If this area did not slow the oncoming charge, it would give the enemy clear access to the castle grounds which had been left undermanned. Princess Camila would be back there to fend for herself with only one division and the citizens of the kingdom.

"Knights, mount up. Knights, mount up," the commands were relayed as Celestino attempted to meet the second wave head-to-head. Gerardo's division was ready. He rode at the center with Daniel by his side.

The attacking marauders were able to see the king's knights on their horses from a distance. The enemy knew that their momentum could only give them the advantage to overtake them as the king's army was standing still instead of meeting their charge.

That's when the rainstorm finally arrived and began to pour down upon them; this made the ground muddy and even more slippery, adding to an already bloody field.

Among the attacking marauders rode a beast of a man. He was a large, fierce barbarian of European descent, with the look of a Viking; his armor was painted black and displayed battle scrapes and dents from many close combat struggles. His armor was equipped with big spikes protruding from the shoulder guards and from his gauntlets.

He wielded a spear on his strong side and a smaller shield on his protective side. His secondary weapon was a Mammen axe, and his presence on the battlefield was enough to petrify the average man from fear, many of whom thought they had spotted an actual demon. Suddenly he yelled aloud, "Charge in the name of our Lord!"

The enemy's intent was to overtake Celestino's knights once and for all; the king's men were retreating and the remaining archers were scattered and not ready to counterattack, as they had done with the first wave.

"Form a line. Prepare to attack," Pablo began to line up his Green Dragoons to meet the enemy face-to-face on the battlefield.

"Hold," the king raised his hand, and the knights waited as instructed.

The enemy approached them at full speed as their barbarian demon knight led them.

"Hold the lines," Celestino commanded once again. They stood on their horses, waiting, at a huge disadvantage from the oncoming charge.

"Bring out the pikes now," the king roared and the men that were by the trenches hastily complied.

The enemy was taken by surprise. Having been focused on the calvary, they did not notice the defense of the sharp poles hidden and supported by the trenches that Celestino's troops had prepared for them, until it was too late.

Heavy losses were taken by the enemy as fixed spears stabbed the horses through their chests and necks and went straight into the riding knight's chest and out their backs. Others flew off their horses, breaking their necks or limbs after the brutal momentum had stopped.

Even their fierce demon warrior was killed in the charge, although he didn't go down easily even after being mortally wounded. Those that remained alive from their wounds were getting picked up by Celestino's knights. Furthermore, the following incoming waves were blinded by their charge leads. Now they were blocked from moving forward by their many fallen comrades.

"Archers, fire," Celestino commanded the archers to target the next advancing waves of attack. Immediately, the enemy took several losses by the arrows rained down upon them. The enemy's spirit was all but broken, and their will to fight was low. Their numbers kept taking a severe hit, and the body count rose steadily.

King Celestino sought the opportunity to reverse the momentum and crush their spirits entirely. He wanted to decimate them so that they would never return to attack them ever again.

"Prepare to charge!" the king roared.

"Prepare to charge," his command was echoed by his captains.

His cavalry lined up ready to charge onto what remained of the enemy's attackers who awaited with anticipation the final charge of their own. Even the horses were anxious to move forward as their knights struggled to keep them from breaking ranks until they were told to do so.

Celestino moved to take his place in front of his knights to lead the counterattack and, once he finally saw the proper opportunity, gave the command.

"Charge!" he roared.

His Green Dragoons charged in formation and protected the king as they finished off what was left of the enemy. Specifically, those that were not able to escape. It was a devastating blow for the remaining attackers. A loud horn was heard, sounded by the attacking marauders; the call to retreat. Anyone who remained alive and able proceeded to head back.

More than half of the remaining warriors were stuck, trapped between all the fallen bodies, leaving them nowhere to take cover.

King Celestino's strategy had worked. They had made the enemy pay for their hubris. He stopped on top of the cliff, victorious. He noted with pride his handiwork below, how he had personally defended the enemy's attacks. He looked towards the faris lord who had started to turn away from the battlefield.

Before riding away, he stopped his horse which pawed the muddy ground uneasily.

The faris lord took a last look at Celestino, his face angry and his eyes glaring at the king. After a few seconds he routed his horse to ride away and joined what remained of his defeated army in their full retreat.

Celestino had led his knights to another well-deserved victory, one that would indisputably affirm him as the rightful ruler of the land. His people, his kingdom. He gazed over the battle scene, transfixed by the gruesome display before him.

The battle replayed in his mind, each key moment from the battlefield surfacing with intensity. He also recalled the face of his enemy across the battlefield glowering at him before taking his leave. The man looked familiar but Celestino couldn't recall where he'd seen him before. If indeed he ever had.

Nevertheless, he could relax now for the attack was over. However, as he basked in the victorious high, he did not notice one of the enemy's fallen knights behind him; mortally wounded and completely camouflaged with the other dead brethren.

The wounded knight regained enough strength to notch an arrow into his bow. He drew the bloodied shaft backwards and released it, sending it whistling forth, flying straight and true into the king. The arrow struck Celestino, piercing his armor and chainmail and entering into his rib cage.

"Nooooo!" his Green Dragoon commander yelled in desperation. That enemy warrior paid an immediate price; his entire head was swiftly lopped off by Duke Pablo's sword. Celestino's knights looked on in horror; they saw, as if in slow motion, their king fall off his horse after being struck by the arrow.

"The King has fallen," the cry echoed throughout the mountain top in despair. "Protect the King!" they yelled.

His strength was leaving him as he tried hard to keep his eyes open. Celestino knew he was in trouble. His captains hurried to his aid to get him out of the body-littered field as soon as possible.

"Quickly, get him back to the castle," Prince Gerardo commanded.

The remaining enemies were retreating, and a line of defense was left behind to ensure there were no returning attacks and to attend to their injured. The Asturian soldiers had won a victory, but it was a bittersweet one in the end.

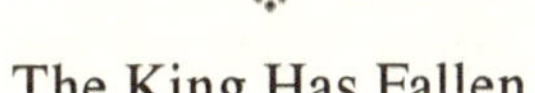

The King Has Fallen

King Celestino was taken back to the castle; a unit of knights rode ahead of them to notify the division left behind to protect the castle. Baron Gregorio Gutierrez, who commanded the castle's division, was aware of the king's emergency status and immediately made preparations.

"Ring the chapel bells to announce our king's return," he commanded. "Prepare the medical advisers. The King is in need of medical attention."

"Yes, Lord Gregorio," they replied and began to mobilize themselves accordingly.

Queen Joanna and Princess Camila came out of the castle to find out what was happening. "Baron Gregorio," the Queen commanded, "I demand a full report."

"Your Majesty, King Celestino returns and he requires immediate medical assistance," the baron reported.

"What? What did you just say?" The Queen answered with a cracked voice as she clutched her chest with both hands.

Princess Camila ran to her mother's side. "Momma, Father needs us to be strong right now. Baron, please see that everyone is in place and ready when the king arrives."

"Indeed, Princess Camila, everyone is ready," he assured them both.

Upon the king's arrival, he was immediately swarmed by his medical advisers. Servants scurried around them preparing the way.

"Hurry, bring him to his bed," Camila frantically instructed the servants as she ran to receive them. Queen Joanna scampered towards her husband in desperation and held his hand as they moved him to his room.

Archbishop Nicholas Loftus and Mildred Miller, the castle's wise woman, were already waiting to assess the king's condition. The king's armor and clothing were soaked in blood, which dripped out as they begun to peel it off of him in order to attend to the wounds.

"He has received a deep and severe wound that could easily become infected, Your Majesty. He also has broken ribs, and I believe he could have a punctured lung. He has lost a lot of blood," Mildred said anxiously.

"What can you do to make him better?" Queen Joanna desperately asked her.

"I am cleaning the area to help with the risk of infection, my lady," Mildred responded. "And I am going to try to stop the bleeding by putting these herbs on his wounds. The herbs should adhere to his ribs, keeping them intact to heal on their own."

The king yelled out in severe pain and squeezed Joanna's hand until her knuckles were white.

"In nominee Patris et Filii et Spiritus Sancti," Archbishop Nicholas began to pray over the king while they took care of him.

Celestino was a strong-willed individual and gave full effort to show no weakness. But, nevertheless, the strain of it overtook him, and he was in and out of consciousness as his medical team labored. The nobles waited quietly for the outcome just beyond the privacy curtain.

Gerardo walked in. He pushed right past Camila and his mother, straight up to Pablo and jammed a finger against his breastplate. "What happened out there? Your sole purpose of commanding the elite division was to make sure Papá was out of danger. I cannot be in two places at the same time. I was routing the enemy."

"My deepest apologies, Your Highness. There was no way to see in all of those bodies lying on the ground that there was one injured man. He'd been left for dead. There was no way he should have been capable of hitting any target."

"Except that he did," Gerardo growled back at him.

"Yes, sire, I take full responsibility as the First Command—"

Gerardo held up a hand to silence him. "You have failed to do your job, and if Papá dies you will no longer be a duke in my kingdom. I will make sure of that."

Gerardo turned around and scornfully looked at all the nobles. "Out. All of you!" They scurried from the room to avoid his full fury. Then he calmed himself and joined his family at the king's bedside.

In the hallway, Count Daniel casually made his way over to the duke and said with a twinkle, "Looks like there will be a new Green Dragoons commander, Pablo. May I remind you who is next in rank?"

"Keep dreaming, Daniel. You may get the title, but you will never be their leader," answered Pablo as Daniel continued on his way. The halls became full of speculative whispers as the men waited for news.

Inside the king's room, Mildred was finishing up attending to the king. "I have done all that I can at this time. I was able to seal the wound and keep him from bleeding out. For now, it will depend on the king's strength and his will to live and to get better."

"Thank you, Mildred, please continue to watch over him. I need you to stay here for as long as it takes," Camila said.

"As you wish, Your Highness," Mildred curtsied.

"Papá va a estar bien, Mama," Camila comforted the queen. "Mildred has stopped the bleeding, and he will be better now."

"Yo sé, hija. I do not know what I would do if he died," Queen Joanna cried softly while Camila put her arms around her in a loving embrace. Gerardo hung his head and walked out of the room.

"Why are you crying, Joanna?" It was the king who spoke with raspy breath. They both looked towards him immediately, surprised.

"Mi Amor," Joanna moved to his side.

"Papá," Camila did the same.

"I still have things to do. I am not ready to leave this world yet," Celestino said and then grimaced from the exertion.

"We are glad to see you conscious." Camila continued with some concern, "Papá, you must get some rest for now. You must build your strength and let your body recover." She turned to the door and encouraged her mother to do the same.

"Pablo!"

"Yes, Your Highness, I am here," the duke answered, quickly entering the room.

"Let everyone know that my father is conscious and that he will address them as soon as he is able."

"I will, my lady." Pablo looked towards Joanna to acknowledge her. "I am relieved to see him recovering, Your Majesty."

"The king goes through his toughest battle now, the battle for his life," lamented the queen.

A few days had passed by, both the queen and the princess were asleep. They were seated near a corner of the king's bed with their heads laid down, resting peacefully. Mildred entered to check the progress of the king's wounds and tried not to disturb them all.

"Your Majesty, how are you feeling? Your ribs are steady and not moving. It looks like the opium and the honey are doing their job."

Celestino coughed as he stirred. This woke Camila and Joanna, and they stood immediately to help Mildred dress his wounds again.

"Nicholas," the king called out with a raspy voice for the archbishop who snoozed in a chair in a nearby corner.

He snorted awake and rose to attention, straightening his robes. "Yes, Your Majesty, here I am." He approached the bedside. Celestino waved him closer. The archbishop placed his ear by the king's mouth briefly before returning to the upright position. "The king is requesting for everyone to exit the room to talk to me in private."

Joanna, Camila and Mildred looked at each other in surprise and stood up to walk out of the room, as requested by the king.

❖

"I wonder what it is that they are talking about? A confession? It has been over ten minutes now," Queen Joanna paced back and forth.

"I do not know, Mama. Whatever it is, Papá will let us know one way or another."

The archbishop came out of the room to talk to them. "The king wants to address his people. Marshal Diego, prepare the king and, when the people are gathered, be ready to help him over to his throne. Send a notice that the king will be making an announcement. On his successor."

Everyone looked at each other, surprised.

"Yes, Your Excellency," the marshal replied.

So it came about that King Celestino was set to address the nobles, the allies and his subjects. Word had spread that he was to present them with his decision on who he would appoint to be the successor of the throne once the time came. Archbishop Nicholas stood with him; his presence was not only symbolic but much needed, since it showed Rome's support.

Everyone gathered in the royal reception room and faced the king's throne. They were anxious, wondering who the next appointed ruler of the land would be. This was a crucial announcement as it would define the peace or chaos among the neighboring kingdoms.

A few of the allied kingdoms had sent their representatives to the castle to show support. Among them were Count Walter Gallegos, representing King George Sanchez of Segovia; Count Carlos Montes, representing King Juan Velásquez of Salamanca; Marquess Albert Collins, representing King François du Basque of the Basque kingdoms; and Count Mullah el Hassan of Granada, who was an emissary of peace and a liaison throughout the kingdoms.

The king was assisted into the grand room and helped onto the throne. Although he looked weak and pained, Celestino knew it was vital that he make it through the address for the sake of his citizens and everyone in attendance.

The king was surrounded by the members of his elite Green Dragoons, who were charged with his protection. These included: Duke Pablo Cervantes, Count Daniel Lemus, Baron Edward Preston, Baron Christopher Varney, Baron Gregorio Gutierrez, Marshal Diego Skaggs, Marshal Miguel Valente, Marshal Saul Torres. Most other members of the King's high court, including the archbishop and many of King Celestino's nobles, were present as well.

Archbishop Nicholas stepped forward to address everyone in attendance. He raised a hand and blessed them, "Dominus vobiscum."

"And also, with you," everyone replied.

Nicholas continued, "The king acknowledges everyone here and thanks you for partaking in this important meeting. In the name of Rome and in accordance with this king's high court and the nobles' support, I, Archbishop Nicholas Loftus, present His Majesty King Celestino Garcia the rightful ruler of Galicia and Asturias."

"Hail to the King!" and "God save the King!" everyone chanted.

King Celestino nodded to Duke Pablo, who ordered everyone to silence. Then the king's royal baron Edward Preston stepped forward and presented them with the king's declaration.

———❖———

The Reigning Oaths

The royal decree stated…

> *I, Celestino Garcia 'The Just,' King of Galicia and Asturias; Son of Casimiro Garcia, King of Navarre and Aragorn, Duke of Castile and León -*
>
> *Having made all these people my subjects and ruling over these lands which I took from the strongholds -*
>
> *I am ready to give my soul to God and the Holy Spirit. I hereby entrust that which I have received from my father to my firstborn. Following the customs of the kingdoms, my son Gerardo Garcia will be named King of Galicia.*

The baron stopped and waited for the king to address the prince. The king looked at Gerardo, who was present. Then he coughed some before being able to continue. "You, my son, will receive the taxes from Coruña and Santiago de Compostela." Gerardo bowed his head in acknowledgement.

Baron Edward continued with the declaration.

To my daughter Camila Garcia, I grant the most distinguished Kingdom of Asturias.

A collective gasp arose from the audience. Even Camila was shocked, as she had not expected for her father to make such a generous decision in her favor. It was not traditional. It was a complicated decree to administrate. And she loved it.

Everyone murmured among themselves. Gerardo's mouth fell open. He shook his head, not believing his own ears as he watched everyone's reactions. He felt anger and embarrassment because this did not make sense to him. The nobles were in shock and disbelief after hearing such a proclamation.

"Is the king purposely splitting up the kingdom?" Count Daniel commented to those around him.

"Not to mention that he is leaving a kingdom to his daughter. A woman?" Marshal Miguel responded to the count.

"A woman with no husband to be called a king. And a kingdom that has been so hard to protect and unify," Count Daniel continued to question aloud.

"If the king wants the princess to be the reigning queen, so be it," Duke Pablo answered the count.

The two sides quickly became apparent, who was loyal to the king's decision and who was opposed to it. The allies and emissaries simply watched and awaited the outcome. Then the archbishop stepped in, splitting up the two groups that had formed and raising his hands as a sign for them to stop, so the address could continue.

Everyone settled down. The archbishop looked at both sides and stated, "This is indeed the will of God. And Rome accepts it. Praise be to God."

Some of those present still wanted to show their dissatisfaction, but, before they could continue, a command was heard. "Silence," said Duke Pablo. "Silence. The king's declaration will be heard."

The duke's action was critical, as this displayed his loyalty and his will to back up the king and what he had to say. Everyone complied and returned to listening to the rest of what the king had to say. Celestino looked towards Camila. Her heart raced, and her mouth was suddenly very dry.

The king was saddened by the general reaction of those that were opposed to his will. He coughed some more and overall appeared to be weaker and discouraged. Yet he continued, "You, my beloved daughter, will receive the taxes from Oviedo." Camila bowed her head with humble acknowledgement and gratitude. With those words, order returned. Everyone had calmed down, and the ceremony was able to proceed.

King Celestino continued to instruct his heirs. "Kneel, my children, and swear to accept my last will and testament." He gasped for air and coughed again before proceeding. "Swear that you will never raise a hand against each other. Swear before God. Before your King. Before your Father."

And they swore it. With these words, King Celestino would fulfill his oath to unify and protect both kingdoms. To keep the unity that was earned from a legacy that went back to his fathers before him.

The new king and queen were very nervous and confused. They still had not fully comprehended what this new co-regency would hold for either of them. There was a heavy silence over the whole room. Celestino's son Gerardo took a knee. He looked at his younger sister in disbelief of what was given to them. But mostly of what was given to her.

The young prince replied, "I swear to obey the will of my King and my Father. I take my place as the new King of Galicia."

After Gerardo finished accepting his pledge, everyone remained still, pending the outcome from the daughter of the king. Camila held her chin high. She responded with bravery and class in her pledge.

"I accept the legacy which you, My King, have bestowed upon me. I swear to keep the same motto that you, My King, have taught me. I swear to enforce it for the protection of the kingdom. To be just. To be kind. To look out for the well-being of the people of the kingdom. I swear it on my life."

King Celestino signaled for them both to stand, and they did. The archbishop held a hand high.

"The king has spoken," his voice echoed through the halls. "The king and queen have taken their reigns, and Rome supports it."

Baron Edward followed, finishing with this declaration: "Long live the King and Queen." And the entire assembly answered vigorously, "Long live the King and Queen."

Next, while a stringed quartet played some regal music on the balcony, the nobles one by one approached the new king and queen and kissed their hands as a gesture of acceptance and respect. There was, however, a silent discomfort in the mannerisms of some of the nobles who were not pleased with the decision.

In particular, those who simply took issue having a queen without a king to rule over them; not to mentioned that most were closer to Gerardo than Camila. However, others thought the decision was not only just, but it was also correct, and they embraced it as such.

Then the allied representatives proceeded to pay their respects to the new monarchs in anticipation of their acknowledgement and continued alliance.

Daniel approached Pablo chuckling with his arms wide open, as if he was to give him a hug. "Well, it looks like there is no place for you in Galicia, Pablo. Like I told you before, there is a new commander of the Green Dragoons."

"It is that kind of ignorance that shows why you can never be their commander, Daniel. The Elite are loyal to their one and only leader, which you apparently don't understand. No, Daniel, they will stay in Asturias under my command to protect their queen as they always have. That is your reality - being the commander of King Gerardo's knights." He said before turning and walking away, leaving Daniel seething in anger.

After the coronation ceremony, Gerardo and Camila returned to their father's chamber, where they stood watch over him together with their mother.

Chapter 2
The King's Lineage

King Celestino was known as a good and kind lord like his father King Casimiro Garcia before him. Celestino's earliest ancestry could be traced to King Garcia I of León ruling in 910 A.D. His father had taught him the old traditions and true ways by which to run a prosperous kingdom; he had taught him to make good use of the land and, very importantly, how to win the hearts of the people.

Casimiro had successfully defended the kingdom against the aggressors of his own time, even as his father had done before him. Celestino's lineage went back to the times where the land was under constant provocation from the Moors and since then many other enemies had threatened the peace of the kingdom.

His father's guidance gave Celestino the proper leadership foundations. Because of that, he became a well-respected monarch. One who also had won the confidence and fealty of the people of the kingdom, just as his father had done. Wanting to pass down his father's teachings, the king had also given orders to raise his two children to be chivalrous and to look after the well-being of the people of the kingdom. "Noblesse Oblige" was the French saying, which meant that their noble status obliged their royal family to do better and provide for those less fortunate.

King Celestino made his children learn the way of the sword, to be able to protect the land. This was the same training by which his father had raised him as well. Yes, that also included his beloved daughter Camila. Training his daughter in the same way as his son was unique. Women, and particularly ladies of royal or noble lineage, were traditionally never to be exposed to any source of combat. For it was considered a man's duty to do so; it was never fit for a lady. Nevertheless, he also knew that, as his heirs, they needed to learn to protect themselves on their own.

As King Celestino watched his children kneel before him, he thanked God he had been able to live long enough to watch them take over their lands as king and queen. He felt proud as only a father would be. Yet, he also knew the hardships that awaited them ahead, as the full weight of royal responsibility bore down upon them. His children would now need to depend on their mentors and rely on the protection of their loyal nobles and knights. The protection of the church represented by the archbishop and the blessings and support of Rome were always a powerful asset.

After their crowning ceremonies, King Celestino retired to his chamber, where he was laid on his bed. Alongside him was his beloved wife, Joanna. His children Gerardo and Camila were also nearby.

Gerardo stood by the right side of his bed and Camila to his left. Camila reached out to touch his hand and softly caressed it. The top was soft like goose down, but she knew the palm was rough and calloused. His beloved Queen Joanna sat at the head of the bed and cradled his head in her arms. They knew their time together was fleeting. She held him tight, and they looked into each other's eyes.

The king shifted his gaze to his two beloved children and smiled at them, proud and full of joy to have them by his side. Celestino then returned to look into Joanna's eyes. He kept his eyes fixed on her until he could no longer keep his eyes open. He could barely talk; nevertheless, he made the effort. He managed to say his last words directed towards Joanna.

"I love you, my love," the king whispered hoarsely.

"I love you, too," Joanna replied. She continued to whisper comforting words in his ear, most of which only he could hear. "I love you, My King. My beloved husband. My love."

The king's arms finally lost their grip and both Gerardo and Camila saw his hands slowly drag down towards the bed. Celestino could no longer look at Joanna and slowly closed his eyes for good. Queen Joanna was devastated, and she wept for his passing. Camila and Gerardo simply knelt as tears welled up in their eyes. They, too, continued to hold him and began to pray for him all while trying to comfort their mother.

"Requiescat in pace, King Celestino," the archbishop lamented in his Latin tongue. "The king will be remembered for his legacy. The way he lived as a just king. In life and in the face of death. He will be missed..."

"Adios, Papá, vaya con Dios," Camila whispered to her father as he slipped away on his final journey.

Queen Camila

Queen Camila, the youngest heir, now had her own kingdom to reign. She was the king's beloved little girl, who had also loved him very much. She symbolized the love that flowed throughout the kingdom.

She was referred to as the queen with the good and kind heart. This was a right match for the new queen, the land, and its people. She, as her father before her, always looked out for the well-being of the people.

This was a virtue that was rare in any kingdom and was also frowned upon by some of the more stingy and self-serving nobles. In their minds, nobility and peasants were not to interact freely at any given time according to their long, time-honored customs.

These actions, however, won her the immediate support from both the church and the people of the land. Even during her father's reign, she had opened the royal storehouse to provide everyone in the kingdom a bag of rice or sometimes a meal. This upset the stingy nobles, but she always had the respect of her people.

Shortly after her father's passing, the people of the land gave her an amazing welcome to the kingdom. The citizens gathered at the entrance and courtyard of the castle, cheering and celebrating. "God save the Queen! God save the Queen!" they chanted. As she stepped out to acknowledge them, the people bowed and kneeled.

"Please rise," Camila would tell them.

"Praise God for having sent you to us, Queen Camila," they would say. Inside the castle, a public welcoming ceremony was underway where everyone —nobility and clansmen alike—were present. They all bowed and swore their fealty to their new queen.

"Hail to the Queen," they all chanted, including those who had come to witness the celebration, blue bloods, and the people from their village alike.

"This is overwhelming, Mama. I was not expecting quite this big of a welcome. I feel the love of the people."

"Claro, Mija," the queen mother answered. "The people love you, always have. You have always been kind and sweet to them, and our people have always looked after you in one way or another."

"Even though it seems as if I've inherited a huge burden, I feel like it is my right to carry on with my father's legacy. At least I could look out for everyone's well-being."

"You are precisely what the kingdom needs," Joanna answered.

Her faithful court was always near her to make sure order was kept. "Marshal Diego, can you please make sure that the people have enough food and shelter. I need an inventory of the resources you need to accomplish that please."

"Yes, of course, My Queen," Diego bowed and walked towards the door.

"Thank you again, Marshal," Camila smiled back at him. "It is going to take some getting used to being called Queen," Camila and Joanna laughed together.

"Duke, can you please take care of the allies and guest arrangements for tonight's feast? I want to make sure that everyone is taken care of and that they enjoy themselves. I also want to coordinate a merchant exchange with them. Please let us start to list our goods and theirs so that we can start the import and export as soon as possible. Oh, and one more thing. Please send word to Commander Juan Carlos and Captain Ivan to join us in our meeting."

"Yes, Your Majesty. It shall be done."

"Thank you, Pablo. Oh, and by the way, I did not have a chance to thank you for staying with me instead of going with my brother."

"My Queen, I have served your late father, and I have always been assigned to your protection. I am not going to start serving someone else now."

"Thank you, Pablo, it means a lot."

Baron Gregorio Gutierrez was assigned to the Galician division, however after the sovereign detachment he chose to serve the queen. Marshal Diego Skaggs was a loyal knight to her and stayed under her service along with Archbishop Nicholas Loftus, especially since Gerardo did not care to have him in his court.

As a resourceful administrator, the queen was well-known throughout the nearby kingdoms. She had met most of the lords and ladies from a very young age. She took great care of her kingdom, and those qualities made it hard for anyone to not want to be under her reign or honor an alliance with her.

The queen noted with some hesitation that some of those so-called alliances were romantic advances on the part of some opportunistic lords. However, finding a man whom she could rule alongside was not a priority for her. She was a dependable woman, and her focus was completely on the tremendous daily burdens of her reign. Besides, having a king rule alongside of her would also mean sharing authority over the kingdom.

The lands of Asturias were lush and fertile, making them prime real estate for nearby rulers to claim as their own. That sort of encroachment was common. Fortunately, the queen's leadership and good will elicited the support of her loyal knights and her people.

The queen cared to waste no time sitting around and waiting for trouble to come to her. She thought it was best to go on the offense early. So she requested a meeting with the key members of her court.

"I appreciate everyone for their attendance even though this meeting has only just been called together. Your expedience is noted. And we've got work to do. So, thank you all."

"Thank you, Your Majesty," the men responded in unison.

"This is all happening so suddenly, but I know that we have been sort of paired to each other, as it were. You served my father so faithfully as well as the kingdom, and for that I am ever grateful. I should like to discuss the continued well-being of the kingdom. First, I want to formally thank you, Duke Pablo, Baron Gregorio, Marshal Diego, Commander Juan Carlos and Captain Ivan. Your loyalty is invaluable."

"Thank you, Your Majesty," the men replied.

"I understand many of your men have sacrificed their families and their lands for many generations; constantly on guard against other kingdoms, as they sought to disrupt and disinherit us from our territories."

The seasoned noblemen nodded at each other gravely, perhaps recalling their own sacrifices along the way for the kingdom's sake.

"Now, I want to know the status of our merchant exchange proposal with the other kingdoms."

Duke Pablo rose to address the queen. "Your Majesty, the exchange that you have proposed is already well accepted. Segovia, Salamanca, León and as far as the Basque territories are already on board. We are pending news from the Portuguese territories, Your Majesty."

"Excellent news, Pablo. I thank you for the job well done."

"Thank you, Your Majesty," Pablo answered. "In regard to the citizens of the land, we have already provided aid to the neediest families as you wished, my lady."

"Wonderful, Pablo. And Commander Juan Carlos, please submit a list of whatever your needs are as well."

"Thank you, Your Majesty, will do."

"Very well, then, please let me know if anyone, including yourselves, need anything. That is all I have for now. Thank you again for your trust and loyalty, and may the Lord bless us all."

"Amen," the men stood up and appreciatively thanked the queen.

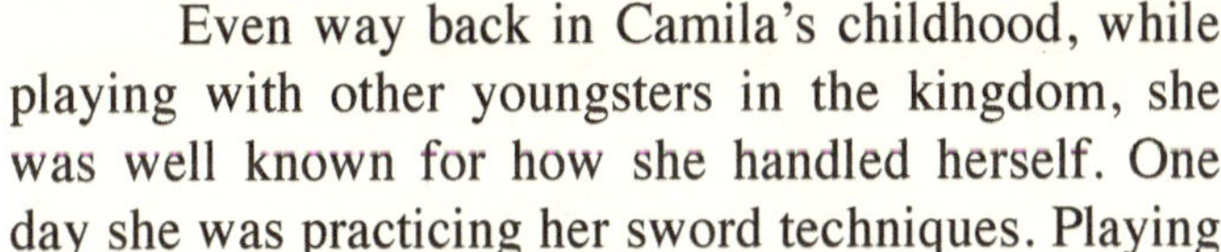

Even way back in Camila's childhood, while playing with other youngsters in the kingdom, she was well known for how she handled herself. One day she was practicing her sword techniques. Playing nearby were the other noble youths who had gotten used to having her out there among the boys.

A new lad had come to the kingdom and began to watch them play. He sat there without anyone paying him much attention. He had a slender build with brown hair and hypnotizing hazel green eyes that reminded Camila of a cat.

Camila invited the boy over to play with her, and he amiably accepted her invitation.

"Hi, there. What is your name?" Camila asked cordially.

"François," the lad answered nervously with the hint of a French accent.

Camila curtsied a bit, "Bonjour, François. I am Camila. Do you want to play with me? I could use a partner to practice my sets."

François broke into a huge smile of relief. "Sure, I'm willing to give this a try."

"Very well, then," Camila said pointing to a barrel of wooden swords nearby. "Grab one of those practice swords and come on over."

François did so and they partnered off. As they practiced, Camila showed François a set of combinations she had learned; François was a fine student and picked things up remarkably fast.

They were so engrossed in their one-on-one, they didn't notice the attention they were getting from the other teens of nobility; in particular, a couple of her childhood friends George and his good friend Juan. These two were always a real terror for the younger and weaker lads.

The troublemakers stopped what they were doing, and George said extra loudly, "Oh, look what we have here, Juan. Looks like we have another girl to add to our group."

Juan picked up the older bully's taunts. "Great. That is what we needed... another girl. Maybe she is here to watch the men play. What is your name little girl?"

François got a little red around the neck but decided it best to ignore their comments.

Camila raised the tip of her own sword to the two loud mouths. "Hush, you two. Leave us alone. Don't you have anything better to do than to give others a hard time?"

George put on an innocent face, "Oh, take no offense, my lady, we just want to see what this new kid is made of."

Juan moved closer, too, to turn up the heat. "That's right. We want to see if he can really wield the sword with men and not just with girls." He turned to François and asked, "What do you say, little girl?"

Camila stepped in before François could answer. "What is that supposed to mean? You guys know very well that I am as good as any of you, if not better. At least I am better than you two brainless goats."

Now it was Juan's turn to go red around the gills, "Oh, you may train with your father's Green Dragoons, but you know they are really going easy on you, right? You really don't honestly believe that you can really take on full grown men, do you?"

George had a little more sense than Juan and held his friend back, "Easy, Juanito. You do not want to get kicked out of the castle if she decides to go and tattle to the king, do you?"

Juan reconsidered a little, "All I'm saying is that she has not been tested in a real challenge by real men. That's all. Besides why isn't the lad saying anything? He is hiding behind the princess's sword. Or maybe her skirt?"

Camila took another step towards Juan and raised her sword in an en garde position. "Alright, that is enough! To begin with, I do not need to go to my father as if I was some helpless little toddler, like you. I can take care of myself. If you want to test your blades, come and put your skill to the test, I will take care of both of you!"

François stepped up beside Camila, "It's alright, m'lady. Please forgive me; I was not aware that you were the king's daughter. It would not be right to let the princess of the land fight on my behalf."

François turned to the bullies and pointed the sword's hilt at them both. "You two lads want to know who I am and what I can do? My name is François, and I am ready for either one of you that wants to challenge me and see what I am capable of."

George and Juan looked them both over like they were crazy and laughed out loud. François and Camila were about three years younger than George and Juan and therefore smaller.

Camila turned aside to warn François, "Be careful. These lads like to take advantage and pick on the smaller and younger kids instead of fighting someone their own size."

Juan raised his own wooden practice sword into an en garde position opposite of François. "Alright kid, let us see what you are capable of. I am going to send you back to France or wherever you come from."

George was excited for the beatdown he knew his friend would dish out to this little peon. "Give him a pounding Juanito. Comment allez vous his butt back to the north."

Juan lunged at François and aimed his sword tip straight for François's midsection in an attempt to scare François and finish him right away. But François adeptly side-stepped it and deflected Juan's strike.

Juan recovered quickly, "Do not run, little lad. Stand still and face me like a man."

François stood en garde and then lifted his sword above his head like a scorpion and waited for the next attack to come. Juan took the bait and ran towards François again and executed a downward strike towards the head. François tilted his sword sideways to receive and block the strike. Juan followed with a left side, low sweeping strike towards the legs. François swung his sword to intercept that strike as well. Juan spun around 360 degrees to come out swinging his sword across the smaller kid's eye line. François pulled his sword towards his left side and once again blocked the strike.

After seeing François hold his own, George realized that he was making Juan look bad. George jumped in to assist Juan in teaching this little French brat a lesson. He ran towards François from behind, striking him across his back when he was not looking. François looked back at his attacker in pain.

Juan took advantage of this and kicked François in the stomach, dropping him to the ground. George swung his sword down towards François, and Juan did the same with his own sword, and they pounded the poor boy from above.

François was able to dodge and block some hits, but more of them broke through his meager floor defense and throttled his chest, stomach and arms. The pain was excruciating but he endured it, until his sword was completely knocked away. Now he was completely vulnerable.

Finally, Camila could watch no longer from the sidelines and charged in with her own sword, striking George on his back the same way he had done to François. George immediately cried out and dropped to the ground in pain, rolling away from her. This put him back in range of François, who managed to strike him with a back fist to his face while he was lying next to him.

Next, Camila charged Juan with a lightning-fast left strike and right strike combination towards his head. Juan was able to block the first strike but got hit with the second, and he too dropped to the floor yelping in pain.

Camila stood above François in the ready position to defend him in case either one of his attackers got up their courage again. She watched them both writhing on the ground in pain but spoke to François. "Are you okay, François?"

"Oui, m'lady. Je vais bien, merci," he smiled up at her. "Thanks to you."

"Can you stand?" she asked.

François stood up slowly with a limp and grabbed his right arm with his left hand. He was bleeding from the nose and had several bruises on his arms and legs. Camila saw his condition and turned furiously back to the other two. "Get up, you two barn rats. Juan, would you say that I have now been tested by real men? Or perhaps you are not considered real men but lazy rats with big mouths."

Juan was struggling to his feet, "Camila, you attacked me by surprise, so you had the upper hand."

"Perhaps I should challenge you to a one-on-one duel in front of the people to make it fair? By the way, do you think that you and George were fair by attacking François, who stood his ground before you cheated?"

Juan was helping George to his feet, and both were backing away, leaving their swords where they lay on the grass. "N-no, that will not be necessary Camila. I gotta go now. Come on, George, let's get out of here before our families find out about this. We were fine until we got ambushed and got these bruises; that is what my report will be."

George added, "Camila, you and I have known each other since we were little kids. I cannot believe that you would side with this stranger. I am out of here."

Camila finally began to relax her sword, but her eyes were still blazing fire. "When you act dishonorably and hurt people, I will not sit back and allow it to be done, George. You, out of all people, should know that about me."

Both George and Juan hobbled away and got on their ponies with difficulty, since they had received a good beating from Camila. They rode off to find a sympathetic house servant to nurse their wounds and their egos.

Camila helped François to the castle and called for her own royal court to give him assistance.

"I thank you, m'lady," François said with a nudge to Camila from his good shoulder. "I will never forget you for this. I am in debt to you. By the way, I am very impressed with how you took care of them."

She smiled back at him, "Do not talk now, François, everything is going to be okay. My father's caretakers will tend to you. And don't worry, we'll tell them we were surprise attacked by twenty marauding mongols all at once." François laughed at the outrageous idea.

From that point forward, Camila earned the respect of any young adult in the kingdom when word got out of her actions and her skill with the sword. From time to time, she was seen in armor riding alongside the royal court throughout the land, ready to protect the land and engage in battle, if necessary.

There were even some rumors that the brave princess would don some generic, nondescript armor and venture off into battles, without anyone's official knowledge, to defend the land against the enemy's attacks. But all of that was another time, another page in history, prior to her father's passing. Now that she was a ruling queen, that was not to be. As queen she could not afford to be so reckless with her personal safety when the whole kingdom was at stake.

However, Queen Camila was definitely not a traditionalist when it came to women and their societal limitations. Nor was her father. History would have to decide whether they were right in the end or not. But now, as the sole ruler of her kingdom, she needed to make sure all of her people were defended from sword and famine. And sometimes, that took a warrior, but most times it took a diplomat.

———◆———

King Gerardo

King Gerardo was Celestino's primogeniture. They had fought in many battles together, side-by-side, including in that final, fateful battle where his father became mortally injured; he was known to be a fierce and ruthless knight.

So, that was how Gerardo ended up as the Lord and King of Galicia. Counted in his ranks were Count Daniel Lemus to lead his army, Baron Edward Preston, and his Marshal Miguel Valente. He did not want to take Archbishop Nicholas Loftus with him, and, in all reality, he did not care if he had Rome's representation in his kingdom.

After his coronation, he was approached by his royal court to receive their orders and expectations regarding his new monarchy.

"Congratulations, Your Majesty. If anyone deserved to be our new king regent, it is you, sire," Count Daniel said.

"Have I not demonstrated leadership and strength every time we have gone into battle?" Gerardo questioned him.

"You have, sire," responded Daniel.

Gerardo turned towards Baron Edward and stated, "Am I not the first born to my father the king?"

The baron's first reaction was to try to understand the reason behind the question. "You are, Your Majesty," Edward replied, although he couldn't help feeling that the king was questioning his personal loyalty, and it made him uneasy.

"Am I not a fair ruler?" he looked towards Marshal Miguel.

"Of course you are, Your Majesty," Miguel replied.

"And yet, my Papá decides to give my little sister—who does not know anything about reigning —half the land that should have been part of my kingdom," Gerardo roared. "I have demonstrated to be a powerful man, a patient man—even more so than my father—and for what? It did not matter to him."

"What would you like us to do, sire?" asked Daniel.

"As much as I feel betrayed by my own family, I will honor the king's dying proclamation. For now. I realize that if I try to do or say anything in the matter, it will make things worse, since the people would think I am a sore loser and possibly a traitor to my father."   Gerardo reclined back on his seat and rested his head against his big fist, pouting. He was very upset and dissatisfied with the outcome of the kingdom's distribution. It was eating away at him like a pesky little piranha.

"Sire, if I may make a suggestion as your army's commander? You are a wise man that has established respect and fear from everyone. I think that it would be best if you were to distance yourself from your sister. By doing so, she would have to fend for herself. Surely, she is capable. Your father thought so. And if not, the queen would then be vulnerable without your direct support," Daniel explained carefully.

Gerardo looked at the count and knew what his underlying intentions were. "To wait for a siege on her land and then move in and take over from whatever new hostile enemy stakes a claim. That is what you mean, Daniel?"

"It is, sire," the count answered.

Baron Edward looked towards them and added. "By these tactics, Your Majesty, you would be able to legitimately claim the whole kingdom as your own. If she has lost her kingdom and you win it back, then your actions would be considered noble and chivalrous."

"You will be a hero and be recognized as such by the other kingdoms, sire," Count Daniel stated excitedly.

"I like it," Gerardo smiled at the plan. "I have decided that such a way would be the best way of obtaining my sister's kingdom."

"Indeed, sire," Daniel, Edward and Miguel agreed in support of the king's decision.

"For now, we need to be certain that no friend nor foe comes near our own border without our knowledge. We will decide who enters and whether to allow them access to Camila's territories. Make sure our borders are well protected with a visible show of force."

Daniel snapped his heels together, "Of course, sire."

Gerardo was an opportunist. And a realist. These actions made him not much different, in the end, from any other lords in the nearby lands.

"I want to begin a higher taxation. We shall call it a home protection endowment," the king added.

"As you wish, sire," Count Daniel replied. "Edward, I want you to oversee that task. Start to let everyone know when you do your patrols."

Edward nodded. Gerardo paused for a moment and stood up to pace back and forth as he thought up even more ideas.

"I want to lower the battle age from 18 to 16, so more men can join our security mission to guard our expanding borders. Some may not return but my father paid that price enlisting me into the army. Why should anyone else in this kingdom do any less for our safety and well-being?"

Gerardo turned back to look at his men who were listening intently, nodding in agreement, and taking notes of what he was establishing. He then sat down on his chair, leaning into the high, leathery back that creaked against his armor. "Furthermore, from now on, whenever we find ourselves in the situation of an encounter or war, I want to be presented with all of the spoils instead of distributing them to the people, as my father had done. In this way, we can build a war chest."

"Of course, sire. Will do. We can send a decree at once with all the new rules. Is there anything else, my lord?" Daniel prodded him.

"Yes, let them know that the punishment for stealing from my stock will be death. Hanged from the bridges for all to see."

The men looked at each other with surprise, but did not comment. They had mixed feelings about such harsh punishments. But there was one more new and surprising decree which added some interesting benefits. You see, Gerardo was also known to be quite a social lady's man, and he loved to be part of large gatherings held in his own honor, which allowed him to feed that enormous ego.

Therefore, he immediately ordered the creation of a royal harem. As the young men would be called upon to serve their king on the battlefields, the most beautiful young women in the kingdom would also be called upon to serve. In other ways.

At the end, the king stood up and so did his court, to pay respect; he left the room abuzz in speculation.

Once, as a young adult prior to becoming a king, Gerardo decided to go hunting for female companionship. A sporty, hedonistic past time he enjoyed. He took his royal escort as usual, to be used not only for his protection but also as his muscle in case anyone refused his orders. Fathers and older brothers could be quite unreasonable at times, until the gold coins or the sword resolved their petty objections. They rode out to one of the nearby villages of the land. When he arrived, the people bowed in respect and welcomed the prince and his entourage.

Gerardo scanned the village and saw a fair, flaxen-haired maiden by her father's side.

"You there, come here," he commanded her. The girl shyly looked at her father, who was next to her and waited for his approval.

The father discreetly pulled his daughter closer to him and took a knee placing his right fist across his chest to address the prince. "My lord, my name is Gregorio Gutierrez. I am a loyal servant of the kingdom who has fought alongside your father King Celestino and served under his dynasty. This young girl is my daughter who is a mere doncella with an innocent child's mind. I ask of you, my lord, to please spare her."

"How dare you speak to me directly and, if that were not enough, to refuse a direct order of the prince?" Gerardo bellowed angrily at the peasant.

"My lord, I beg of you, again, please do not take my daughter," pleaded Gregorio.

A division of horses was heard approaching at a fast clip. The prince and his court looked to see who was coming their way.

"It's your father King Celestino and Duke Pablo and the royal escort of the Green Dragoons, Your Highness," announced Marshal Miguel.

The prince stood by and waited for his father's arrival. When the king arrived at the scene, all citizens of the village took a knee and bowed their heads to honor him. Gerardo's knights also bowed their heads to honor the king.

King Celestino noticed Gregorio with his hands and knees to the ground and approached him, maneuvering his horse between Gerardo and Gregorio.

"What has this man here done to be begging favor and mercy from you?" asked the king.

"Papá, I did not know you would be out this way today," Gerardo responded, trying to change the subject. "We could have ridden together."

"That sounds charming, Gerardo," the king pressed in again. "Now, what has this man done to be so humbled here before you?"

"He decided to interfere with my directions, Papá. All I wanted to do was talk to the young lady next to him," he lied. "I was going to bless her with some coins."

The king, of course, did not believe a word of what Gerardo was saying. Celestino looked towards Gregorio. "Rise, old friend. I see little Karina is growing. And how is your son, Danny?"

Gregorio stood up as commanded by the king. "Thank you, my lord. Yes, Karina and Danny are both fine, Your Majesty. You honor me by remembering my family, sire."

"What kind of monarch would I be if I did not remember the former Captain of my Royal Green Dragoons and his family?"

"Thank you, sire, I am deeply humbled," Gregorio replied.

"My son," Celestino looked towards Gerardo. "I do believe you were about to give Karina a sack of coins?"

Gerardo was confused at first, but then quickly jumped to it. "Of course, Papá. Daniel!" Daniel quickly approached them with a sack containing coins.

"Yes, my lord, I have it right here," replied Daniel, covering for his friend.

"Very well, then, what are you waiting for? Give it to her," Gerardo commanded the count.

"Here, girl," Daniel tossed her the sack of coins, which jangled loudly when she caught them.

Celestino looked back towards Gregorio and smiled at him and his lovely daughter. "Do not stay away for too long, old friend, I may call upon you sometime, again," Celestino told him.

Gregorio bowed again, "As ever, I am at your service, Your Majesty."

"Everyone else, back to the castle," Celestino commanded.

The king's escort led the way. Gerardo looked towards Gregorio and sized him up before joining his father to head back.

Once the army was out of earshot, young Karina approached her father. "Look, Daddy, we have some gold coins. This has got to be more than two years' wages. So, why did I feel so scared by the prince today, Daddy?" she asked watching after them.

"Always follow your intuition, Karina. Even when it comes from royalty. The father is indeed a great man, but the son is not cut from the same cloth. I am afraid that one day we may have to leave this kingdom, to protect ourselves from the prince," Gregorio shook his head sadly.

Indeed, on the very day of the new monarchs' coronation, Gregorio packed their belongings and took his family to Asturias and followed the queen.

❖

Gerardo hid his aggressive desires less and less and became well-known for his bawdy demands. But if he was ever questioned about them by his father, he produced a scapegoat or would have a sudden and convenient religious enlightenment to keep out of trouble.

In fact, this now made him twice as dangerous, since his sister Camila loved him dearly and would never suspect him to do her or her country harm. After all, she figured that, as her blood brother, they had both promised their father before God to hold a peaceful alliance. She assumed she had nothing to worry about.

Gerardo was well known throughout the kingdoms. He figured he would pick up where his father left off with alliances, so he was not worried about establishing any new ones. For now, he simply wanted to live life at its fullest by feasting and having royal consorts attending his beck and call. He was characterized as a man of strong temper who had the means to fight anyone, be it a one-on-one skirmish or a battle against another kingdom, army to army.

For the most part, his allies would much rather stay out of sight and avoid that famous temper. Contracts and alliances be damned, they knew he would simply pick a fight with very little provocation and attack them or their cities. Especially since he now had a significantly larger army of young lads conscripted into service, fodder for a zealous war machine.

They obeyed his wishes out of fear of retribution. The brutality of these actions created divisions among his ranks, although those that did not agree with the king remained silent.

Gerardo had known some of the other neighboring kings since childhood—like the current Kings George of Segovia and Juan of Salamanca, the same ones who had tormented a feisty Camila and François as kids. But Gerardo was older than they, so he had never had a strong connection to them like his sister had had. He did, however, make a connection with Lord Mullah, who seemed to always be visiting Galicia and establishing a rapport with all of the monarchs of the surrounding kingdoms.

Mostly, Gerardo would simply distance himself from everyone, as he was not much of a people person, unlike his sister. He could barely put up with the nobles and couldn't abide the commoners and peasants and all.

Chapter 3
Count Jacob Cedillo

King Celestino's death caused a definitive impact throughout the kingdoms and surrounding lands. He had worked so hard to unite his territories and had long hoped to continue that legacy through his children.

His passing caught the attention of ambitious and nefarious lords near and far, who wanted to take advantage of the country's shifting power dynamics and swing things in their favor. Lord Jacob Cedillo was from Seville and the current protector of León in his king's absence.

At León's castle, a lone rider thundered into the courtyard and reined in his sweaty, breathless stallion. As he dismounted, an attending squire took the reins from him, "Welcome back, my lord. I will take your horse to the stables to get fed and cleaned."

It was Baron Henry Johnson, who had just returned from Asturias. The baron simply nodded his head and walked away at a fast pace towards the castle.

Once inside the castle, he continued across the main hall and into the dining room where Count Jacob was eating roasted suckling pig and lamb.

"Your Excellency, I bring news from abroad," he said, quite winded.

The count looked up to see who was so eager to interrupt his dinner. "Ah, you finally manage to return, Henry. Are you suffering a palpitation?"

"My lord, King Celestino split his kingdom before his passing," the baron informed him while trying to settle his gasping breaths.

"Interesting. Do tell me more," Jacob sat back on his chair and paused from eating. "How is the kingdom split, and who reigns the land now?"

"King Celestino's son and daughter, my lord. Gerardo, the eldest, reigns over Galicia and Camila now reigns over Asturias."

The count stopped to think about this curious news. "It's very interesting, indeed. And has the queen chosen a king to reign alongside her?"

"No," the baron leaned in conspiratorially, "the queen reigns alone."

Jacob jumped up, "This is perfect. A chance to secretly… explore."

"Yes, and that would give my lord the opportunity to scout the strongholds and weaknesses," responded Henry.

Jacob smiled at the thought. "Get the army together, and leave one division in charge to protect the castle. I think we need to pay a visit to this new lady-monarch," Jacob commanded.

"Very well, my lord. I will notify Marshal Robert Alvarez to get things started," said Henry.

Count Jacob had taken nearby villages from the southern territories and was working his way north in his campaign of expansion. He claimed to be expanding these territories in the name of King Alfonso XI of León, under whom he was currently serving. But his plans were bigger than that. The king had assigned the count to the protection of his territory while he was out on a mission to the Kingdom of Aragon to give aid to the people in the face of a devastating and mysterious illness.

Jacob had a unique opportunity to take advantage of his king's absence, all while using his name to flex his muscle and power. King Alfonso XI had been very active in various campaigns. He was credited with the restoration of order. He gave new powers to the municipalities in exchange for their support against the nobles, and he furthered the long shadow of his crown by choosing officials without aristocratic affiliations in the year 1325.

He had then turned his attention to the Marinid Kings of Morocco, who had seized Gibraltar and routed the Castilian fleet at Algeciras in 1340.

More recently, he joined King Alfonso IV of Portugal and defeated the invaders at Rio Salado in 1340. Alfonso was assiduously courted by both France and England; both wished for an alliance that would give them the support of his powerful fleet, although he would not commit himself to either side.

Count Jacob busied himself as Alfonso's trusted guardian while the king busied himself with building and strengthening his vast territories and their allies. The way Jacob saw it, if the king were to die while away from his kingdom it would allow Jacob to keep ruling over the land as the appointed steward in his king's absence.

Interestingly, the Kingdom of León was once under the reign of Garcia's lineage, when their grandfather Casimiro was made a duke of the land by his cousin, King Sancho.

So, after a few days of preparation, the count and his large army took to the road and began their journey towards Asturias. During King Celestino's reign, the territory had been secured by different posts along the way to intercept any oncoming forces. However, along the way, Jacob had neither been contacted or experienced anyone occupying the borders. Jacob's arrival to the main roads leading into Asturias was met with no resistance. Nary a scout.

"My lord," Henry approached Jacob's carriage and rode alongside of him to inform him of the tactical oddity. "There is no military presence overseeing these roads. There are usually patrols by now. This could be a trap, my lord."

"They wouldn't dare," Jacob answered and snickered derisively.

"Very well, my lord," Henry said. Then they took advantage of the unrestricted passage and crossed into the land without any resistance.

Unbeknownst to them, Jacob *was* being watched by stealthy lookouts, and a message had been reported back to King Gerardo. Count Daniel was speaking with King Gerardo as Baron Edward entered to announce the news.

"Pardon, Your Majesty," the baron knelt to pay respects. "An army from the south has crossed the border into the Asturian territory. Do you wish to have the assigned division intercept?"

The king shot Daniel an 'I told you so' look before answering, "Do not trouble yourself with them. The time will come when we face them. For now, keep me posted on their movements, Edward."

"Yes, of course, my lord," the baron answered.

———————❖———————

Back in Asturias, Camila's knights also detected Jacob's advancement from a high post and sent the alert back to the city. When the news arrived at the castle, Duke Pablo had them ring the bells to alert everyone. He then proceeded to notify the queen who heard the alarm.

"Your Majesty, we received news of an army heading our way; they just set foot onto our land, crossing the borders from the south," Duke Pablo reported to the queen.

"Well, are they friendly? My brother should have intercepted them in that area," Camila said a little confused as they would have had to cross through Galicia to arrive at the Asturian border.

The duke responded without hesitation, "Your brother's intent is unknown, My Queen. The reality is

King Gerardo's men were not in the area. My advice is that we prepare ourselves for a possible attack."

"Yes, I agree, Pablo. Prepare for battle. Have all of my knights join us for the protection of the kingdom. And alert the clans. Their presence is mandatory, as well. I will personally ride out with you."

"As you wish, ma'am," Pablo said. "I'll be along presently with your royal escort."

Camila wasted no time. She armored up and rode out, surrounded by an escort of Duke Pablo and his mighty Green Dragoons to meet the invaders.

Crows could be seen circling overhead at the breaking point. Camila arrived at the defensive hilltop to prepare for the enemy's attack. This was the very same hilltop where her father had been mortally wounded by an enemy arrow. Camila could still see where her father's armies had fallen by the thousands. The grass hadn't even fully grown back yet. Mass graves were now present along the road to honor the fallen. Dark clouds were forming above, all very ominous.

The clans were present upon her arrival and were led, as always, by Commander Juan Carlos and Captain Ivan. Her second division was led by Captain Gregorio Gutierrez, who had already established the first defensive line. Gregorio was currently assigned to the southern border post, having transferred himself from Galicia to distance he and his family from Gerardo.

Gregorio approached the queen as she dismounted next to their mobile headquarters. "The enemy is already here, Your Majesty," he led the way into a command tent with a table underneath it to finish the briefing.

Camila noticed that Gregorio was wearing a braided lock of blond hair from his daughter and a leather gauntlet with his son's name engraved as good luck charms.

"Baron Gregorio, I am so glad to have you in my ranks," the queen touched his arm sincerely. "You have been a loyal member of the king's Royal Guard and decorated member of the original Green Dragoons." He nodded back at her, his eyes smiling warmly. And then it was back to the business at hand. "Tell me, what has taken place?" She gestured to the territory border on the map before them on the table where the enemy markers had been placed, "Are they ready to attack us?"

"If they were here for a fight, we'd be fighting, My Queen." Gregorio replied. "No, it does not seem so. Something else is at play. They seem to be holding their lines for now. Perhaps they want to talk about terms first."

"Very well, then, let us hold our ground and reinforce our defensive position right here," commanded the queen. "I will personally contact their leader. Do we know who we are dealing with?"

Pablo stepped in to answer, "If I am not mistaken, it looks like Count Jacob, my lady. He is the steward to King Alfonso XI from León. Do you concur, Gregorio?"

Gregorio immediately agreed, "Yes, Pablo, you are correct."

Camila, positioned in between Gregorio and Pablo, looked from one to the other, considering the implications. "You two have served my father for as long as I can remember. One thing I know is that you both know these territories and their monarchs. Very well, then, let us discover what this Count Jacob wants."

"Your Majesty," Pablo moved forward quickly to partially block her. "It is not advisable that you meet with him personally. Please allow me to make the contact for your safety."

"Pablo, as the monarch of this land, I have no problem speaking to the count of another kingdom or anyone for that matter. As Gregorio noted, if they were here for a fight we'd be fighting." Before he could object again, she moved back outside to mount up and swung her leg gracefully over the giant stallion. She kicked a heel into the horse and moved forward.

"Captain," Pablo paused at the entrance, "stay behind. You have the command of the army until our return."

"Understood, sire. And know that our arrows will be aiming at Count Jacob and whatever delegation meets with you," Gregorio assured him. "Juan Carlos and Ivan will help me flank them."

Pablo nodded back at him, "It is good to be fighting alongside my old brother in arms again, Gregorio." He then mounted up and clucked his tongue twice, and his horse sped away to catch up to the queen.

The queen galloped her horse expertly down into no man's land between the two armies. At her side was Duke Pablo and her marshal Diego who had selected a mid-point that offered them protection. Jacob also rode up from the opposite direction into the meeting area together with Baron Henry and his own marshal Roberto.

When Camila arrived, she and Jacob were at the front and center of their armed escorts. They kept forward of the Dragoons behind them as a show of good faith and in order to talk freely.

Count Jacob bowed his head with respect towards the queen and began, "Your Majesty. It is my pleasure to finally make your acquaintance."

Camila was less cordial in her response. "How dare you invade my lands and then form up here in such an offensive way. You break the treaty among our peoples for which there will be consequences," her horse pawed the ground, almost as angry as his queen. "You will stand down your army immediately, or I shall have my archers open fire on you for such an insolent act of aggression."

"Yes, Your Majesty, you could do so. I am grateful that your virtue and patience have steadied your hand, thus far, from such an egregious— although completely warranted—action. For that, I owe you my life, My Queen."

Camila was intrigued by Jacob's response. Her horse snorted, though. He was a war horse, and he wanted blood. She patted his neck soothingly and turned back to Jacob. "Speak your terms, then. Why do you present yourself on my kingdom soil with the entire force of Toledo marshaled behind you, if not for war?"

Count Jacob demurred and said, "I am here before you to offer my service and that of my army to you, My Queen. The word throughout the land is that you are a kind and just ruler. And that your kingdom is a place where your subjects are as strong and loyal as your iron will. That is enough for any lord to want to be a part of that kind of kingdom, ma'am. My sword is yours. My army is yours. We only move by your command, I assure you."

Queen Camila studied him carefully. She looked up to the sky as a bird arced high overhead. But that was just to buy a little time to glance sideways where she could see Pablo relaxing his own hand on his leg beside her. It wasn't much of a signal but enough to show her that he perceived no foul play or imminent danger. She turned her attention back to the smooth-talking peacock before them.

"I have heard of you, Count Jacob. I know of your conquests and battles in the south lands. Namely the keepsake Kingdom of León." She paused a moment to let her family connection sink in and then continued, "I have heard that you also claim to take lands by your king's orders. Tell me then, would your king order such an atrocity? How much loyalty do you have towards your king? Not much, I daresay, as you now speak of abandoning him."

Jacob looked at the queen surprised by the fire she had in her words. She was no push over. "You are wise and fair, My Queen. Hence the reason for me to defect. I also do not agree with the orders I have been asked to follow. Again, I do apologize for the way I entered your kingdom, but..." he paused as if searching for what to say next. "It was necessary to get your attention, my lady."

"I assure you, you have my fullest attention," she leaned in closer.

"Ahem, of course," he stammered. "Well, like I said, my lady, instead of fighting an army like mine, you will have it as your own to defend your kingdom and to embolden your rule of peace. No one will dare attack you with two armies at your beckoning. That is an enviable position of strength."

"No one dares attack me now," Camila countered. "To attack Asturias is to attack Galicia, and to attack Galicia is to attack Asturias. You see, I already have two armies."

Jacob was growing more and more anxious, fiddling with his saddle. He obviously was used to getting his way more quickly. Camila let him stew in awkward silence as she considered his brazen proposition for a moment. In the end, she realized that acquiring allegiance from these men made good sense, considering how other kingdoms would view her. Plus, more groups might come to do the same. She could certainly use the military numbers.

And the most troubling part of it all was that, despite all of her blustering on about Galicia, her brother had not set one foot out to intercept Jacob. Not even an advance squad. And that did not bode well for their family alliance. She knew that even if there was no encounter with Jacob's army here and now, there would eventually be a war with some other despicable, royal toad. "Better to keep your friends close and your enemies closer," her father had always counseled her and added with that wry twinkle of his, "under your heel, preferably."

"Very well, then," she said finally and heard Jacob release the nervous breath he'd been holding in. "I shall give you the opportunity to prove yourself and your fealty to my kingdom. Lay down your arms and fall in along with my knights, and let us envision together a new corporate beginning."

Jacob wiped a trickle of sweat from his brow, flashing that weasel smile of his at everyone, quite relieved. "I am forever in your debt, My Queen. My humble men and myself are at your service."

Everyone throughout the entire battlefield celebrated the news. More knights and a stronger, firm presence meant a smaller chance they would be attacked in the future. And if they were attacked, it meant a greater chance of success. But, it also meant more mouths to feed and bodies to quarter. The queen and her army returned to the castle with their new knights and citizens.

⸎

Just as Count Jacob had predicted, his whole army had been invited right into the kingdom. And they didn't even have to make a dumb wooden horse to gain access. And now from within, they could build a better understanding of their host's weaknesses as well as her strengths. He signaled his men to fall in behind he and their new queen.

As they calmly rode back to the castle along with Jacob and the men, Pablo approached the queen to be able to talk to her in private.

"Your Majesty, I dare not question your decision to invite these men into our land and give them full access, but may I know the full extent of your plan? That I may offer some counsel as your loyal servant and commander of your army?"

Camila listened to the duke's concern and smiled back. "Yes, Pablo, I thank you for your concern. I am not a fool. Of course, I have reservations about Jacob and saw this as an opportunity to get to know his true intentions better. So, I opted to study the count up close and personal and make him feel welcomed."

Pablo looked at her with a surprised and embarrassed look. "Forgive me, my lady, I promised your father I would always look after you, and for that reason, I appreciate the full confidence of your intention."

"Pablo, I need you to be alert for any foul play that Jacob or his men may attempt. It sounds like he sincerely wants to join the ranks. Nevertheless, keep him on a short tether. I am not going to let him weasel his way into the kingdom like a wolf in sheep's clothing. We know how that story ended. On the other hand, I am not going to start a war if I can defuse the situation and turn it to my own advantage."

"Consider it done, ma'am. I will make sure that the men are watched and held accountable. I don't mind telling you, I thought it rather odd that your brother would not—"

She held up a hand to stop him. "I had the exact same thought. Thank you, Pablo. You, sir, are a shrewd fox, and this kingdom relies heavily upon your vigil and counsel. I do not need to tell you your job. But, please continue to be my eyes and ears, as you were once for my father."

"Of course, My Queen. I shall get back to leading the way," Pablo answered before heeling his horse off into a canter.

The queen looked over her shoulder and caught Jacob staring at her. He quickly sat up taller, smiled and then looked away. But what was that first look? It wasn't scornful or even angry. She would have preferred either of those. No, she'd seen this look before somewhere. The way he looked at her was like a schoolboy with a fresh strawberry tart. Or a dog with a juicy hambone. She blushed a little around the collar and then clucked her tongue, kicking her horse into high gear.

❖

Lethal Acquisition

Baron Henry, Count Jacob's second-in-command, and Marshal Roberto, his third-in-command were not happy to hear Jacob was smitten with the new queen. This dramatically complicated and altered the whole strategy they'd agreed upon from the time they'd left León. Baron Henry was an older noble and Jacob's army captain who had been in every campaign with him. In addition, he also served as an adviser because he was such a man of information. Henry and Roberto approached Jacob from each side of his horse to be able to converse without raising suspicion.

"We fail to understand what it is that we are doing exactly, Jacob. The original plan was a great one. A hostile takeover of Asturias," Henry questioned him pointedly but smiled as if they were discussing the foliage.

"Our objective has not changed, Henry," the baron exclaimed, also with a big, fake smile. "In all the campaigns that we had together, we were able to accomplish what we set out to do by sticking to the plan, Jacob."

Jacob snapped, "Take it easy, Henry, and mind your tone," the count threatened. "I know what the initial plan was, I made it. But now I have a better plan. The queen has allowed us access to the kingdom without a fight. We now have alternative options that had not been possible for us to foresee."

"Alternative options? What do you mean by alternative options?" Henry didn't like the sound of that.

"The only part of the plan that's changed is that, instead of taking the land by force, I will take it by a more romantic approach," Jacob responded confidently. Of the three, his smile was the only one not forced. He was smitten very badly.

"Forgive me, but are you loco, Jacob? You think that the queen will just fall into your lap like a tavern girl? You will be wasting your time; you'll be wasting everyone's time. If it's just a matter of getting your wick wet, accommodations can be made. I've seen two or three striking milkmaids on this journey alone. Pick any one of them. Or all of them," Henry pleaded.

"Hush, you whine like a mule. To hell with your heifers. I want the Queen of Asturias. And why would she not fall for me?" Jacob asked. "I intend to charm her and treat her as no man has before. And as a king, she would be my queen. Queen Camila, my sun and my moon," Jacob responded wistfully.

Roberto was staying quiet for now, just listening to their points of view. Something that was impossible for Henry. "Do you not see that the original plan was the most direct approach and with much faster—and certain—results? Since when do we deviate from what we set out to do?" insisted the baron.

"Patience, Henry. Perhaps the original idea to take the land by force sounded good at first, but this way, as Camila's husband, I will be king," Jacob declared with anticipation. "We can have the whole kingdom and enjoy some perks as well." He let that sink in for the moment before he continued with their mutual benefits. "Of course, you would become a count or higher yourself, and you, Roberto, will be a baron or more," Jacob added with a flourish.

"Very well, then. I don't suppose we had fully thought through our end of this deal," Henry replied. "Nevertheless, it is not wise to keep me out of the plan just like that. Miscommunication is bound to take place when you least expect it, Jacob, and it is never a good thing."

Marshal Roberto was loyal to Jacob, and he often saw the conflict between the count and the baron. But he usually aligned himself with Jacob's final decisions. For the most part, he watched and waited for the count's final order, and he followed it without much conflict.

"What I need for you to do is this, send word down the ranks to scout for weaknesses and structural vulnerabilities in the castle itself. We can use that information if we need to take that road in the future."

"As you wish, my lord," they both answered and slowed their horses, dropping back to direct the ranks. Jacob held Roberto back one more moment after Henry's departure.

"Yes, my lord?" the marshal asked.

"Keep a close watch on Henry; let's make sure he's not going to be trouble."

"As you wish, sire," said the marshal.

------------◆------------

A short time later the queen and the combined armed forces arrived at her castle, the Castillo del Eliseo, where the citizens and the remaining division of knights were waiting anxiously for their return. The people cheered and celebrated their victorious venture.

The queen entered the castle as soon as she was able to hand off her horse to the stableboy. Her mother Queen Joanna glided elegantly towards her to welcome her back. "Camila. Mi hija preciosa. I was worried about you. The only thing I could do is pray at the church with Archbishop Nicholas and the other ladies waiting for their men to return," Joanna said through happy tears.

"Ah, Mama. Thank you for your prayers. They must have worked because, instead of battling a foe, we returned with an ally," Camila informed her.

"Oh, that's lovely, Camila. Come tell me all about it." The queen mother hurried her inside where Camila could talk to her while offloading her bulky armor. She was ready to be in something more comfortable for that evening's festivities.

At the castle dinner banquet, Jacob arrived bearing gifts of gold and precious jewels, and conducted himself in every way as a perfect noble gentleman. Everyone enjoyed this moment of having a new alliance. The people of the kingdom looked at it as a great asset. The count had a respectably-sized army, and they could certainly gain strength from the alliance.

Jacob entered the ballroom where the celebration was to take place. He stood in the receiving line, awaiting some time with the queen. As he watched her, he noted that, not only was she very diplomatic in all of her dealings, but she was also highly intelligent on a host of topics and could speak at length with anyone about their expertise. Finally, it was his turn.

"Your Majesty," he approached her. He leaned forward and bowed to her with his right hand across his chest. "You have a magnificent castle, and your citizens seem to be delighted to be around you. I am fortunate to be among them, as we all are."

"I thank you for your compliments, Count Jacob. Yes, the people of the kingdom do show sincere appreciation; they are my priority. A duty and a privilege," Camila answered as she acknowledged others that passed by her, bowing in respect.

"I can see why your people love you, ma'am; may I offer my services to personally make sure your kingdom is well patrolled, thus keeping the people of the kingdom safe? Of course, all under your personal command."

"Why thank you, Count Jacob," she happily answered. "I will discuss your offer with Duke Pablo. He is my commander in charge of the kingdom's safety."

"I appreciate it, My Queen," Jacob inclined himself again to pay his respects and moved away to allow others to talk to her as well.

The queen, although appreciative of Jacob's good will offerings, was apprehensive and understandably so. She went along with some of his ideas, but her intuition was to follow protocol and have him follow the chain of command. In the meantime, they enjoyed the celebration, which included dinner and copious amounts of wine. The entire court took part that evening's festivities.

Later, into the dinner and celebration, Lord Jacob addressed the queen again.

"I thank you so much for this welcoming gathering, Your Majesty. I have never experienced such a celebration in my honor. Not even in my previous kingdoms," the count smiled with a hand over his heart and the slightest of bows.

"The festivities are not just for you, Lord Jacob; they are for everyone within the kingdom. You are as much a part of it as all these guests, so let us simply enjoy this moment." The queen raised a goblet of wine in the air.

The count grabbed his own goblet and clunked it against hers adding, "Yes, My Queen."

This supper celebration carried on all night, and for a moment there seemed to be peace and harmony.

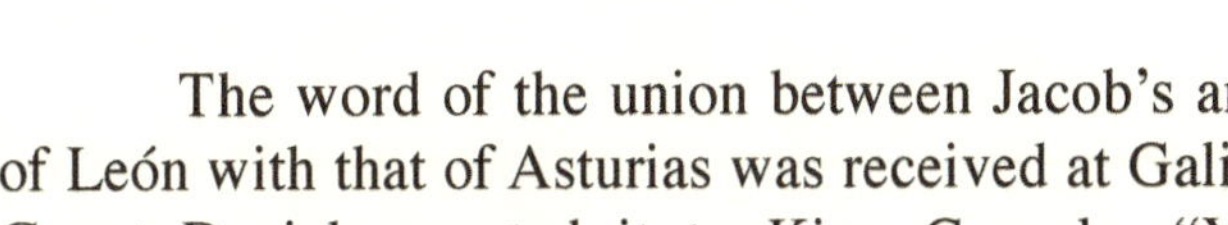

The word of the union between Jacob's army of León with that of Asturias was received at Galicia. Count Daniel reported it to King Gerardo. "Your Majesty, we have received a notification from

Asturias. It seems that the incoming army from León has joined Queen Camila's stronghold."

"How so? How is this possible?" said the king, his entire expression soured by the news.

"Our sources stated that there was an agreement for the Leónes army to defect from León, and Queen Camila allowed them to join her own armed forces, sire," responded the count.

Red-faced, Gerardo stood up from the chair in a in blustery rage. "Como carajo. So now Camila has a bigger army, and she will be more capable of defending herself. This is not what I had in mind. Camila thinks she can attack me? Double up the border defense and have them stand alert for any aggressive movement coming our way."

"Yes, sire. Right away," Daniel left quickly.

"If she wants to attack me, I will make her pay dearly," he seethed.

Chapter 4
The Count's New Direction

oving forward with their daily routine, Camila's knights noticed heavy activity within their borders. Marshal Diego reported it to the queen, "Your Majesty, Captain Gregorio sends word of heavy armament and divisions being moved from Galicia to our border lines."

"What exactly are my brother's knights attempting to accomplish?" asked the queen.

"It seems that they are preparing for combat. Captain Gregorio believes that such force of numbers and tactical deployment could only be due to preparation for a better defensive position and even an offensive advantage, My Queen," Diego advised.

"Please let Gregorio know to stand his post. We will send additional divisions directly, but we do not want to have my brother's army interpret our response as hostile. Not until I've talked to him about it, anyway."

"Yes, ma'am," the marshal replied.

"I need to call a meeting with Duke Pablo, I will also need a small group of skilled emissaries that can deliver a message to my brother," the queen said.

"Yes, right away, ma'am" Diego paid his respects with a courteous bow and departed to take care of the orders.

Camila hurried to the courtroom to discuss the current predicament with her other captains. Pablo was there waiting for her arrival.

"Your Majesty," he greeted her.

"Pablo, we have a potential situation on our hands. It seems that my dear brother is reinforcing the border areas with heavy armament and more divisions, as reported by Baron Gregorio. I have sent a team of skilled knights to scout out the purpose of his movement."

"Excellent, ma'am," said Pablo. "That is exactly what needs to be done for now. It could be nothing more than an exercise. Nonetheless, I also suggest that you send an extra division to back them up until we find out what the king's intentions are."

"Yes, I thought the same thing," Camila said, "but I do not think that their presence needs to be exposed, yet. Perhaps they amass at the second outpost, where they can be ready to engage, if necessary. What is your counsel, Pablo?"

"Perhaps this is the time for you to use Count Jacob and his army, My Queen? Their presence alone may be enough to dissuade your brother from making a hasty move."

"Okay, have the count patrol the region; but he is not to go beyond the tree line closest to our border post," the queen insisted. "And who do you recommend we send to deliver my message to my brother?"

"I will go and will make sure to speak to him directly. I will coordinate with Gregorio and tell him to hang back in case your brother misses the point. But first, I will send five of your elite knights to deliver our invitation to His Majesty."

"Good, I will compose the message, and you make contact with Jacob. I will notify you when the message is ready."

"Yes, Your Majesty," the duke responded and left the room.

Count Jacob was contacted by the duke who assigned him to help patrol the border and assist the baron in his security detail, as specified by the queen.

Shortly thereafter, Camila handed over the letter to Pablo to give to the emissaries for Gerardo.

———◆———

While the border armies were sizing each other up, they were making sure not to provoke an encounter. The elite patrol of emissaries departed on their trek to give King Gerardo his message.

Upon the emissaries arrival, they were taken before the king, where Miguel announced their presence. "Sire, messengers from Queen Camila have arrived and they are requesting an audience with you, my lord."

Gerardo looked at the men before him. "Speak," he grunted at them, fussing more with a hangnail on his hand, as if he had no interest in their news.

The emissaries took a knee and bowed in respect. The leading knight at the center extended his hand out holding the sealed letter. "Your Majesty, my name is Diego Skaggs. I am one of Queen Camila's marshals. I was also a loyal servant to your father, King Celestino. We bring a sealed message for you from your sister, my lord. I am to return with your response to this letter."

The king looked at him and stated simply, "I know who you are, Lord Diego." Gerardo then gestured to Count Daniel who in turn approached to grab the letter and handed it over to the king. Gerardo then broke the seal and began to read the letter.

My Dear Brother,

I have received news that your military activity along our borders has been increased severely and that it includes heavy armament, which you've sent to locations where it overlooks my lands. I do hope that these actions are nothing but a simple misunderstanding and not a potential aggressive threat to my citizens nor me.

Rest assured, that I have no intentions of fighting you, and if I have offended you in any way, I would covet your forgiveness, as I had not intent of doing anything to offend you.

Please, I ask of you not to jeopardize our oath to our father. Please stand down and recall the forward divisions that you have assigned to the area. If you care to discuss this issue one-on-one, please let me know, and we can arrange a meeting.

Gerardo, our men and our lands are deeply interconnected. The citizens of our kingdoms are even related, just like you and I. Please reconsider any foul thoughts you may have towards me, as I have none towards you.

Much Love,
Your Sister Camila.

Gerardo admired his sister's loopy and ornate calligraphy. She always was better at that sort of thing than him. He folded the letter and paused to consider his response. He then looked towards the messengers.

"I am aware of your queen's new alliance with an army from the south. I know everything that happens throughout the territories. So, it is not I who jeopardizes our oath to our father. Tell your queen that I will stand down my additional divisions in good faith. However, if she attempts to attack my land, I will personally conquer Asturias and reign over it myself. Ah, and tell her that there will be no mercy."

He then waved his hand at them, dismissively, to signal their leave.

"We will report your message, my lord," Marshal Diego responded. The men rose, and Count

Daniel ordered them to be escorted out of the castle, and they headed back to report the news.

The marshal returned to give Queen Camila the message, and Gerardo gave the order to stand down and remove the additional divisions from the border, hence de-escalating the threat. In return, Camila sent word for Count Jacob to go back to his normal patrols of the land, instead of acting as border support.

Camila went to her royal courtroom and called for Duke Pablo to meet her there.

"Your Majesty, did you call for me?"

"I did, Pablo, thank you for coming. I need to ask you; you have been a loyal servant to my family for a long time," Camila said with dismay. "I am confused by my brother's demeanor towards me and his aggressive actions. Can you believe he feels threatened by my taking in Jacob's army?"

"Yes, ma'am. I have been, as you have stated, a loyal servant to you and your royal family for quite some time. Absolutely, yes, I can see your brother reacting in such a way."

"Pablo, I realize that even though Gerardo is my brother, I may only know a fraction of his true self. Perhaps you can shed some light on this for me, since you've known him as a child, as a man and as a warrior. What are his thoughts?"

"My Queen, as long as I've known Gerardo, he has been a lone-wolf survivor who thinks only about himself and his needs," Pablo explained. "He always benefitted from your father's glory and rose from under his shadows. Now he wants to establish himself as a supreme leader, to whom people need to bow down and yield right away at his every demand."

He paused momentarily to consider his next words very carefully. "My Queen, people will bow either out of respect or out of fear. To monarchs like yourself, we bow out of respect. People bow to your brother out of fear."

Camila had taken a seat and simply listened to Pablo's brutal, but honest, response. "Thank you for your candor. I do not know why I fear the potential of a bigger problem with my brother more than with anyone else at this point." She stood and nodded at Pablo gratefully, "Please, I should not keep you from your duties any longer. I thank you for your input."

Pablo bowed to her before leaving, "I am at your service, Your Majesty."

A couple of months went by, and there were no confrontations between the kingdoms. By now, Jacob had gotten to know the territory very well. He had met most of the knights under the queen's sovereignty, built a rapport with the nobles, and gotten to meet some of the supporting clans spread out in towns and villages across Asturias.

The count was also able to establish trust with the people of the land who, in return, looked to him as a new lord and protector. This was a good thing for his reputation because positive feedback was getting back to the queen. The kingdom was pretty much safe against any foul play from any other armies; the people of the land appreciated Jacob's show of concern and diligence for their protection.

He, of course, followed up with queen, giving her detailed reports of his findings, his conversations with the villagers and their situational needs to be able to attend properly to them. His men were also respectful and followed the commands according to their ranking hierarchy. Duke Pablo would give Jacob a task to test his reaction and willingness to comply, and Jacob carried it out with no hesitation.

By now, Jacob was able to walk around the castle freely. As a count, he could delegate acts which bettered the kingdom, and those actions did not go unnoticed.

One day he saw Camila overlooking the kingdom from one of the tower balconies, and he decided to converse with her.

"I hope I'm not interrupting, Your Majesty," he saluted her with a hand over his heart.

"Not at all," she turned to welcome him. "Good evening, my lord."

"With the setting sun and you poised here in the tower overlooking your castle bathed in light, well, you're just like a painting," he joined her at the edge of the balcony with a hand upon the stone wall.

"I like to be up here because it humbles me. No matter what I do or don't do, the sun will rise and set, with or without me," she said watching the solar edge dip below the mountains. "A good reminder that the heavens are in control, and our tiny problems down here have no more significance than the eyelash on an ant."

Jacob watched her as she reflected. He dared not to break the spell a second time.

Camila took a deep, cleansing breath and then turned back to him suddenly, "I see you have established yourself well in the kingdom. I have heard good things about you."

"I have, My Queen. I have you to thank for that," Jacob answered. "The land is as beautiful and dignified as the queen that reigns over it."

Camila studied him and the corners of her mouth turned up in appreciation, "Thank you, my lord. I appreciate what you do for the kingdom. Are you all settled in now? Does this job and position fulfill what you were searching for?"

"Indeed, My Queen," Jacob replied. "I have for the first time in my life found my true home. I feel alive here. I feel part of something special."

"I'm glad to hear that," said Camila. "You have become a great asset to our ranks."

Jacob smiled and gave her a slight bow. "My Queen, I would like to respectfully request to be considered for membership in your elite Green Dragoons. I want to be assigned to your direct protection."

Camila was intrigued by Jacob's request and pleased by his willingness to excel in the ranks. "I will take your request into consideration and will notify Duke Pablo of your interest. Now tell me, why are you so interested in being assigned to the Green Dragoons where there will be many more demanding expectations placed upon you? Not like the freedoms of a commander of your own division, with the liberty to patrol at your own discretion."

Jacob thought about what to answer for a couple of seconds and said, "I find you to be extremely kind and generous, and I want to fight for you and…if I must, die defending you. I will do so, My Queen. I also want to remind you that I know the lands of León, and, as your loyal servant, I can lead you in the reconquest of that kingdom, which was once lost from your family."

Camila was surprised by the response. "I admire your resolve, Lord Jacob, and your respect to the court and its duties. A knight willing to die for his queen, that says a lot about you. However," Camila looked at him with a concerned expression. "I am not interested in León or breaking the alliance that my family has with King Alfonso XI. Neither I am looking to start a war against a well-known, powerful monarch who means me no harm. For those reasons, I would not have a part of that."

Jacob knew that he had said the wrong thing in offering to lead against León. "My humble apologies, My Queen, it was not my intention to upset you. Perhaps I should have taken greater caution in expressing my innocent intent. For that, I do apologize."

Camila acknowledged his apology with a nod. "I appreciate your sense of duty, and I am sure you would be a good fit for my elite court. Again, I will consult with Duke Pablo, and we will get back to you."

Jacob paid respects to the queen. "I thank you for your consideration and time, My Queen, and again, thank you for your kindness." And then he left the area.

That was not the outcome that Jacob had been looking for from the queen. He thought that she would be swept away by joy and gratitude bordering on endearment towards him at the opportunity to regain the territory of León. Thrice, she had foiled his flirtations and responded to his request as a simple change of duty.

Shortly afterwards, Camila met with Duke Pablo, and he presented her with the day's report. After which she brought up the ambitious count. "What do you think of Count Jacob so far, Pablo?"

"Your Majesty, I believe that when it comes to his duties as it relates to patrolling the land and reporting his findings, his work has more than sufficed," Pablo said thoughtfully. "Regarding his personality, when we are gathered, he seems to keep to himself and watches us from his seated area; well, except for when he is near you, then he is enraptured, My Queen."

"Enraptured?"

"Smitten."

"Smitten?"

"You've bewitched the poor count, I'm afraid," Pablo grinned, enjoying her discomfort.

"Oh, dear. Yes, I have noticed that, also," Camila massaged the bridge of her nose. "Interestingly enough he came to talk to me and requested to be considered as a member of the Green Dragoons. How do you feel about that?"

"Does he know that to be a Green Dragoon requires of him to pass our evaluation test which includes fighting and agility? To even be considered, well, he hardly seems in good physical constitution to even attempt it in his present shape, ma'am. Not to mention that the request would need to be accepted unanimously by the members of the court."

"I did not go into details with him," the queen answered. "I told him that his request would be considered, that I would talk to you, and that you would get back to him with a response. I want you to reach out to him and inform him of the qualifications needed, so in case he wants to pursue a place as a member of the elite Green Dragoons, he needs to prepare himself."

"Will do, ma'am," Pablo answered, "I fear the damn fool is lovelorn enough to try it."

Camila's eyebrows shot up, although she was more amused than anything else. Pablo flushed a little.

"My apologies, My Queen, will there be anything else?"

"No, that is quite enough of that for now. Pablo, please keep me informed as always of the progress, thank you."

"Of course, Your Majesty," he replied.

The duke sent for the count to talk about his request to join the elite brigade under his command. When Jacob arrived, he casually approached Pablo, "You called for me, sir?"

"Count Jacob, the queen has informed me that you requested to join the Green Dragoons.

"I did, indeed." Jacob stood a little straighter at the mention of the royal elite team; even attempted to suck in his gut a bit, as if the testing should begin immediately.

"This is exciting news. As the commander in chief, I am to go over the requirements with you to be accepted as a member," Pablo began. "First, you are to pass our physical evaluation, which includes fighting and agility in order to be considered. Then, there needs to be a unanimous vote by the members of the court."

Jacob reacted, more than a little offended. "Requirements? I see. I was not aware that such requirements also applied to someone of my rank and status. Now that I know, I will ask you to give me time to prepare accordingly."

"Of course, take the time that you need to prepare. Please let me know if you need to train with some of the members to get an idea of what it takes, and let me know when you are ready," Pablo said.

"I am not implying that I am not ready right at this moment," Jacob clarified. "But, I really want to do well, thank you."

"Of course," Pablo agreed. "Take as much time as you need. I am sure the challenges of our rigorous exam will be a non-event for a man of your strong military credentials."

"I'm sure they will," Jacob agreed and then turned to go his separate way.

Jacob met with his captains, Baron Henry and Marshal Robert, to discuss his further intentions towards the kingdom and plans towards their future direction.

"I have met with Queen Camila and requested to be considered as a member of her Green Dragoons."

Henry looked concerned while Robert smiled at the news and said, "Jacob, once again you make decisions without giving us any warning. Are we to also become members of the elite division?"

Jacob looked at them both and gave them a slight chuckle. "In order to publicly show our gratitude, I want to host a gathering in appreciation of the queen for having accepted us as members of the kingdom and for considering me as a candidate for her elite royal brigade."

Now it was Henry's turn to laugh, and he said, "After a couple of months, and still getting nowhere with wooing our fair queen, you are still looking to impress her with the size of your…banquets."

Jacob laughed along before returning to a serious tone, "Okay, enough chatter, let's talk about the details of what I want at the gathering; after all you never have a second chance to make a first impression."

⁕

As planned, a couple of days later, the count hosted a gathering in appreciation of the queen, where the lords of the land and her elite Green Dragoons all attended that evening with delight.

The Castillo del Eliseo was full of glamour, with heraldry banners and torches lined up at the entrance to welcome all the nobles. Jacob's men were assisting as escorts to those arriving in carriages and in taking their horses to the stables.

There were two rows of dining tables at the sides of the dining room, both connected to the head table at the top of the room. The three long tables easily accommodated the guests and had white table sheets to contrast with the red carpet in the room. The tables were decorated with such elegance, filled with lots of food and drinks, decorated with big flower arrangements and stunning candelabras. Jacob had not held back in investing in this good impression.

The count also had his men join the guard alongside the queen's Dragoons, as well as the army, who were posted throughout the different areas to show solidarity in the protection of the castle.

As the guests arrived, they were brought to their assigned seats. The last to arrive was Queen Camila with the queen mother, who was just behind her, and they were both escorted by Duke Pablo and Marshal Diego. The queen's entrance was grand, and of course Queen Camila was escorted to the head of the table, where she took her seat.

Everyone was having a good time enjoying the decadent food and fine wines imported from France and Italy; they feasted on delicacies such as swan meat, wild duck, and stork, in addition to fruits and vegetables.

Meanwhile, outside the castle, during the height of the celebration, some of Jacob's men rose as one deadly unit and struck the queen's army down. Every soldier to a man. Most were stabbed from behind, the ultimate betrayal. These men had grown to trust their brotherhood, even trusted them with their own lives, unfortunately.

Baron Henry led the attack quietly along the city walls, while the others continued to celebrate inside the castle with drunken revelry. It was a well-organized plan which took everyone by surprise.

Most of the queen's guards were killed before they even saw it coming. Others were able to fight back but had no real chance of surviving, the odds stacked against them. There was a small group that was able to escape to the nearby forest to hide.

Others were taken as prisoners with the option to join the count's army or suffer a very public punishment by mutilation. This would be an effective example of horrific consequences to any other rebelling clans.

Meanwhile, the queen and her lords were celebrating with Count Jacob inside the castle. Marshal Roberto led a group of peasants that carried platters overflowing with food. The group entered unnoticed since they were perceived as lowly servers to the nobles who indulged themselves.

Jacob positioned himself near Queen Camila and next to her mother, Queen Joanna. The marshal looked at the count and nodded at him. Jacob nodded back at Roberto and quickly grabbed Queen Joanna, placing a knife to her throat, while simultaneously using her as shield. The peasants with the food platters were now standing behind Queen Camila's lords and pulling out knives and smaller swords to do the same to them.

These servants were Jacob's men in disguise. Everyone was shocked at the sudden chaos around them. Duke Pablo tried to move, and he was struck on the back of the head; he tried to recover but a knife was pressed against his throat, cutting him just enough so that he'd hold still.

Archbishop Nicholas made the attempt to stand, waving his arms to calm everyone. He was kicked behind the knees, forcing him to sit down, and also had a knife put against his throat to immobilize him.

The women were pinned to the chairs, and some were told that if they screamed, they would be dead before they hit the ground.

Marshal Diego was quick to react, but two men were also waiting for him. One grabbed him from behind, and the other punched him in the stomach, causing him to double over in pain. He was then grabbed by his hair and dragged back to his chair. He was thrust down, his throat landing on the flat side of a knife, which pressed against him hard enough to choke him. The top edge bit into his jowls, and he held still after that, as well.

Jacob yelled to them all, "Do not resist, or everyone will die right here, right now, starting with Queen Joanna!"

Camila yelled in desperation, "Please, don't. Please let my mother live!"

The lords looked at her and waited for her command to fight back. Camila glanced at what the ballroom had become and wondered what would become of her mother and her Royal Court?

She looked into the eyes of her Green Dragoons and shook her head from side to side to tell them to stand down. She knew that a counterattack would only lead to their own certain deaths.

Count Jacob looked at Queen Camila and yelled once again, "Do the right thing. You know you have been defeated. Trying anything would be the end of everyone here. Killing everyone is not my intention, of course. Release the castle and the rights to the kingdom, and I will have mercy on everyone. Including your own life. I swear it."

To Queen Camila it felt as if the world stood still. She was in complete shock. In her mind she tried to land on an alternative option, but there simply was none. She scanned the room and saw their bleak situation and the fear in her mother's eyes. This was "checkmate."

Duke Pablo was near Camila, and he was not ready to give up just yet. He implored his queen, "Do as you must, My Queen. Order us to defend, and our lives will be given to protect you."

But Camila just shook her head, sadly. "That's what I'm afraid of," she murmured softly. She then looked up at Jacob. "That is enough. Let my people go. Let them go, and you can have the castle. But, you have committed high treason, and everyone will know that. You will never gain the approval from Rome."

Jacob laughed at her. "Approval? Approval from whom? I do not need approval from anybody," he snorted. "Nonetheless, I will honor my deal. You and your court will be escorted to the outskirts of the kingdom. I will have mercy on you all. However, I better not see you in these lands ever again, because you will not be shown mercy again." Jacob grabbed one of the wine goblets and swallowed a triumphant gulp before he continued.

"But before you go, now, I would like to suggest an even more merciful solution to you, Queen Camila. I publicly propose this to you in front of all of these witnesses here today. My offer is for you to keep your land and your kingdom. All you must do is marry me. Marry me, and rule along beside me." He waved his arm to the crowd and leaned in expectantly for her answer, "What say you?"

The queen looked at him in disgust. "You can have my land. My castle. My kingdom. But you will never have me."

This was no surprise to Jacob. Nevertheless, it did sting a little bit and angered him profusely. He yelled to his guards, "So be it. Get them out of here... get them out!"

"Yes, my lord," his men answered as they escorted everyone out the doors, out of the castle and into wagons awaiting to transport them unscathed to the outskirts, as promised.

The queen and the remainder of her courtiers were now unarmed, alone, and with no place else to go.

"Wherever shall we go, My Queen?" asked Mildred through her tears and sniffles.

"There is only one place that can guarantee our safety," the queen answered, sadly. She felt like a total failure for having trusted in Jacob. She took some comfort from seeing her mother Queen Joanna and the rest of her surviving knights.

Archbishop Nicholas was heard praying the Lord's Prayer aloud and the people were joining him in prayer.

"Pater noster, qui es in caelis: sanctificetur nomen tuum; Adveniat regnum tuum; fiat voluntas tua, sicut in caelo et in terra…"

Escorted from their own lands, they all rode along in silence. Camila could not help but see, scattered by the roadside, her army of knights, dead. They were left where they had fallen, and their armored bodies littered the roads all the way out of castle.

"Camila," Queen Joanna whispered to her daughter as she took her hand. "You acted bravely and made a very important decision as the monarch of the kingdom. You just saved the Green Dragoons and the entire royal court, and they will certainly live to fight another day."

"Oh, Mother, I am such a fool. The greatest fool, for trusting Jacob. Look at all those faces and bodies lying on the ground, dead. People I knew, people I grew up with. How do you explain that or justify that, Mother? How? I wish you knew how I felt right now," she said as tears rolled down her cheek.

"Sí, hija, losing loved ones hurt and, being the reigning monarch, it hurts twice as much. Because you feel responsible, and somehow you will always wonder if you could have done better. Yes, I know exactly how you feel. Your father and I endured more pain than you can ever fathom. But remember that ultimately you did what you had to do, and that no matter how you feel right now, you have saved all these people, and they are still under your care and responsibility as their queen," Joanna comforted her.

"Oh, Mama, I know that Father and you went through a lot and that you both were very wise throughout your reign. But look at me. I was entrusted to reign after you, and I have failed."

"Now, forgive me if I sound insensitive, but you need to focus on taking care of what you have right now in the present time, Camila. You are a true leader, Camila, and your citizens need you right here, right now."

Camila paused for a moment to digest what her mother had told her. "I did not look at it that way,

Mother. How much suffering must you have experienced for all those years. You are right, I need to stop feeling sorry for myself, and I need to focus on the people that remain and that will need to be looked after. Thank you for being there, Mother, and thank you for your support," Camila said with deep gratitude.

"You do not need to thank me. You are my daughter. You are a Garcia," Joanna assured her softly. "And you may slow down a Garcia, but you will never, ever stop us. We are ordained by God."

"Yes, I know God Almighty will never abandon me, or our people and that justice will be served sooner or later."

"That's my daughter," the queen beamed. "And I know this may sound like a bad time to say it, but your father would have been proud of you to see how strong you are."

Joanna gently pulled the queen's head onto her chest to nestle there in peace, security, and comfort as they continued their journey inside their bouncy little carriage until they reached the outskirts of Asturias.

Chapter 5
The Quest for Safe Haven

few hours later, Queen Camila and the remainder of her people were dropped off just across the border of Galicia. As the wagons drove away, returning to the Asturian castle, Pablo approached to check on the queen, "We still have a handful of strong knights to protect you, Your Majesty," the duke told her. "What shall be our destination?"

The queen responded, sadly, "The only way we would be protected, with no expectations of any marital or sexual propositions from a lord, is to head towards my brother's castle, Pablo."

"Back to El Castillo de la Galantería, ma'am," Pablo confirmed. "Very well, then."

"After all," the queen continued solemnly as she began walking, "Gerardo is my big brother, and I am sure that he will embrace me and my people and take us in, just as I would do for him. Besides, Mama is with me, so I am sure that he would be happy to see her safe.”

As soon as they entered King Gerardo’s territory, the queen and her survivors were intercepted by his patrolling knights. They immediately recognized her and rushed to her side. Together, they made haste to the king’s castle to give her and her people some food and relief after hours of dirty, dusty travel.

“My lord, my lord,” Marshal Miguel ran up to the king. “Forgive me, my lord. Today’s patrol has found and rescued Queen Camila and Queen Joanna, sire.”

Gerardo, although surprised by the news, had to suppress a little smile as he turned away from his marshal. He had not expected his sister’s kingdom to fall quite so quickly, and he did not want to gloat in front of his men.

After composing himself, he turned back towards his messenger and commanded them, “Bring in the guests and prepare the necessary accommodations to receive them.”

“Yes, my lord,” said the marshal, who hurried away to fulfill his duties.

Upon the queen’s arrival with what remained of her courtiers, the king came out and welcomed them all. “Camila,” Gerardo greeted her warmly. “Are you hurt at all?”

“Brother,” she broke into a smile of relief upon seeing him. “No, no, I am unscathed but some of my people require medical attention.”

Gerardo took her hands in his. “It shall be done. Immediately. Do not worry about a thing. I want you and your people to clean up and then join me for dinner," he smiled back at her. "We will have plenty of time to discuss what has happened. The important thing is that you and Mama are well."

"Thank you, my brother," she answered with a slight curtsy. Her eyes were a little misty now that she could relax under the safe protection of her brother and his entire kingdom. But she choked back the tears; she had made the choice to grieve only in private.

After dinner, Gerardo summoned Camila to the high court room to talk. "Tell me everything. I want details of all the treachery that has taken place. How did Count Jacob manage to infiltrate and take over the kingdom?"

Camila briefed him and spared no detail. She told him exactly what had transpired and what devious tactics were used to accomplish his plan. Gerardo was intrigued by everything she told him.

Finally, he pounded a fist to the table, "I swear to you. Sister, I swear that I will take the land back. Jacob may think he knows our land, but he does not know it like I do. He does not have the loyalty of the people, and, with the information that you gave me, I now know where your loyal clans retreated to. I will use that information to take the castle and destroy Jacob the traitor once and for all. Te lo prometo."

"Thank you, brother," Camila hugged him in deep gratitude. "I know you are a man of your word and will right this great wrong against our family legacy. Muchas gracias."

Hostile Takeover

Early the next morning, Gerardo gathered his knights and proceeded towards Asturias. Memories of yesteryear, when the land was under his father's reign, flooded back as he saw the familiar territories.

It brought back that same resentment that his father had chosen not to grant the entire kingdom to him. "Had my father given me the land to begin with, we would not be in this predicament," he lamented. "And all those lives would not have been lost."

"Your father would be proud of you for making things right, sire," Daniel encouraged him.

"Daniel, we need to search for Camila's clans, using the information she entrusted to me."

"Yes, my lord," the count replied.

Back in Asturias at the Castillo del Eliseo, Count Jacob held his own crowning ceremony to acknowledge his reign over Asturias.

"Thanks to his leadership and guidance we now have a kingdom of our own. I, Baron Henry Johnson, have the honor to recognize and pronounce thee, King Jacob Cedillo. Hail to the King, long live the King," the cheers were echoed by Jacob's men.

"I, Jacob Cedillo, having served as the count of León and having rightfully taken over the Kingdom of Asturias, I accept the monarchy as the king." The men cheered and banged their chalices on tables to celebrate their new leader.

"Furthermore, Baron Henry Johnson and Marshal Roberto Alvarez, step forward," Jacob ordered. They both did as commanded.

"Take a knee," he added, and they both complied.

"I, King Jacob Cedillo, execute my first decree. In gratitude for your loyalty and your actions in the battlefield, I dub thee, Sir Henry Johnson, Count of Asturias. And Sir Roberto Alvarez, I dub thee Viscount of Asturias. Rise, Sir Henry and Sir Roberto," Jacob commanded. Everyone cheered once again and celebrated throughout the night.

***

King Gerardo and his army crossed into Asturian territory and shortly after that reached the clans' hiding areas within the Tito Bustillo Cave and the Sidron Cave territory. They were located at the outskirts of the kingdom. Immediately, the wounded among them were sent back home to Galicia to be tended to.

"This is King Gerardo of Galicia, brother to Queen Camila of Asturias," Daniel addressed the clansmen. "He takes on the quest of securing our lands back from Lord Jacob, the usurper, who is for now the proclaimed king of the land. Those able to fight, join in the quest in the name of your queen."

Two men stepped forward from the crowd and paid their respects to the king. One of them said, "I am commander Juan Carlos Herrera and to my right is Captain Ivan Escobar, my lord. We would be honored to join you. What do you require for us to do, sire?"

"Your role is to infiltrate the walls of the castle," Gerardo explained "You are capable of blending in and making yourselves appear to be humble and submissive peasants, hard-working men of the kingdom."

"We are honored to fight alongside with you, my lord. We will join you in the quest to get the kingdom back for our queen," Juan Carlos replied.

With that in mind, Camila's clans added themselves to King Gerardo's ranks without hesitation. The clansmen were led by Gerardo who saw the irony of using tactics of infiltration against Jacob, just as he had infiltrated the castle under Camila.

Upon their arrival at the Castillo del Eliseo Asturias, the clansmen split to go on their own mission while Gerardo's army kept moving forward.

While his spies snuck over the back walls, he made enough noise approaching the castle with his army from a distance to assure that his presence was afforded the castle's full attention. He wanted Jacob to know he was coming for him, that he was coming to take over the throne. Most importantly, the diversion was working.

"Lord Jacob! Lord Jacob! My King," Viscount Roberto said, his voice quaking with fear. "King Gerardo approaches quickly."

Jacob was not surprised. "Very well. That hot headed fool Gerardo. No planning or strategy, just walking right up to my front door and banging it down, I suppose. What a clumsy tactician," Jacob laughed and the whole court laughed with him. "It looks like I am going to be expanding my territory again soon. He does not stand a chance with my military prowess. Prepare to defend."

"Yes, my lord," his division captains, Henry and Roberto, replied.

"Are we to meet him in the battlefield, my lord?" Count Henry inquired.

"No, no need. We have plenty of time. We will wait for Gerardo's arrival and defend the castle from within the walls. To bring out the army would be more costly and require a slower defense. Inside the castle walls we have everything we need. An extensive supply of arrows, weapons, food, and water. Not to mention the high ground of the castle garrisons," Jacob explained.

"Very well, my lord. I will get everyone ready for their arrival."

"Let them come," Jacob challenged the room, unruffled and carefree.

Gerardo arrived at the castle by nightfall. His approach was seen from a long distance away because of the castle's view atop the hill.

"Stop here, set up camp but be prepared to attack at a moment's notice," Gerardo told Daniel who was near him. "I would have preferred a battle across an open field, but I knew that would not be the case. So, it is a good idea to let the men rest before tomorrow's combat."

They also awaited the sign that the queen's loyal clans had successfully infiltrated the castle and had reached their positions. Meanwhile, his men finished setting up base camp.

"Bring the catapults forward, and put them in position," the king ordered.

His men brought them forward with mighty heaves, as requested.

———————◆———————

"My lord," called Viscount Roberto. "They're lining up the catapults now, sire."

"Very well." responded Jacob. "Prepare the archers and our own catapults from the courtyard. Be ready to counterstrike."

"Yes, sire," said the viscount.

Jacob's men were in position looking down from the high walls of the castle and led by Roberto, while the inside courtyard ground troops were preparing to defend and counterattack with their own catapults.

The ground defense was commanded by Count Henry, who was delegating the king's orders.

"You, there," pointing at a group of men standing by the catapults, "prepare the catapults. Make sure that they are set to reach the proper distance over the castle's walls and into the enemy's line."

Immediately, the men quickly went to work on the catapults to set the distance, placing the boulders on them and locking them in firing position.

A second group approached the catapults. "Who are you guys?" they questioned those setting up the catapults. "We are the ones that usually set these up," they continued to question.

The men already assigned by the count were agitated by the men questioning them, and a member of the first group answered, "Does it really matter who sets them up? Go get all boulders and rocks that you can for the catapults to shoot. We can take care of this."

Henry noticed them all arguing by the catapults, and, since there was no time for that, he needed to intervene. "What are you men doing?" Henry questioned them. Before they could answer, he interrupted them. "Do not just stand there, go get boulders and rocks to prepare for the battle," Henry pointed in the direction he needed them to work.

The additional men left the area as commanded and went to get the rocks and boulders requested.

❖

Outside of the castle, Gerardo had waited long enough and was eager to start the attack. "Launch the catapults," he commanded.

"Launch the catapults," his command was echoed across the army. Big boulders of rock that had been slathered with oil were now lit up by torches.

They were launched one by one, creating a tidal wave of flaming strikes against the castle walls. Some even launched over the walls and decimated the castle's interior.

Jacob observed the maneuver from a high tower. Once the initial volley had ended, he ordered for his knights to respond in kind. "Release the catapults! Release the catapults," he commanded, as he scanned the castle for damage. "Henry, make sure you keep them aimed at their line of fire and force the enemy to stay back."

"Yes, my lord," the count answered. "You heard the king, fire those catapults."

The night sky lit up again like an odd sunrise as the fire balls began going back and forth, lighting up the treetops and casting strange moving shadows across the ground. The castle was struck again and again with an occasional boulder lobbed over the walls into the interior ballrooms, the main reception area room, as well as the church, killing and destroying whatever was in its way.

Jacob's counterattack was not as effective. The catapults were not quite leveled to the proper distance where they could inflict maximum damage on the enemy.

Jacob questioned the matter, "Henry, what is going on down there? Why are we not hitting our targets like we should?"

"The catapults are damaged, my lord," responded Henry, "it seems that the ropes are not long enough to reach full distance for some reason."

Jacob yelled in disbelief, "What do you mean? Fix them now!"

"We are trying to fix the situation, sire," Henry said. "Roberto, send more men our way to help assist with the situation."

"Right away, Count," the viscount answered. "Quickly, you heard him, some of you need to leave the tower and go down to assist them now."

⟡

Gerardo knew that he needed to take advantage of the situation. "Archers, fire. Focus on sending waves of arrows down into the castle courtyard to take out Jacob's army."

"Archers, prepare to deploy the arrows," the cry was echoed down the ranks by Count Daniel who was by his side and by his lateral division captains Baron Edward and Marshal Miguel.

Rows of archers ran into the field just beyond the catapult range. They lined and stretched back their bowstrings. "Fire," they heard from behind them.

Gerardo simultaneously let loose another barrage of fiery rocks. Alongside the blanket of arrows, they scored hundreds of casualties.

⟡

Jacob watched his men fall to the ground from their balcony posts along their high-walled positions; in addition to those getting killed at the ground level.

Jacob was dumbstruck by how ineffective his defenses were. He was losing the upper hand quickly. At this rate, he would lose the whole castle in a couple more hours.

"Fix those cursed catapults," Jacob yelled to his commanders who flinched at his desperate rage. "We need more distance to be effective."

Henry answered under duress, "My lord, we are not able to do much currently, the enemy's arrows are making it impossible to work freely on the catapults. Someone has seriously tampered with them, sire. Where are those men you sent over, Roberto?"

The viscount went on to look for the men he sent to assist with the catapults and to his surprise he found them killed in the hallway staircase that connected the floors of the tower. "How could this be?" he wondered aloud. "There is no way that any arrows or boulders could have reached them here." Roberto ran back upstairs to gather more men. He surmised a possibility of an enemy infiltration.

When Roberto arrived at the top, his men were cowering behind the wall to not get killed from the aerial attack. Even Roberto withdrew behind an archway as another barrage littered the entire area.

He leaned over the wall and yelled down, "Henry, be careful down there; we have intruders inside."

The count could not make out what the viscount had said due to all the destruction that was being done. He, himself, was too busy ducking for cover, which made it harder to pay attention to Roberto's warning.

"You there, go down and find the enemy that infiltrated our stronghold and kill them," Roberto commanded a group of men.

"Yes, Viscount," they responded and went on their way down the tower stairs, slowly crawling to stay safe from incoming strikes.

The continual bombardment of rocks and arrows was now making it almost impossible for Jacob's army to make any corrections as they had to abandon their posts for safety. Jacob watched as his commanders and men ran to take cover. "Cowards! Get back to your posts," he yelled angrily from the safety of the tower.

The castle's catapults were completely abandoned. The only safe place was indoors and behind the castle walls. Jacob began to wonder what had gone wrong. "Roberto, what are you doing, hiding behind that wall? Get out there, and do your job, and lead the counterattack."

"My lord, every time we stand to shoot our arrows at the enemy, their arrows or boulders take us out by the handful, sire."

"Stop making excuses," Jacob yelled in desperation. "Can't anyone do something right, today? I have commanded scores of battles before. How is it that our catapults are so ineffective? Roberto, gather the remaining men and go out using the tunnels," Jacob commanded. "Set up a stronghold in the west, and flank Gerardo from there. There is no use for us to be pinned in here."

"As you wish, my lord," Roberto answered. "Knights, follow me!" The viscount and his knights mounted their horses once they were able to do so and exited out the tunnels. They then headed the long way around the castle to confront Gerardo's army.

As they came around in position, they were spotted by Gerardo's west flank, which shifted immediately into attack formation, ready to charge.

Marshal Miguel noticed Roberto's approach and announced, "Sire, the enemy has come out, and they're getting ready to charge."

"Daniel, break off, and take care of them," the king commanded. "Take your division and Miguel's men. Miguel will stay here with me with my divisions."

"Yes, sire. I will make sure they pay for their insolence. Vamos. Charge!" Daniel bellowed taking the two divisions and immediately riding down to intercept Roberto and his men.

Roberto saw the action taking place, that Daniel's division broke off and started heading in his direction. "Men, this is our kingdom. Defend it with your life. Charge!" the viscount roared as they rode forward to meet Daniel's attack.

The two units clashed in the middle of the field and began their fierce encounter; swords were swinging, and men and horses and body parts were dropping to the ground. Daniel was surrounded by a group of skilled knights that had served under the protection of King Celestino's Green Dragoons and were now under the assignment of Gerardo's army.

"Follow me, let's make a hole through this enemy's line," Daniel commanded. They began to create a hole in between the enemy, killing everyone in proximity.

Roberto's men were experienced, too. Most of them had seen action in different campaigns with King Alfonso XI and knew how to read combat situations.

"Left flank, left flank," Roberto directed, as the left side of Daniel's army began to weaken.

Roberto's men circled around to sweep their enemies from the outer perimeter, working their way in towards the center of the battle.

Back inside the castle, Count Henry was unable to do much from his stronghold and took cover with the men assigned to his position. He suddenly noticed a large group of villagers passing through the hallway inside the castle. They were killing his men and advancing towards Lord Jacob's location.

Henry immediately shouted at his men, "Prepare to defend and hold our ground. We have enemy men approaching fast. Archers. Fix your sights on the east halls," he positioned himself to defend this area.

His men turned around and retreated away from the front of the castle to relocate, as ordered by the count. The unknown villagers were none other than Juan Carlos and his clansmen. They held their position from the east side of the castle and were preparing themselves to engage in the open fight after having been spotted by Henry.

"Archers, open fire at the enemy," Henry commanded. His men complied. The clansmen took cover within their own stronghold, and they held their positions.

"Attack!" an additional command was heard. Another group of clansmen led by Ivan charged Henry and his men from behind. Henry managed to turn around and take cover from the arrows shot at them.

"Look behind you, look behind you," he warned his men as his division shifted again to take cover from their new threat. Henry and his men found themselves surrounded with no direction to retreat. To the east, Juan Carlos was there; to the northwest, Ivan had come around; to the south the bombardment continued.

————— ❖ —————

Boom...
A loud explosion, which was heard for miles, reverberated from within the castle itself. Jacob ran to a western window and saw one of the walls collapsing.

————— ❖ —————

"The walls are down, my lord," Miguel reported to Gerardo.

"Very well. Miguel, take the fourth division and go to the exit point of the castle's escape tunnels, in case Jacob decides to flee in that direction. If he does, bring him to me dead or alive, it really does not matter at this point. Although I would not mind seeing him face-to-face."

"Yes, sire," Marshal Miguel replied and rode away.

"Attack!" Gerardo wasted no time and ordered a full attack onto the castle. Jacob's knights had taken a big hit and the majority had been killed or had sustained injuries that made them unable to defend their current locations.

The explosion distracted Henry and his castle defenders long enough for Juan Carlos and Ivan's marauders to rush them. Henry was the only noble and trained knight in the stronghold, as the rest of these men were mostly archers and catapult soldiers.

Henry took his sword out, slashing a group of Ivan's men holding his own. He struck the first attacker with a simple overhead swing to the clansman's head. He then spun 360 degrees to evade an incoming attacker and swung his sword towards the clansman's head, taking it clean off at the shoulders.

He then faced another soldier approaching him from the left flank, and he immediately swung his sword at a low rising level, cutting off his leg. Henry quickly moved over to face Ivan's direction and thrusted his sword into a clansman pressing forward.

Ivan saw Henry's quick and swift approach and turned to face him and fight him in battle.

Henry carried on, attacking another clansmen in between the two of them by simply deflecting a strike and thrusting his sword into the attacker.

Henry sensed motion on his right flank. However, when he turned to defend himself, Juan Carlos was right upon him and struck Henry with a hatchet between his eyes. Henry's body instantly dropped dead.

Juan Carlos looked at Ivan who nodded his head in gratitude for coming to his aid.

The rest of Henry's unit was easily overwhelmed and dispatched by Juan Carlos and Ivan's men. The queen's clansmen had done their job. They had blown up the wall and tampered with Jacob's catapults. They were the infiltrators that Henry and Robert had discovered and attempted, unsuccessfully, to intercept.. Instead, the clansmen hacked away at Jacob's army from the inside, decimating their numbers.

These actions opened the castle up like a gigantic front door swinging wide open. It gave Gerardo the opportunity for a direct strike, as his soldiers scurried quickly and efficiently inside the castle walls.

———❖———

Jacob knew this was an unmitigated disaster. The fighting continued, but the battle was lost. The only thing for him to do now was feign a surrender and then make good his escape. Jacob gathered up his remaining defenders. "Come with me," Jacob commanded. "We need to escape through the lower tunnels. Knights, guards, archers, anyone capable of defending me, lead the way to the tunnels."

As Jacob continued to advance to the west wing and towards the lower-level tunnels, they grabbed their horses from the stables and started to charge their way out to in hopes of finding safety beyond the castle walls.

❖

Triumphant, King Gerardo entered through the castle breach with his second wave. The remainder of Jacob's army was either dead or in the process of dying or surrendering. Most threw down their weapons and welcomed the opportunity to join King Gerardo's army in surrender.

Gerardo's knights rounded up all their prisoners, all that was left of the enemy inside, and corralled them into the main courtyard littered with bodies and burnt debris and pockmarks from the assault.

❖

The battle outside the castle also was impacted by the explosion which startled Roberto's horse, since he and his men were closest to the outside walls of the battlefield. The startled, bucking horse threw Roberto from the saddle.

Roberto bravely fought from the ground. As an attacker rode near to run him over, he ducked his head while swinging his sword and cutting the attacking horse's legs from underneath, causing his enemy rider to fall off his horse.

An additional attacker approached him, swinging his sword at his head, and Roberto rolled off to evade the strike. He sprang back to his feet and grabbed a lance with which he impaled another horse, throwing the rider and breaking his neck.

Roberto quickly spun to his left as he heard another charging enemy on horseback but it was too late. Daniel rode from behind and hit him on the head with the sword's handle, knocking him unconscious. Soon afterwards, those who were left alive had either surrendered or were killed.

"Yes! We have victory," Daniel yelled to his men. "Let us finish this," Daniel and his men crossed the enemy lines, subdividing Roberto's knights, isolating the men, making it easier to annihilate them.

Thomas Diaz, Daniel's under marshal pointed out, "Baron, a group of men on horses is trying to escape from the castle."

Daniel quickly delegated. "Take two squads and finish things up here, the rest of the men, follow me. We need to cut off their escape."

Thomas replied, "Yes, my lord," while Daniel proceeded towards Jacob and his men.

Jacob's men saw Daniel's men heading after them and warned Jacob. "My lord, we have been spotted; Gerardo's men are chasing us."

"Quickly, we have to make it to the forest," Jacob replied. "We can light up the forest behind us, that's the only way we can stand a chance." He and his remaining knights rode at full speed in an attempt to save themselves.

"Wait," Jacob commanded while pulling his horse to stop. He raised his right hand to signal his men to do the same. He saw Miguel and his division were bisecting his getaway path from the front. Daniel was also gaining ground on Jacob, heading straight towards them at full speed.

Miguel yelled out, "Here they come. Swords out."

Jacob needed to decide what to do next. He pulled out his sword and his men did the same. Jacob looked behind and saw that Daniel's division had gained distance and that he was surrounded.

"Alright," Jacob commanded. "Stop. Put your weapons down and keep your hands up. It is over." His men obeyed, wearily.

Gerardo's man circled around Jacob and his men and pointed their weapons at them. Daniel ordered his men, "Drag him down off his horse, and tie him up. We will present him before the king."

They did as commanded and brought Jacob before Gerardo.

❖

"Mercy! Mercy, I beg of you, great king," Jacob skittered forward on hands and knees, groveling. "A king should never kill another king."

Gerardo's eyes narrowed, "You come before me and ask for mercy? But you had none before, betraying my sister."

"Oh, but I did. I allowed her to live. And escape unharmed. I allowed your mother Queen Joanna to live. I allowed for her royal court to live. Show me mercy, as I have already shown to you and your mighty blood line, Good King."

Gerardo knew that, whatever his decision was to be, it would mark him for all of history. Was he to be known as merciful? Was he to totally wipe out Jacob's army and kill everyone to show his power and strength? Gerardo looked at Jacob, still down on his knees.

"You want mercy? I will show you how merciful I am. This land no longer belongs to you. I, King Gerardo, son of King Celestino, have indisputably defeated you," Gerardo responded, indicating the castle around them with a sweep of his arm. Gerardo then turned to all the witnesses there. "Am I not the rightful king of this kingdom? I take claim of it. I claim it as my right for having won in battle. I claim it as such, for this was my father's land, and I am the rightful heir to the throne. It will not be disputed by any means for my word is absolute."

As his words echoed off the walls, he turned again towards Jacob and spat. "As for you, Lord Jacob. You did show mercy to my mother and sister. For them, I will spare your life. I am, after all, merciful. But I hold no sympathy for anybody's army, my sister's, or yours. Your knights shall die before your eyes, for it was you who led them to their doom. Stand him up."

A couple of Gerardo's knights jerked him to his feet. Jacob was now facing his own knights, helpless, defeated, and afraid for his future. Henry, his right hand in everything he did, lay on the ground dead. He didn't know where Roberto's body lay. It was missing among the pile of bodies. A group of his knights was already lined up against the courtyard walls. Gerardo's archers took their positions opposite them.

The king nodded to his commander who bellowed, "Archers? Fire!"

Jacob had been overwhelmingly defeated. He was no match for Camila's brother nor for the wrath that drove him to victory. He was now facing the great unknown of what would become of his life and the lives of his remaining knights. How had he been so quickly overcome? He never did realize that there were men loyal to the queen hidden within the safety of the castle walls. An oversight that had cost him everything he had.

Groups at a time were lined up in front of him, and they were all summarily executed before him. There was nothing he could do but simply watch, horrified and saddened. He tried to put his head down and avoid the gruesome catastrophe, but Gerardo ordered his men to hold his head upright and steady.

"If he lowers his head again," Gerardo warned with an icy stare at Jacob, "remove it from his shoulders."

Gerardo sent a strong, unmistakable message to everyone across the kingdoms that day that he and his family were not to be trifled with and that he would destroy anyone who dared to test that resolve.

Chapter 6
Outcast

Gerardo—having given the order to execute Jacob's remaining knights—needed to redeem himself to his own knights and everyone in the land, for that matter. He had shown his ruthlessness to a defeated and surrendered enemy. Now he needed them to see that he was also a just and fair ruler. His father King Celestino and his sister Queen Camila would have never killed a surrendered knight brigade.

He walked by the fallen corpses towards Jacob. "Gerardo," Jacob pleaded, again, "it is wrong for a king to kill another king. Even if you command another to do it in your stead, it will be by your own hand."

Gerardo scanned everyone's faces and saw nothing but shocked expressions. He looked back at

Jacob and told him, "I will grant you your life. For I am a merciful king. But know this, I will hunt you down, and whoever is with you, if I ever see you within my lands or if I ever find out that you have anything to do with any type of foul doing towards me or towards anyone in my kingdom. Do you understand?"

Jacob looked up at him, greatly relieved. "Yes, I understand," he replied before the king could change his mind.

Gerardo bellowed to his guards, "Get him out of here. Get him off my land, and if he is ever seen here again, as I have announced, kill him. I have spoken, and it is not to be contested. I am Gerardo the Merciful!"

"Yes, sire," Marshal Miguel replied. "Guards, prepare the escort."

Jacob was taken away to the southern outskirts of the land where they untied him and turned him loose to venture about on his own recognizance. As for the rest of Gerardo's men, they began to celebrate their mighty victory and the freedom of Asturias.

The queen's clansmen had gathered off to the side and let Gerardo's men take care of the kill orders, as commanded by their king. They retreated to a different location in the castle, away from any non-Asturians, to discuss what they had seen.

"I do not like the outcome of the battle," Commander Juan Carlos told his clansmen. "I am afraid that we just handed over our queen's kingdom to Gerardo the Demented."

The loyal clansmen nodded in agreement. They looked at each other, uncertain what was to become of them now. Juan Carlos continued, "If what Gerardo said to Jacob is true, he has claimed Asturias for himself. Therefore, he is betraying our alliance, and betraying our queen."

"Que carajo!" Captain Ivan exclaimed. "We should hang him before he leaves the land and spare ourselves a wagon load of future troubles."

"No," Juan Carlos responded. "He mentioned it, but he has not acted upon it. We still need to wait and see what he decides to do since the announcement could very well have been just an act of showmanship for Jacob's benefit. After all, he is our queen's brother, and she would not want us to make such a brash decision without her consent. We will wait for the queen to decide what is to take place when the time comes."

Ivan immediately replied with his concern. "Comandante, our hiding places. The king knows of their locations, our women and children are compromised."

"I am glad that you, too, have the same thoughts, Ivan," said Juan Carlos. "We will move our camps to the Holy Cave of Covadonga territory and will use its blessed anointing to defeat anyone who dares to attack us. Just like our ancestor Pelagius defeated his enemies and claimed his victory in the end."

"How would the queen find us?" Ivan asked.

"My friend, how else do you think that I know to go there?" Juan Carlos said with a twinkle in his steel blue eyes. "From the time of our Visigoth ancestors, that has always been our safe haven."

———————◆———————

Gerardo returned to his Kingdom of Galicia, where his sister Camila anxiously awaited him. Upon their arrival the king and his knights passed before a crowd of ecstatic citizens ready to receive them home victoriously. Flowers and petals littered the streets, being tossed by the adoring crowd, eager to bestow their affections upon their returning heroes.

Camila was delighted to see him again and ran to him as he entered the castle. "My dear brother, I am so glad that you are well." She threw her arms around him. Their first hug in a long, long time, longer than he could remember. It was nice.

"It is good to be back, sister," he smiled down at her. Then, they retired to the high court room to talk in private.

"Tell me, what happened," Camila prompted him, eagerly anticipating the details. "The knights you sent back gave us the great news that you defeated Jacob."

"Of course, I did. Of course, as I promised you. I swore that I would take the land back. And so I took the land that belonged to our forefathers." Gerardo filled a goblet with mead. He was famished from the long, dusty ride.

"Oh, thank you so much, my brother," she gushed, throwing her arms around him tightly again for another hug.

Gerardo gently pushed her back to be able to see her eye to eye. "Now, understand, I have reclaimed it as the new king," he said plainly, while watching her expression closely.

Camila released him with a confused look on her face. She walked away thoughtfully, and then turned back to him. What Gerardo had said did not make sense to her. Cautiously she probed, "You have claimed the land as the new king? What do you mean by that?" She paused momentarily, searching his face. "What you mean to say is that you reclaimed the land in order to give it back to me, correct, brother?"

Gerardo, took a few steps up to the throne and sat down upon it, swirling the drink in his goblet. "Look, Camila. Did you really think I was going to expose my life, my kingdom, and my people and then simply return the land back to you as if nothing had happened? All while you waited here so comfortably in my castle. Were you not taken care of here? Were you not fed and catered to as a queen? All while my men and I lost so many of our brothers and knights in battle? Is that what you thought?"

Camila could not believe what she was hearing. "Gerardo, what are you saying?"

"What I am saying is, well, were you?" Gerardo raised his voice even more. "Speak, woman."

"Of course, I was here, just as you said," she was now in tears, both from a sadness and from an anger rising from deep within her.

Gerardo was sympathetic to his sister but would not budge, "Look here, Camila. I will not abandon you. I will not abandon my own sister, nor will I make a mockery of her. But *you* had your chance to rule, and you lost it. You joined with that snake Jacob as your man and you slept with him. And who can blame him for wanting to take his place as the king of the land. You did this to yourself, and I will not allow you to lose our father's land again. Do you understand?"

Camila wiped away some tears and jabbed a finger angrily at him, "I *understand* that you always wanted my land. You were never happy for me. You were always jealous and upset that father knew better than to allow you to keep Asturias. And how dare you claim that I slept with Jacob! How dare you say that it was okay for him to take the land from me! I always knew you were ambitious, brother, but this? What you are doing is shameful, and if our forefathers were looking at you right now…"

"But they are not," Gerardo interrupted her. "They are not looking at me right now. We each do what we must to survive, and we do what we must to expand. That is the reason why you were never a good leader of the land. A good leader would know that. That is the reason that you cannot be a queen any longer. A queen in name, maybe, but not a queen with power."

Camila was devastated and had no words to express the pain of such betrayal from her own brother. She turned around and started to leave the room.

Gerardo called after her, "Camila, listen." He caught up to her and grabbed her arm. "I have not forgotten who you are. You are my sister, and I will not abandon you as I have already told you. I will allow you to go back to Asturias. You will oversee the kingdom as the queen. You will have my full protection from everyone. I will make sure of that. I swear it."

Camila paused momentarily to compose herself and pulled herself loose from Gerardo's clutches. She took a step back to gain some distance before pointing her finger at him again, "You make it sound so good, Gerardo. You make things sound so good that you think you can bewitch anyone with your words and that they'll follow you even to their death. Not out of loyalty or love towards you. They will follow you because of your deceptive delusions."

Gerardo walked away to a table that had a map of the whole land on it and started messing with the army and horse figurines, as if planning for battle. He only half paid attention to Camila as she continued, "The problem for you is that I know the true you. The scared you and, yes, I know that you live in fear."

Gerardo looked at her, upset at her accusation of being afraid. Camila continued to go off on him, waving her arms passionately. "Of course, you will protect the land and make sure that no one takes it. It is in your best interest, since you think it all belongs to you, anyway." She tapped an index finger to her temple. "Up here in your land of make-believe."

Gerardo looked back at her with cold, dark eyes. Camila knew she was on to something, so she continued, "As for me, continuing to rule as a queen overseeing the kingdom?" She turned slightly and chuckled with sarcasm. "Of course, you would do that. It would be idiotic, not to have me there under your thumb. I would tend to the daily reign, and you will not have to worry about a thing. But you know what, brother? I know exactly why you want me there."

"Why is that?" Gerardo's interest was genuinely peaked now.

As she came close to him again, she pointed at his chest. "Because in all your ruthless, bloodthirsty ambition you still want to look like the merciful hero. The people's king!" And she looked at his eyes, waiting for his response.

Gerardo stood quiet, weighing her words. He wanted to refute them, but deep down inside he knew that Camila spoke the truth. "So, will you rule as my queen or not?"

Camila turned away in disbelief. Nothing she said was getting through to him. She might be the queen in name but she would evermore just be his pawn. She took a deep breath and finally answered, "Very well, brother. I will go along with your unconvincing charade. I will take care of the land, my land, and the people of the Kingdom of Asturias. It was, after all, our father's dying wish."

She knew that, if she did not acquiesce, the people in the kingdom would suffer greatly and that Gerardo would always find ways to overtax them and use them to fight his wars, always mistreating them. First to the battle, last to be compensated with table scraps. She was not going to be responsible for having her people go through any more tribulations.

Gerardo smiled, "I knew you would come to your senses." He walked to the nearby table laden with fruits and snacks. He perched against it as he grabbed a couple of grapes and began to bite them in half. "I knew you could never resort to becoming a peasant. But know this, sister. I will now receive the taxes from your capital Oviedo as the true ruler of the kingdom." He watched her slowly comprehend the fullness of the command.

Camila opened her arms in disbelief, "How do you expect me to rule your kingdom, brother, if I cannot collect the taxes?"

"Leave that to me. I will send you the resources to move forward, but the taxes will first come to me directly. And then you will get the share that I think you shall need in order to govern." Gerardo proceeded back to his throne and sat down.

"An allowance," Camila leered. "How quaint. Very well, just remember, I know you plan to send me nothing but the crumbs from your precious taxes. But if the land decays and the people rebel with no hope and no honor, it will be on you."

"No, sister. That decision and choice will be on you," he stared at her, daring her to say something else. But she knew better than to poke a bear. He barked into the silence, "Miguel! Send word to prepare for the queen's escort back to Asturias."

"Yes, sire," the marshal bowed and then exited quickly.

When he left the room, Camila looked up at Gerardo. "Take care of yourself, brother. May God and the souls of our forefathers have mercy upon you."

She walked away to prepare for their imminent departure, while he remained in the room by himself. His shoulders sagged the minute she was gone. That last battle had been as wearisome as some of the wars he had fought. Plus, he was not totally convinced he had won it fully. Only time would tell.

Chapter 7
Lord Mullah El Hassan

Queen Camila prepared to return to the Kingdom of Asturias. She began with a letter that she wrote at the table in her room. Afterwards, she sealed the letter with the royal seal on her ring and then went to talk to her duke. "Pablo, please have our court and all our citizens readied to return home. Make sure the proper arrangements are taken to bring enough food and water for the road."

"Of course, Your Majesty. I will distribute your Green Dragoons to set a perimeter of defense around the caravan, My Queen."

"Very well, Pablo, however, do keep in mind that we are going to be escorted by my brother's knights, so do coordinate carefully."

"Of course, my lady," Pablo replied.

"Thank you, Pablo. One more thing. Please select a small team and have Marshal Diego lead them. I have a special assignment for them. I need them to deliver a message to Juan Carlos, and my brother cannot learn of it."

Pablo agreed, "I know just the ones to send, ma'am. I would trust them with my life."

The queen continued, "Here is the letter I want Diego to deliver to Juan Carlos. I want to let him know of our arrival and intent. Now, if I know Juan Carlos, he will not be found in the usual hiding spot. They will have moved to their safe haven at the Holy Cave of Covadonga territory. Diego knows how to get there."

"He does, indeed," Pablo confirmed. "I personally had him go with me before."

"Very well," said Camila. "I will need the full report from Juan Carlos and Ivan. Diego can bring it back to me. Please remind him that discretion is of the highest order."

"Will do, Your Majesty."

Camila was anxious to meet with her loyal clans who had survived the siege and the takeover of the kingdom from Jacob, but she could not risk giving away their involvement and expose their whereabouts. She knew they'd be waiting there with pertinent and timely information for her.

After her meeting, she went to alert her mother. She quickly cracked her door open and poked her head inside, "Mother, start packing and grab all the valuables we may still have in Galicia. We need to leave now, and please bring that portrait of father hanging on the wall. We will return it to its rightful place of honor." Camila did not wait for an answer;

she left her room as soon as she gave her the message and quietly closed the door.

Her mother was seated on a vanity chair, unsure of why they were leaving so soon. A thousand questions in her mind. But the curtness of her daughter's instruction was enough to invigorate her to quickly comply.

Within the hour, Pablo had returned with an update and met with Queen Camila in her chambers. She was there, packed and ready, along with the queen mother. "The citizens of your kingdom are ready to depart, Your Majesty."

"Thank you, Pablo, I will be out shortly. Please escort my mother down to the carriage."

"Yes, ma'am. Pablo then turned towards Queen Joanna, "Your Majesty, please come with me. I will send someone for your things."

"Thank you, that would be nice," Queen Joanna answered. Her cheeks were a little flushed, and her eyes were misty.

The queen mother and the duke began to walk down the corridor of the castle. Joanna commented, as tears rolled down her cheeks, "I feel like this is going to be the last time I ever set foot in these corridors."

"As your loyal servant, ma'am, I can relate to your feelings," Pablo patted her arm at his elbow to comfort her. "One never knows. Perhaps a day will come when you will be welcomed back to visit your son."

❖

Gerardo had a large army ready to escort them home. Once there, the garrison was to remain in Asturias in the protection of the land. Equal protection from without and within its castle walls.

Then the king summoned Lord Mullah el Hassan. Lord Mullah was a Saracen Knight, proclaimed to be an emissary of peace throughout the kingdoms. Sources said that he had hailed from the Moorish Kingdom of Granada, and that his place of service was Malaga.

Gerardo remembered overhearing Lord Mullah speaking with some of the nobles at the reception on his coronation day.

"The battle to reconquer Malaga was fierce, but it only took an hour to clear it from any danger," Lord Mullah stated with pride and confidence. "We had the enemy running scared for their lives."

"It is impressive, Lord Mullah," Count Walter Gallegos replied with deep admiration. "In Segovia we do not see much action, but it is good to know that in case we ever run into any confrontation, King George can call upon you as his ally."

Count Carlos Montes also agreed, "It sure is impressive. Wow, I don't know how you overcame the enemy so fast, must have been quite the storm the way you routed them, Count Mullah."

"Yes, of course," Count Mullah shrugged matter-of-factly. "If Allah wills it, my men and I will be there when your kingdoms call upon me; that's why we have an alliance."

King Gerardo loved this concept of having influential lords as allies and wanted to join their growing coalition. Mullah had simply made a big name for himself, and the reigning monarchs had heard of his legendary accomplishments.

For today's meeting, Gerardo had his court standing by, serving as witnesses. Lord Mullah entered the throne room and presented himself before King Gerardo, taking a knee. He placed his right hand across his chest and slightly bowed his head. "As-salamu alaykum," he greeted the king.

"Wa-alaykum-salaam," Gerardo responded. "Rise, Lord Mullah, thank you for being one of the first to show me support when I became a king."

"Of course, sire. I am at your service, just as I was for your father."

"I have known of you for some time now, and I saw you visit my father; your loyalty inspires my trust in you. Allow me to ask you," the king continued. "I have always seen you with quite an army. And I always wondered how it is that you have grown such a force?"

"Sire," Mullah explained. "As you are aware, I travel from placc to place, promoting peace across the territories of the different kingdoms. In return, the monarchs of the kingdoms assign men to me, to represent them in the name of peace and happiness in the lands."

"Well, in that case I find it very exciting to offer you the following: how would you like to become a lord in my kingdom?" Gerardo held up a hand and continued, "Now, before you answer that question, I am aware that you currently hold the rank of a count. Am I right?"

"That is correct, sire," Mullah answered.

"If you were to join me and be one of my trusted captains, I would bestow upon you the rank of duke. What say you?"

This was an interesting situation for both Gerardo and Mullah. Lord Mullah saw the opportunity to grow closer to the monarchy, and this was what he had been longing to achieve.

"Sire, you are too kind, and I would not want to offend you by declining your proposal. I will humbly accept your offer and know that my army and I are now at your service."

"Kneel before me," Mullah did as commanded. "Do you, Mullah el Hassan, promise to join me as my loyal servant and be a protector to my kingdom?"

"I do," Mullah responded.

"I, King Gerardo Garcia, and by the power invested in me as the King of Galicia, bestow upon thee, Lord Mullah, the royal title of Duke. Rise, Duke Mullah."

Mullah stood up as ordered and waited as the impromptu ceremony continued.

"Lord Mullah, you are the first person appointed by me since my coronation. Until today, my army was composed of stewards I inherited from my father. Having said that, I believe that their loyalty was initially made with my father. However, you, your loyalty is strictly directed to me, given that you never served my father."

Mullah bowed his head and responded. "Indeed, this is correct, Your Majesty."

"I have a very special task for you, Mullah. I want you to take your army division and escort my sister Queen Camila back to Asturias, where you are to remain to protect and serve that territory."

"As you wish, sire. The king honors me with the privilege of protecting his family. For that I am grateful, sire."

"There is one more thing, Lord Mullah. You are to report everything that goes on in Asturias, that includes my sister's actions. Do you understand?"

"Of course, as you wish, sire."

Gerardo smiled and wished him off, "Very well, go on, and do as I have commanded you."

With another sweeping bow, Mullah left the meeting to prepare for his imminent departure as escort to Asturias.

Gerardo met with his court thereafter. "We have expanded our forces," he exclaimed joyfully to the courtiers and told them of his agreement with Mullah.

Count Daniel was the first to congratulate him. "That is great news, sire."

Baron Edward echoed, "Congratulations, my lord."

"Your kingdom will have much superiority, sire," Marshal Miguel added.

The king waved his hands for them to calm down so that he could continue passing down the information. "Hence, I have bestowed the rank of duke upon Mullah."

Gerardo's men murmured among themselves.

"Your Majesty, up until today's promotion in rank, I was the highest-ranking member of your court," Count Daniel observed. "If I may, with all due respect, My King, you do not know much about this

Moor. Yes, we understand your father met with him during his reign, but he never trusted Mullah.”

“Silence,” yelled the king. “I am not petitioning the council. It is done. Are you questioning my actions, Daniel?”

“Of course not, sire,” Daniel answered. “Your Majesty, I have been your most loyal protector and adviser. My intent is never to question you, but rather to act in your best interest.”

“I need Lord Mullah to hold the title of Duke if I want him as head of my army in Asturias.” Gerardo answered. “Now, my sister has a duke in her court, and I was not going to have my own captain be outranked by one of her own.”

Daniel gave a slight bow. “Yes, my lord. I apologize for the misunderstanding.”

“I will need you by my side, Daniel, I do have other plans for you,” Gerardo said with conviction. “You see, giving him this title will also keep Mullah in check since Camila would not allow him to enact mischief upon the land.”

“Thank you, my lord,” Daniel replied.

“Daniel,” Gerardo continued. “I need you to take a division back to Asturias and finish off the clansmen. Leave no one alive.”

“My lord,” Daniel answered. “Again, I dare not question your actions, but I would like to learn of the reasons why this must take place, sire. The clansmen were a valuable foundation of our victory.”

Gerardo rolled his eyes and placed a hand over his own forehead as he was running out patience towards this man.

“Daniel, you have much to learn. Your questions are childish. I understand that you have always received guidance because the calls of action always came from a higher source. Now that you are a leader you will have to start thinking as a leader. You are not in the Green Dragoons, where men simply obey blind orders. But I am a patient king, and I will tell you the reason."

Daniel placed his hands together in gratitude, "You are too kind, sire."

"These clansmen are commoners, but they now know the secret ways into the castle. I do not need people coming in and out of our secret entrances or blocking our exit. So, Daniel head over to the f territory first and take care of Ivan's clansmen. That will give you an advantage when you come after Juan Carlos at the Tito Bustillo Cave camp."

Daniel stood up and responded, "You are very wise, My King. I will leave immediately."

"Now, that's all I have to say to all of you for now, so leave and take care of your assigned areas," the king made his final statement before leaving the room himself.

"As you wish, sire," the men responded, as he was departing, and each went on his way.

———————✦———————

The caravan, on its way to Asturias, was led by Lord Mullah and his army. As had happened to so many before him, when he met Queen Camila, he became enraptured with her. However, she never paid any attention to him at all. To her, Mullah had always been the wildly dressed stranger that came to visit her father as an ally and a strategic asset. And now he was her babysitter.

Inside the royal carriage were both queens, Joanna and Camila. Pablo and his Green Dragoons surrounded them on their horses for protection. Mullah approached the carriage as they were riding.

"As-salamu alaykum, Queen Camila. That means, 'Peace be upon you,' Your Majesty."

"Wa-alaykum salam. That means, 'And unto you peace,' Lord Mullah," she responded flawlessly.

"Forgive me, My Queen, I did not know you understood our customary greetings. It is clear you are well studied," Mullah smiled, impressed. "Please know that your brother the king has assigned me to be under your command. You will be safe under my protection, ma'am."

"Count Mullah—," the queen began but was quickly corrected.

"It's *Duke*, My Queen, I apologize for my intrusion. I am Duke Mullah now. Head of King Gerardo's army and lead escort to his most precious family. And your humble servant."

"Oh? Curious. I was not aware of your new title, Count Mullah. It must have happened recently, as word of your promotion had not reached me. Of course, I have known of you. You used to attend my father's gatherings."

"Ah, yes, I remember now, you were the little child in the dress swinging a wooden sword around at invisible monsters," he recalled.

"They were very real at the time, and I have the scars to prove it," they both laughed at the old memory of bygone days.

"I have been a loyal ally of your family for some time now. I am a liaison between the Muslim countries of the south and the Christian kingdoms in the European lands. Namely, those in the Iberian and French territories. That *was* the case anyway. Now I serve your brother, the King of Galicia and you, of course, My Queen."

"Very well, then," replied Camila. "I thank you for your escort and for your loyalty and service to my family through the years."

"It is my honor, My Queen," Mullah replied. "I shall give you time to yourself now; the road is long, and you should have your rest," Mullah gave a slight bow and then galloped his horse forward to the front of the army's formation.

⁂

Back in Galicia, Gerardo was still in a celebratory mood, and that evening he had a feast for himself, his nobles, and the members of his court.

"Eat and drink everyone. We celebrate today and every day," the king yelled, lifting his chalice.

"Salud, sire," his men and their women replied, lifting their chalices in return.

Gerardo had yet to choose a wife and had a couple of his concubines seated next to him. He raised his hand to have everyone silenced, but some were distracted in celebration.

"Galicians," Baron Edward yelled to get everyone's attention, banging a dagger against a silver goblet loudly. As the room quieted down, all heads turned expectantly to the king.

"We are now a very powerful kingdom," Gerardo slurred just a bit from the abundant wine. "I have easily defeated Lord Jacob. And now I have a new ranking captain in my court in Duke Mullah."

The room exploded in cheers, and they banged their chalices onto the table to show their feverish assent.

"I am on a clear path of expansion. No lord would want to engage in any battles with me. I am a force to be reckoned with. So, tonight we celebrate the glory of kingdom expansion!"

The cheering and stomping continued even louder. Gerardo reached for his women and pulled them towards him with each arm, kissing them lustily as a show of power and machismo. And they enthusiastically kissed right back. The music and raucous celebrations continued throughout the night.

⎯⎯⎯⎯⎯ ❖ ⎯⎯⎯⎯⎯

Halfway to Asturias, night overtook the queen's caravan. A loud command was heard from Count Mullah. "Halt. We will camp for the night here!"

"What's going on?" said the queen mother. "We're not stopping here, are we?"

"I believe the Count just gave that very command, Mother," Camila answered. "I'll peek out to see what's going on."

When Camila looked outside the carriage to see what was taking place, she saw Duke Pablo approaching Duke Mullah. Pablo said, "Lord Mullah, we're too exposed to stop here."

"Exposed?" Mullah snorted at the question. "Do not worry, my friend; no one will dare attack me or my army. Now, why don't you see to the queen's comfort and allow me and my army to handle the strategy and defense. Before you go, remind me your name, sire."

"I am Duke Pablo, adviser and first commander of Her Majesty the Queen and of her Green Dragoons. Protector of Asturias and wherever her monarchy reigns."

"Yes, I knew you were King Celestino's loyal court adviser before you moved into service of the queen." Mullah said. "Just so that there is no mistake about it, Duke Pablo, the one in command here is me. Not my words, those are direct orders from King Gerardo himself."

"I have no issue with you taking the lead, sire," responded Pablo. "My principal task is the queen and her safety. So, when her safety is compromised, I will step forward and take my principal with me. As is my primary objective."

Pablo then turned around and rode back to be next to both of the queens.

"I can see we may have to work on this one," Mullah had his eye on Pablo, but he addressed Jibril Asbat, his baron and commander who had settled nearby.

"If he insults Saracens, he insults Allah, my lord. I will take care of him, Allah wills it," Jibril threatened.

"No, not yet Jibril," Mullah shook his head at him. "Allah will tell us when the time is right. Keep a close watch on him."

"As you wish, my lord," Baron Jibril replied with a slight bow.

———————◆———————

Pablo approached to check on the queens. Camila had been so attentive to his interaction with Mullah, and she quietly asked him so nobody else could hear, "Is everything okay, Pablo?"

"Yes, Your Majesty. It seems that we will be setting camp here. Please do not worry. I will make sure that you are safe."

"See that you do," answered the queen with a wry smile. "Thank you, Pablo."

He then bowed to her and rode on to give them privacy while camp was being set up.

After he was out of earshot, Queen Joanna harrumphed, "That Mullah is a blathering peacock. Your father and I never trusted him, Camila," Joanna said, pointing a thin, bony finger in Mullah's direction. She sat back again in the carriage, fanning herself while they awaited the time to retire to their tent. "He bragged with his stories of glory and the size of his army all the time, which made him annoying. But for the most part, people just accepted him as the silver-tongued pompadour that he was."

"Yes, I know, Mother," Camila sat up looking for her robe. When she found it, she also grabbed her mother's robe and handed it to her. "It was not my idea for him to come and provide us with so-called protection. This is all Gerardo's doing. He even promoted him to the rank of Duke. Can you believe that?" Camila said, frustrated. "I can only imagine it was so that he could outrank and have command over Pablo. Why else would he promote him over Daniel who has been his loyal commander?"

"Well, if we thought he was flashy with his fashion and ego before," said the queen mother, "it will be multiplied now that he is a Duke. Can you believe that he also wanted all the recognition and the best seats in the house, as if he was a king among kings, back at your father's gatherings?"

Camila chuckled, "Mother, I remember seeing father talk to him from time to time. But even then, I knew father was not as welcoming towards him as he would be with others."

"You are very perceptive, Camila; I am proud of you. Yes, your father knew that Lord Mullah also had a reputation for his short temper. A large man could get away with it; but a short man with a short temper just seemed like a petulant crybaby. It was a bad combination all around." Joanna waved a hand to flick the memory away and forget about him.

"Well, I have a feeling that having him around can put my kingdom at risk again," lamented Camila. "Gerardo let a snake into the garden, and something tells me that Mullah, left unchecked, will become big trouble sooner or later."

They both sat silently stewing over their current situation. Pablo's voice called out a few moments later. "Your Majesties, your tents are ready."

Camila responded, "Thank you, Pablo. Come on, Mama, it is time to get some rest now."

They were assisted from their carriage and escorted to the base camp.

The following morning, they broke camp and embarked on the remainder of the way to Asturias. Meanwhile, Marshal Diego and his men arrived at the Holy Cave of Covadonga territory to meet with the clansmen. Juan Carlos and Ivan were already waiting for their arrival, together with the rest of the men.

Diego addressed them accordingly, "Greetings, Commander. Hello, Captain."

Both Juan Carlos and Ivan replied at the same time, "Marshal."

Diego raised his hand to acknowledge them before proceeding. "On behalf of the queen, we are glad to see that you followed your better instinct and rode out here."

Juan Carlos smiled, "Yes, we figured it was the best precautionary measure."

Diego nodded, "I bring you a message from our queen, and I am to bring her a response back. Also, my men and our horses are hungry and thirsty. We would appreciate some friendly hospitality, Commander."

"Yes, of course, as always, my friend. Please come on down. We will have our women feed your knights, and my men will feed and care for your horses."

Juan Carlos looked towards his captain, "Ivan, will you make sure that you show them where they will be welcomed to get some rest?"

Ivan responded, "Of course, Commander. Men, please follow me." Diego nodded his head in approval to his men, and they followed Ivan.

"Marshal, in the meantime, you and I can go to my humble base camp, where I can offer you food and water while I read the queen's message."

Diego's squad got off their horses and were fed. It wasn't a feast but it would suffice for the evening. Meanwhile, Juan Carlos attended to the queen's letter.

Commander Juan Carlos,

Words cannot express enough gratitude for your and your men's loyalty to the kingdom. I am afraid to say that without you and your brave men's actions the Kingdom of Asturias would be under a new monarchy by now.

Unfortunately, my reign is still not out of the darkness yet but rather under duress from wolves.

For that reason, I fear for your life and that of my beloved clansmen.

Please maintain your position, and I will contact you once I arrive at the castle. We are living in a new, corrupt age where loyalties are uncertain; therefore, I ask you to use your

*judgement when trusting emissaries, even
official ones.*

*I will seek a long-term solution for the
betterment of our kingdom. For now, please
know that your actions have not gone in vain,
and that you and the clans have my forever
gratitude.*

I will call upon you when the time is right.

With Gratitude,
Queen Camila Garcia of Asturias

Juan Carlos finished reading the queen's letter
and proceeded to write back. Once he did, he
entrusted the letter to the marshal.

"Marshal, I give you my letter responding to
My Queen. Please see that she receives it. We also
send with you fresh water for your way back to the
castle."

"Commander, again, it is good to see you and
to have you on our side. May the Lord be with you
always."

"And also, with you, Marshal."

———— ❖ ————

On the other side of the land, Count Daniel
arrived with his division to the Sidron Cave territory.
To their surprise they found the camp empty.

"They must have heard us coming and left," the count sneered to his men. "The king will not be happy to find out about this. They must be heading over to meet with Juan Carlos's camp at the Tito Bustillo Cave territory. We must ride on and try to intercept them before they get to it."

"Sire, we have been riding without any rest," Marshal Miguel said. And indeed he looked exhausted. "This was to be our resting point before moving to the next camp. Should we not give the men and horses a rest before taking on the next challenge?"

"I fear that we will have a bigger challenge if both clans unite against us," the count responded. "However, I recognize that perhaps we should take a little rest to give the horses a break. Everyone be ready to leave at a moment's notice. Mount off!"

❖

Back in Asturias, Queen Camila was finally arriving at her castle. The royal guards, who had remained behind to protect it, now lined up with their swords drawn to give her a royal welcome and salute. The trumpeters played from the high terrace overlooking the turrets, as the remaining men of the division cheered in unison welcoming them.

The citizens of Asturias who returned to the castle were also celebrating with cheers, and the children jumped up and down playfully; some of the old-timers dropped to the ground, relishing the very grass and soil of their homeland, while others were embracing each other with tears of joy.

Duke Mullah led the rank and file escort on point to showcase his heroism for bringing them back.

"We are home, Mama," Camila gushed.

"Gracias a Dios, Mijita."

Pablo rode in closer to their carriage to deter any unwanted crowds near them. "Welcome back to your reign, Your Majesty."

"Thank you, Pablo. Please make sure that everyone gets back to their corresponding living areas tonight, and tomorrow night we will celebrate. I will need to meet with you sometime to talk about the many things we need to do. Please stay vigilant, and watch your backs."

"Of course, Your Majesty."

"Look at Mullah, that peacock, I tell you," Queen Joanna said in disgust. "He acts as if he is a hero. Even his armor is not battle ready but parade ready; you would think this was more about him than about your return, Camila."

"Okay, Mother, thank you for pointing it out, as if I did not notice it; but please don't let him ruin this moment for you."

They waved as they passed by under the castle gateway arches and were much relieved to be back home. Camila was saddened to see the devastation done to the different areas of the castle, inside and out. "There are a lot of things that need to be fixed to restore the castle back to its beautiful former glory, Mother. Not to mention to basic functionality and security."

"Primero Dios, you will have it done in no time, my daughter." They waved at the people welcoming them before retreating into the castle.

————— ❖ —————

Later that evening, Marshal Diego returned to the castle. Immediately upon his arrival, he was met by Mullah and some of his men.

"Where have you been?" asked Mullah. "Why were you and these men broken off from the group?"

"As usual, someone runs point, My Lord. We took the outside perimeter route to get here for security purposes, and, of course, it took us longer to arrive."

"From now on, know that all decision-making goes through me, do you understand?" Mullah barked back at him.

"My decision and actions are in direct protocol with the queen's tactics, sire. If you feel you were disrespected in anyway, you may bring it to her attention. If you have no further quarrel with me, I will take my leave. I need to go check in with the queen now."

"Very well, Marshal, I will not stand in your way. But know that I will have my eye on you, so tread carefully."

"Of course, Count Mullah, and I you."

Diego went immediately to report to Camila, who was walking past the ballroom.

"Your Majesty," he bowed.

"Marshal," she looked around to make sure the coast was clear. No one else was in the hallway, but she still pulled him in closer just to be safe, "What news have you for me?"

"Commander Juan Carlos and his men are well, ma'am. I bring back a letter from Juan Carlos."

"Great job, Diego. Did anyone see you or question you upon your return?"

"Yes, Mullah did, My Queen. Met me at the front gate, practically. I do not think he was pleased to realize that we were missing from the group. I told him that it was your standard protocol to send a patrol ahead of the army and conduct an exterior perimeter check."

"Excellent. I need you to go get Pablo and, both of you, meet me at the high court room."

"Yes, Your Majesty," Diego bowed and walked away to go look for Pablo.

Camila hurried to her chambers, where she sat on a chair and anxiously broke the seal to open the letter from Juan Carlos.

Your Majesty, Queen Camila,

I am delighted to receive news that you have returned to your castle. We are honored to hear of your concern about us, your loyal clansmen.

Please, I ask you with all due respect to be careful with your brother King Gerardo. I believe that he attempts to keep Asturias to himself. He claimed your lands as being under his reign and told everyone that his decision was not to be contested.

He executed all of King Jacob's men, while making him watch, and threatened to cut his head off if he looked away. Only then did he spare the count's life, while having him exiled to the outskirts of the southland to fend for himself, with a standing order to have him killed on sight, if ever seen again within our borders.

Your Majesty, please be well and stay safe from harm. Worry not for us. We are self sufficient despite our meager resources. We will remain invisible and await your call. We have served, and we will continue to serve, you.

Commander Juan Carlos Herrera

Camila held a candle to the letter, and let it burn into a silver bowl. "May God protect us from my brother's insanity," she said watching the last of it burn to a blackened ember.

The next evening, the queen hosted the homecoming celebration of which she had spoken. A feast was given in her honor. Mullah, of course, pretended the whole affair was on his account., as if they were honoring and welcoming him into ranks as the new duke. He reveled in the moment of finally getting a full dose of what it meant to be a high-ranking lord.

The people of the kingdom were loyal to the queen and her royal court, which now included Mullah as a protector and adviser to the land. While they were dining, Mullah stood up and raised his chalice and exclaimed, "A toast!"

Everyone stopped talking and raised their chalices. The queen mother put a hand upon Camila's lap, whispering, "Here we go."

"I, Duke Mullah, head of Her Majesty's royal high court, as appointed by King Gerardo himself, along with our beloved Queen Camila, want to give all of you my most sincere gratitude for your welcome."

The attendees applauded with great enthusiasm. The queens courtiers applauded as well to go along with him, but aside they wondered why he was speaking on behalf of them.

Mullah continued, "Many of you have not met me yet. I will personally make sure that the Kingdom of Asturias is safe from all enemies." The applause continued, and then he added, "My loyalty and my army stand strong with all of you."

The people cheered again. The duke held his chalice high. "Cheers to Queen Camila and for her safe return to the kingdom. May your safe return and my protection be a relief to you, My Queen. I say unto all of you, no friend nor foe will dare to attack us now."

Everyone jumped and cheered in response with a chorus of "Cheers! Long live the Queen! Cheers! Long live the Queen!" His toast was echoed by the court and all present.

The queen smiled and nodded in gratitude. "This man is smarter than I thought," she mused aloud. "He has the audacity to speak before me and establish his position for everyone to know; to flex his rank and power. All the while, making it seem as if he were honoring me. Clever, very clever," Camila seethed through a fake smile to Queen Joanna.

The queen's high court simply observed and listened as everything took place. They needed to stay quiet as the queen had commanded them, for it was dangerous to say anything to interfere or oppose Mullah. In addition, there was always the chance that some of the lords had already been influenced by either Gerardo or Mullah. Political alliances were being formed and had been formed, and allegiances became agents and double agents. Quite the mine field to navigate.

Queen Camila rose and held up a hand to calm the crowd. "Thank you for that touch of confidence, Duke Mullah. It is very kind of you to offer your protection to the kingdom. Time will tell if our true threats will come from without or from within. Perhaps mankind has finally battled itself out, and its warring days are all behind us. I pray they are," she chuckled, and many others did as well.

Mullah nodded to the queen and got a little red around the ears from the humor in her statement.

The queen continued, "For now is not the time to glorify ourselves as individuals. Rather, this is the time to restore Asturias to its former glory. *Our* former glory."

Everyone applauded and yelled happily at the queen's tribute. Also, with that statement she had outmaneuvered Mullah and taken the attention away from him, and had done so with high class.

Mullah, on the other hand, glared at her now, the way that a child looks at another for taking away his favorite toy. He quickly covered his hatred with a plastic smile to mirror his nemesis. He did not like it a bit, and, in fact, took her little speech as a personal attack. Jibril also stood by quietly but noticed Mullah's foul reaction as they exchanged a look.

Back at the Sidron Cave territory, Daniel and his men had finished a meal and had had some restful downtime. They were now ready to move on. "Mount up, Galicians. We have a task to do, and it will not be long before we meet face to face with those primitive clansmen. We will annihilate them once and for all as the king commanded."

The men mounted their horses and went on their way. Sometime later, Daniel's division finally arrived at the Tito Bustillo Cave territory, where they looked for the clans. To their surprise and confusion, again there was no one to be found.

"Joder, con un carajo," Daniel kicked at an old, long-cooled firepit. "The king will not like it when he hears about this. Let us waste no more time. We need to head home and report back to the king immediately. He will not want to be kept waiting." The men mounted up and headed back to Galicia.

Upon their return, Daniel immediately went to present himself before Gerardo.

"Sire, Count Daniel has returned from Galicia, my lord," Baron Edward notified the king.

"It is about time. Send him in immediately."

"Yes, my lord."

"Your Majesty," Daniel entered the throne room, and as he approached him, kneeled to show his respect.

"Rise, Daniel. Tell me, did you accomplish your mission as I commanded you?"

Daniel stood up. He was dirty and visibly exhausted from his mission, "Sire, we followed the trail as you commanded, but when we arrived at their given territories, the clansmen were no longer there, my lord. And had not been for weeks by the look of it."

Gerardo stood up and walked towards Daniel. The king raised his voice and pounded one fist into his other hand, "What do you mean, they were not there? Did you search the area, hombre? Of course, they must have heard you coming, and those cowards were surely hiding."

"We searched, my lord. The camp was cold, I assure you. We swept the area and all surrounding areas with intent of capturing anyone. But there was nary a track left behind."

Gerardo turned back towards his throne and climbed wearily up the stairs to plop back down upon it. He had begun to put on more and more weight from all of the feasting and lascivious living. Just that short walk had almost winded him. He caught his breath and then continued his attack, "How can this be then? Como carajos did they know you were sent to kill them?"

"We wondered the same, my lord. It just does not make sense. They simply vanished from both areas."

"Hijo de—," Gerardo cut himself short, he was so angry. "You have failed me. There is no changing that. However, perhaps they realized the powerful force that my kingdom has assembled around Camila, and they have abandoned Asturias all together." Gerardo paused to make sense of the many possibilities ahead of them.

"In either case it does not matter now, for I have Mullah securing that territory, and he will take care of anyone who he identifies that does not belong. Go ahead and get cleaned up, your duty now is to protect me and Galicia."

"Thank you, sire, you have always been my principal responsibility, and I am grateful to continue your protection."

Chapter 8
Establishing the Kingdom

A couple of months passed by without incident. Then one day King Gerardo called a meeting with the members of his court and his ranking captains. "I am becoming wealthier than ever, now that I am collecting the additional taxes from Oviedo, and only sending back minimal funds to maintain Asturias. I feel empowered, gentlemen. Now is the time for further kingdom expansion."

"Expanding the kingdom would not be an easy task, sire," Commander Daniel replied. "When we defeated King Jacob in Asturias, we had a lot of leverage in the way of trust from Queen Camila's nobles and her clansmen, who were eager to retake the kingdom for their queen. However, conquering another territory without inside help is going to be a lot harder, my lord."

"What are you saying, Daniel? Do you not believe that we have the capacity to expand?" Gerardo asked pointedly. "Explain yourself."

"Of course, we do, sire. I do not mean to question you. It is my responsibility to give you advice on the difference in the two situations. However, to explain further," Daniel paused for a moment and gave Gerardo a slight bow to show him respect. Gerardo waved a hand at him, and so he continued, "To accomplish your expansion, it will require siezing enemy territories without the help of nobles and countrymen and spies on the inside aiding in our cause. It will be more difficult and costly to orchestrate."

His captains Edward and Miguel nodded their heads in agreement with Daniel.

"I will tell you what I need," Gerardo yelled. "I need leaders. Leaders that can produce victories and who are not afraid of the little challenges involved in carrying out the king's instructions. I give you the strategy, and you carry it out. Very simple." The king stood up and left the room while his court stood up to pay their respects towards him. "That is all I have for you today!"

After he had left the room, Daniel let out a long anxious breath. "The king's thirst for wealth and power is growing unbearable," he said to the others. "He will not rest until he finds a way to conquer more lands. He lives under the shadow of his predecessors' mighty accomplishments, and now he wants, more than anything, to make a conqueror's name for himself."

The Castillo del Eliseo had made great progress under limited resources these past few months since the queen's return. The fallen walls had been replaced, reinforced, and beautified with the queen's family crest as accents. The castle and its surroundings were cleaned up and looked to be prospering once again, even under the meager allowance from Gerardo.

"Mother, how do you like the remodeling to the castle? I just finished hanging father's portrait here in the hall of ancestors and look how amazingly it fills the room."

"I love it, Mija. Yes, I love the way the castle has been fixed up and the nice flourishes you added to make it even better than before." The queen mother clasped her hands to her chest, her eyes welling up with emotion. "I agree that your father's portrait looks so much better here. Like you told me back in Galicia, you do take care of it much better than Gerardo could ever have."

"Thank you, Mama," Camila said, rubbing her back lovingly.

A familiar voice behind them interrupted their bonding moment. "As-salamu alaykum, Your Majesties," Duke Mullah approached them and placed a palm to his chest, waving blessings towards them.

Joanna didn't not immediately turn to look at him. Instead, as her daughter moved towards Mullah, she took a couple of steps away and dabbed a kerchief at her eyes rather covertly so the Duke would not catch her vulnerability. Such was the cat and mouse games they were forced to play, living in close quarters with an undercover wolf.

"Hello, Duke Mullah," Camila broke into a radiant and all together fake smile that she had perfected. "What news have you from the kingdom today?" The queen mother sat down on a velvety cushioned bench nearby without so much a word to Mullah. At her age, she hadn't the energy to muster the false pretense that her daughter could. So, her dark eyes scanned him up and down rather sourly.

Mullah didn't even feign to notice. He was completely focused upon Camila. "I have personally contacted each of my captains, and we have finished the defensive communication system, Your Majesty. I was personally there when we tested it."

"What?" Joanna asked. "What is he talking about Camila?"

"Mama," Camila held out a calming hand to settle her mother, "the Duke established a series of command posts across the countryside and sent knights to their designated areas and protectorates." Camila sat down on the bench beside her. She took her hand in her own, squeezing out a little warning as she explained. "These strategically located command posts also provide a new avenue of communications from mountain top to mountain top across the land where the men can send a fire signal to to announce the need for additional men to fend off enemies, should an attack take place." Satisfied her mother would not blurt out something confrontational, Camila turned towards Mullah, "Was I correct in my explanation, my lord?"

"Outstanding, ma'am," Mullah pressed his hands together with sincere admiration. "I could not have explained it any better."

"I would like—," the queen mother began before Camila spoke over top of her.

"Mother, I'm certain that the count has a ghastly amount of administration duties to attend to now." Camila motioned with her right hand indicating the door. "My lord, we would not want to keep you from attending to them any longer. Thank you for stopping by with the most encouraging report."

"Your Majesties," Lord Mullah bowed and retired from the room.

They waited for the click-clack of his boot heels to recede in the distance before the queen mother spoke again. "I was going to behave," she said.

"Mm-hm," Camila replied, not believing a word.

"Really, from a defense standpoint, the peacock seems to know what he is doing," Joanna explained. "Of course, he sees this kingdom as his own and takes every opportunity to undermine you, Camila."

"That is not behaving, Mother. But, yes, he brings vast tactical knowledge from different areas of the world. I think it is in his nature to seek out glory for his deeds. He is trying to impress us."

"Do what you must, dear, I shan't coddle him," Joanna replied, and that was that.

"Oh, Mama," Camila laughed at her mother's grit. "I've had Pablo assess Mullah's work and tactics, and he agreed that since Mullah has skilled knights from different kingdoms, they're a collective repository of military stratagem from field battles to survival skills."

"Is our army retaining these new ideas they're being trained in?"

"They are, Mama. I have sometimes watched them from the north bartizan, and they greatly appreciate the opportunity to learn new skills from each other. To compare notes, as it were. Especially since they will conceivably be battling side by side against a common foe."

Queen Joanna simply remained silent as she soaked up the explanation. Camila patted her hand. "I must go, Mother; it is getting late, and I need to receive Pablo's report at the high council room."

"Go on, Mija, I know you have things to do. I don't mind sitting here with your father."

They both smiled up at the large, endearing portrait of King Celestino watching over them.

Camila entered the high council room where her courtiers and the Green Dragoons awaited her. They rose from their seats and bowed their heads to acknowledge her.

"I apologize for my delay. Please take your seats. Pablo," she gestured to her right hand man.

"Your Majesty," Duke Pablo spoke for them all. "You do not have to apologize to us." They all mumbled agreement.

"I know it has been some time since we last met, but I am grateful for returning to these meetings," she began. "I know it has not been easy. As a matter of fact, I know it has been very difficult having to rebuild our rank and structure and our small-sized army. Nevertheless, now that we have some basic kingdom defensibility back in place, I do believe it is time we began to envision our next immediate steps."

The men acknowledged her words with hearty head nods peppered with a chorus of "Here, here!" and "Amen!"

Camila nodded gratefully and continued. "What news have you from throughout the kingdom and your designated posts?"

Pablo rose and began his report. "Thank you, Your Majesty. I called Baron Gregorio Gutierrez and Marshal Diego Skaggs to help me select new leadership to establish the infrastructure of the ranking system, my lady."

Camila nodded her head and gestured him to continue. "We have called upon the following nobles who were awarded, with your permission, the rank of under-marshal, and who will lead as captains and will oversee the different squad divisions, ma'am."

"Great," Camila looked around the table at some new faces, "I would love to meet them."

Pablo introduced the men who rose to their feet when their names were called. "James Wise," he began.

"A great honor, Your Majesty," James bowed. He was an older man with a battle-hardened face. He had a raspy voice, full beard, and stocky build. She nodded at him in acknowledgement and James bowed, again.

"Timothy McCarthy," Pablo said.

"At your service, Your Majesty," Timothy stood and nodded. He had a medium build, a closely shaven beard rather than the thick, long bush on James's neck. Timothy had a quiet but not shy demeanor to him and every little action radiated confidence.

Pablo continued the roll call with, "Christian Balian."

Christian stood up and replied, "My sword is yours, Your Majesty." He looked to be the youngest of the group so far. He had a fresh face, not much facial hair, and a slender body type. He looked very fit and sharp. He bowed to the queen, and she acknowledged him.

"Matthew Boyd."

Matthew stood up immediately. "It is my honor to be a member of your court, Your Majesty," he said. He sounded a bit nervous but excited to be there. He was tall with a medium build and had a goatee. He was probably in his mid-30s. Camila recognized him from having seen him around the stables from time to time.

"Yes, Matthew, I believe we've met," she said. "Is the ornery grey mare still kicking like a mule?"

Matthew smiled sheepishly, "Yes, ma'am, and I have the scars to prove it."

"Always the old ones giving the most trouble," Pablo winked across the table at the grizzled old bear, James Wise.

"We know what we know," James conceded with a twinkle in his eye.

There were some chuckles around the table. Pablo swept a hand across at the newest recruits. "They will join Gregorio, Diego, and myself, my lady."

"Excellent, welcome," the queen exclaimed, looking each one in the eye again. "I am grateful to have you here, and grateful to each of you for your wisdom and stewardship within our kingdom's leadership."

"Thank you, My Queen." they all responded.

Pablo signaled for the under-marshals to be seated, again. "These squads form a platoon, and they will be overseen and commanded by your loyal and experienced commander Gregorio."

Camila looked towards Gregorio and nodded at him, "I am indebted to you, my lord. Speaking of our leadership, I believe it is only proper to recompense you for your years of loyalty and good deeds." The queen rose and stepped aside from the table. "Will the following come before me when I call your name?"

The men looked to each other, uncertainly. "Gregorio Gutierrez, Diego Skaggs, Juan Carlos Herrera, Ivan Escobar." They each rose upon hearing their names and proceeded to present themselves before the queen. "Please take a knee."

The men did as commanded. The rest of the men simply stood witness. The queen withdrew her father's sword from its sheath and touched Gregorio's head and shoulders as she promoted him. "For your loyal service and diligent duties to our kingdom, I,

Queen Camila of Asturias dub thee Sir Gregorio Gutierrez Count of Asturias."

Camila then turned towards the other three and did the same. "Diego Skaggs, Juan Carlos Herrera, Ivan Escobar." Each time she mentioned their name she looked at them in the eye to acknowledge them. "I dub thee Barons of Asturias. Rise and be presented as such."

The newly promoted officers rose and turned to face the men who broke out in cheers, pounding their fists to the table and stomping their feet in celebration before settling and returning to their seats.

Gregorio lingered a moment. With a tear in his eye, he said, "Thank you, Your Majesty. This is such a surprise. I never thought I would see the day of becoming a count, especially since your father's service days are behind me. As I served him, I am in your service, My Queen."

For a moment, Queen Camila side-stepped her royal decorum and offered him the warrior's handshake. Beyond the civilian grasp of a hand, this was a forearm to forearm clasp that brothers-in-arms would use. "I cannot express my gratitude for your lifetime of service, Count."

Juan Carlos and Ivan were equally as surprised by the queen's actions. Juan Carlos raised his hand to get the her attention. As Gregorio returned to his seat, Camila noticed the hand, "Juan Carlos, did you want to add anything?" She took her seat again, as did they all.

"My Queen," Juan Carlos began carefully. "We are but loyal servants of your kingdom.. You do not have to pay us to defend our own lands." He and Ivan lowered their heads in a stately bow.

The queen smiled at them and then addressed the room. "Not only have you earned your recognition for your service, bravery and for going above and beyond in the defense of the kingdom, but..." she paused for a moment, "you have earned the right to be recognized as members of nobility, and nobles have fiefdoms."

That won her another standing ovation from the entire room. After the recognition, everyone sat down again. The queen took a drink from her chalice before her and then turned to Pablo. "Should we continue with the report, Pablo?"

Pablo rose again, "The squad captains are ready to give their full reports, ma'am. James, we will begin with you."

"Thank you, Commander," James rose to address the queen. "Your Majesty, the north reports no incidents or any threats. The citizens are stable and the fishing shores have been productive."

"Thank you, James," replied the queen. James took his seat again.

"Timothy," Pablo called him up to his feet. Timothy rose to speak. "Thank you, Commander. Your Majesty, the east reports no incidents, however the neighboring regions of Santander report rumors of some infighting and hardships. As a result, our borders are sealed for our protection, ma'am."

Camila nodded to acknowledge the report and motioned for Timothy to take his seat. "Pablo, we may have to send an emissary to see if we can be of some aid to them. Make sure our delegation brings some food and water to assist them in their needs."

"Of course, as you wish, My Queen." Pablo proceeded, "Christian, please report your status."

Christian stood up, "Thank you, Commander. Greetings, Your Majesty. The south has no incidents to date. Lord Mullah's forces patrol that area, and our men are shadowing them."

The queen nodded at him, "Thank you, Christian."

Pablo called the last captain, "Matthew, your report, please."

Matthew stood up "Thank you, Commander. Thank you, Your Majesty. There are no incidents initiating from the west division to report. However, Lord Mullah has been seen traveling from Asturias to Galicia, back and forth."

"Interesting," the queen shared a look with Pablo and then added, "Thank you, Matthew."

Matthew was signaled to return to his seat, he acknowledged. "Thank you, Your Majesty."

Camila steepled her fingers together in deep thought, "Duke Mullah has shown military readiness in his tactics. He could keep guard against any enemy attack, but if the duke considers my brother his enemy now, he may be deterring my brother from gaining access back without his permission."

Pablo glanced at Gregorio and then addressed the queen, "Your Majesty, according to recent observations, Mullah's knights have all of our country's entry points well covered. In preparation for this meeting, we have discussed and agreed among ourselves that Duke Mullah, of whom we know very little, has too much control, by any measure."

Camila looked at Pablo and then to Gregorio, who nodded as he rose to explain further, "Your Majesty, we have heard the reports, and having personally been assigned to your father's royal escort, I am vastly familiar with your brother's ways. King Gerardo's kingdom goals are very different from yours, My Queen. It is my most humble opinion that he should not be trusted."

Gregorio scanned the room, and Pablo gave him a nod. Gregorio added, "It is not wise to have someone like Duke Mullah going back and forth to talk to your brother and bring the king information of your every move, my lady."

Gregorio then sat back down while the men around him nodded their agreement. Camila sat quietly for a moment with a pensive and sad expression on her face before she composed herself and said, "I believe I do owe you all an apology." The men were immediately intrigued by this. The queen searched for the right words and then proceeded, "I can only imagine how you must feel. Mullah was assigned to handle all of the military tactics and protection details by my brother. In most part because we did not have an army to do so after Gerardo laid claim to our land."

All the men rumbled in shock and disbelief at the queen's revelation that Duke Mullah had been assigned by the king.

"I did not have the heart to tell you this before," continued the queen. "But I need to keep you apprised of our dire situation." The men looked at each other trying to understand what the queen was referring to. "When my brother took Asturias from Jacob, he did not claim the reign to return it to me as our Father would have wanted. He claimed Asturias for himself."

There was instant chatter from most of the men, Diego asked, "What? What do you mean, Your Majesty?"

"I knew the king was not to be trusted," exclaimed Gregorio.

"Listen up," Pablo urged them and added more patiently, "Please, gentlemen. Allow the queen to continue."

"Thank you, Pablo," she stood up now and paced the room.. It was easier to explain and talk that way. "By Gerardo's decree, he took over what remained of my army. His plan was to send each of you out to war somewhere for his personal kingdom's expansion. He worries not for your well-being, nor for our corporate well-being, but is driven by his thirst for more and more power. And more land is more power. More subjects is more power. And he will certainly not allow anyone to get in his way."

The queen scanned from face to face as she circled around from behind them. "The only thing I was able to do was to make a deal with him that I would administrate over the land—demoted to be the king's regent—while he maintained full military control of the kingdom. Hence the reason why he sent a Saracen lord with us and bestowed upon him the title of Duke, so that he could claim authority over Pablo," she explained with a bit of irritation in her voice.

The men were in silent shock from the news; they pondered her words as the full predicament of their kingdom dawned upon them.

"My Queen," Pablo said, "we are so sorry that you have had to endure this terrible underhandedness alone. We are your protection and have failed to protect you. Yet, your kind and benevolent actions have preserved us all. However, we do live to fight another day, and we are here to tell you that you are not alone in this fight. Your loyal men, your council, and your Dragoons stand with you."

The men heartily agreed. They stood up as one unit and withdrew their swords to salute their queen.

"I thank you all," Camila answered, truly touched. She took her seat again, and they followed suit. "You do not know how much your support means to me. Now, I agree that we must take control again, but whatever it is that we do, it has to be subtle, precise and tactically sound. We only have one shot at this. Gerardo and Mullah both imagine that dutifully marching to their drumbeat. So, we cannot make a move until we are fully ready to go all out. If anything goes wrong, we will have not only Mullah's army to contend with, but my brother's forces, also. And, make no mistake, despite your fancy new titles, we shall all be flayed open and strung up from the garrison."

The men chewed on this carefully. "Pablo?"

"If I may, there is a clear and very present danger in staging a coup within an occupied land," responded Pablo. "If Mullah controls the access points to get in and out to the kingdom, he also controls the kingdom." Pablo looked at Gregorio and deferred to him. "Sir Gregorio, you have more common knowledge about both King Gerardo and

Mullah from being assigned to his escort when he was a prince."

"Take heart, Your Majesty, because interesting opportunities emerge. As we speak, Mullah and his army are training our men in their every military tactic. As we shadow them, every day they set patterns, and we learn more about the way he thinks; we will continue to be alert to any suspicious deviations," Gregorio said thoughtfully. "In time, I believe a weakness will be exposed, and a course of action will present itself, if we are patient."

"Agreed," Camila smiled back at him with some relief. "Again, it's an impossible job well done so far, everyone. Keep learning and keep probing."

The men nodded their agreement.

"Thank you, ma'am," Pablo said in gratitude.

"Very well, then, as always, please take care of yourselves and your families," encouraged the queen.

"Thank you, Your Majesty."

Everyone stood up and paid respect to the queen who left the room first. Everyone else followed thereafter.

The Invitation

High in the castle, Queen Camila found herself overlooking the kingdom from her bedroom. The sun was beginning to set. A handful of people were carting goods through the cobblestone streets below. There were thatchers mending the last of the holes in people's roofs. She could see hope in some, despair in others.

Camila was unaware of her mother Joanna, who carefully approached her while she was deep in her melancholy sadness.

"Camila," Joanna called out.

Startled, Camila sucked in a breath of air, forcing a smile as she turned, "Yes, Mother."

"Where have you been? I have been looking for you, I have not seen you all day; have you eaten yet?"

"No, Mother, I'm not hungry."

"What is wrong, Mija? I see you are stressed, what is going on?"

"It's nothing, Mother, I just have to sort out a few things, that's all."

"My poor child. I know you too well for you to try to hide things from me."

"If anyone knows me, Mother, it is you. I just feel imprisoned within my own castle. I dropped my guard with Jacob. Because of that, now I am responsible for upending everyone's future, and I hate to think that my choices have increased my people's burdens and unhappiness."

"Oh, hush, Camila. You have a big heart and there is nothing wrong with opening it when you feel you should. That is what makes you very special. That is a gift from God. Do not blame yourself for someone else's bad intentions. Besides, what makes you think that people are so unhappy?"

"But, Mother…"

"No, do not 'but, Mother' me, Camila. Ever since you were little, you always wanted to skip to the end of the book. You don't get to know the ending while you are in the middle of the story, Camila. At the right time, you will know what to do; you always have. You are Camila the Just," Joanna proclaimed with a warm, happy smile.

"Alright, Mother, I will follow your advice. But this book we're in is a child's horror fable," they both laughed at that. "Anyway, now I know what father had to endure. I always wondered how he managed to deal with it all. I guess, because he had you. Thank you for cheering me up. I love you, Mama."

"I love you, too. Now come, and get something to eat, dear. You can't save the world on an empty stomach."

Camila hugged her mother closely as they walked out of the room.

———————— ❖ ————————

Meanwhile back in the land of Galicia, Gerardo summoned Mullah to another meeting. They would not risk notes and scrolls and third party relays, no matter how trusted their messengers were. They took a walk around the vacant castle gardens while they talked.

"What news have you of my kingdom of Asturias, Mullah?"

"Excellent news, my lord. Very quiet! No one dares to cross your lands since they know I provide its protection."

"Very well, I like that," he smiled. "What news have you of my sister?"

"The queen is safe and well-kept under my watchful care, as well, my lord. She is doing wonders for the morale and the industry of her people."

"*My* people," Gerardo reminded him. "Excellent. I have decided to head into the southlands. Word is that Jacob is attempting to re-group and re-form his defeated army. But if I can attack him now, he will never be able to recover, and I can expand my territory. I will need you to extend your watchful protection to Galicia, as well as Asturias, while I am away."

This was all very big news to Mullah. "Yes, my lord," he placed a hand over his heart and then pointed it to the sky. "Consider it done."

"Very well, then. I shall prepare for my departure. I cannot wait to finish what we started with Jacob once and for all. And to add his territories to my own."

"And his taxes, too," Mullah smiled a toothy grin.

"Precisely," the king nodded with a glint in his own eye.

"As always, I am at your service, should you need me to come along at any point, my lord."

"No, Mullah. I need you here. Besides, Jacob is so dim-witted, he cannot possibly foresee an attack coming, so it will be a quick field trip, if anything. For now, I need you to protect your king's land until I return triumphant from my quest."

"Of course, sire," they finished their walk, and Mullah bowed to Gerardo and returned to meet with his men.

"Allah yursil barakatih, Jibril," Mullah said to them.

"Allah will send his blessings onto you as well, my lord," Jibril answered.

"Make the necessary preparations. We were just handed over another kingdom. I have control of both territories, Galicia, and Asturias."

"Allah is mighty, my lord," Jibril answered.

"I will be staying here with this division. I need you to take a squad and return to Asturias. Brief Khalid on the current situation, and come back with two divisions. You and I will focus on the larger area of Galicia, and Khalid will stay with the fourth division in Asturias," Mullah ordered.

"If King Gerardo returns, he would be suspicious to see three divisions on his land, my lord," counseled Jibril.

"True, *if* the king were to return, he would encounter our forces. However, between you, me and the horse stables, I doubt that he will come back," Mullah said smugly. He waved a hand dismissively. "Many bad and unfortunate things could take place along his journey; it would mean that Allah wills for me to keep the reign," Mullah gave a humble shrug.

"Yes, my lord. Liakun Allah maeak," Jibril paid his respects to Mullah.

"Mashallah Allah," responded Mullah. They each headed their own way.

At the Kingdom of Asturias, a short time later, Diego arrived to the Castillo del Eliseo at a moderate clip. His horse was sweaty from their travels. He quickly slid off the horse and handed the reins to a squire who eagerly attended him. Diego rushed in to speak with Queen Camila who was just exiting the chapel, "Your Majesty. Your Majesty."

She turned back and waited up for him. "What is it, Baron?"

"I bring news from Galicia, Your Majesty," he approached her and took a knee before her.

"Rise, Baron. Now tell me what is so important that you come rushing towards me so out of breath?" the queen asked curiously.

"You might prefer someplace more private, my lady," Diego suggested.

Camila signaled him to follow her back into the chapel. They entered and sat at the lobby's reception area. "Have a seat, Diego. What news do you have for me?" Diego sat as told, and leaned in to speak almost to a whisper.

"King Gerardo has departed to attack Count Jacob and take over his lands in the south. He leaves Duke Mullah behind to oversee both kingdoms, My Queen."

The queen couldn't contain her surprise. Her eyebrows arched high, and she let out a low whistle. "Thank you, Diego. You have done well. Now, I should like to speak with Duke Pablo immediately, if not sooner. Thereafter, get yourself a little bit of rest, and get something to eat, you must be exhausted."

"Thank you, Your Majesty, as you wish," Diego hustled away to notify Pablo, while the queen stayed to pray for the well-being of both kingdoms, as well as for her brother's impending battle.

Less than ten minutes later, Duke Pablo entered the chapel to see the queen. "You called for me, Your Majesty?"

"Yes, Pablo. How much longer before our new and secret army is ready for battle?"

"My Queen, the new troops are ready for your command. The new subjects have been training and picking things up very quickly."

"Oh, good to hear," Camila sat back on the couch, clasping her hands and crossing her ankles. She took a deep breath, "Please have a seat. I have a bad feeling that something is about to happen, Pablo."

"My brother is preparing to attack Jacob. Gerardo's attack is just an excuse to fulfill his blood-thirsty desire for kingdom expansion and make a name for himself."

Pablo's eyes went wide, but he kept quiet. Camila took a deep breath and grabbed Pablo's forearm, squeezing it tight. "But he leaves that snake,Mullah in charge of his own kingdom and ours. And if Mullah ever sought an opportunity to increase himself and his own power—and when has he not—it would be now. So, I need you to have everyone on high alert, Pablo. Send word to all my nobles and clansmen. I think we should have everyone close by and ready to defend the land in case of an attack."

"I concur, my lady," Pablo agreed. "I am aware that Jibril took two additional divisions to Galicia which makes three divisions there now." Pablo paused and scratched at his chin, pensively. "It's a little sooner than we had hoped, but beggars can't be choosers. I have already sent word to the captains to be on full alert; the enemy has to know that moving so many divisions away from their posts would draw some attention. Anyway, I was already headed here to give you the full report, My Queen."

Camila's eyes danced across the floor, drowning in a thousand thoughts all at the same time. She spoke some of them aloud, "Mullah will be splitting his time between Asturias and Galicia, so he will not be able to focus on our land as much. If I know him at all, he will choose to prioritize Galicia and will likely close the borders from that side."

Pablo nodded in agreement, "That would be the most logical course of action, ma'am. May I recommend that we reinforce the borders to Galicia for now?"

"Yes, and with Mullah occupied in Galicia, I feel that this is the perfect opportunity for me to seek alliances," Camila said. "I need to get help while Mullah is not scrutinizing our every waking breath. I think Gerardo is making a big mistake by chasing Jacob. This could be very costly to him."

"What do you suggest, my lady? Would you like to send emissaries across our borders to seek assistance?"

"No, not yet, Pablo. We have an even greater opportunity. I have received an invitation to attend a ball held by the Kingdom of Segovia. It's just the cover we need to build a strong alliance and obtain their support."

"I think it is a great opportunity, ma'am, we can certainly make this happen."

"Very well, I shall attend the ball. Go on, make all the preparations necessary to leave," she said excitedly.

"As you wish, Your Majesty," and, with a bow, he stood and left the room.

Camila hurried off to find Joanna and give her the news. She found her in her bed chambers. "Mother," Camila called out cheerfully. "Get ready, we are going to a grand ball."

It took a second for this news to sink in, and suddenly Joanna's face lit up, "Oh goodness. Maybe you will find love there."

Camila froze in shock. "Oh, Mother, really? I cannot believe you. You are a one-tracked mind. Shall we bring a priest, just in case?"

"Well, it can happen, you know," Joanna said with a chuckle. They both laughed and then busied themselves with preparations for the big gathering ahead.

Camila sent word for her royal escort to be readied for the journey, and she practically waltzed about the castle in high spirits for the first time in a long time. Her mother had it all wrong. She wasn't courting for a king; she was courting for an *army*.

Chapter 9
The Alliances

There were many kingdoms that surrounded Asturias. Many had sworn an alliance to Queen Camila, and many others had at one time or another joined her father in battle against their common enemies during his reign. The kingdoms that Camila trusted the most were governed by King George Sanchez of Segovia and King Juan Velasquez of Salamanca, who had been friends of hers since they were young. King George was hosting the gathering that she currently planned to attend.

And, by the way, George and Juan were the same mischievous friends that had bullied Camila as a child and that would pick fights with the younger lads. Thankfully, they had outgrown their ornery stage. George went on to inherit the monarchy from his family, and Juan acquired his kingdom by his actions on the battlefield. He was awarded the rights to his land by John II of France as part of the Order of the Star.

Massive festivity preparations were underway in Segovia. George and Juan sat in the castle's reception room eating and drinking. From time to time some servants would drop in and show some fabric samples or present party decisions for approval and exit again in a flurry.

"Do you think Camila will decide to visit?" Juan asked him.

"I do believe she will," said George as he thoughtfully swirled the wine in his chalice. "She could use the time away from her family drama."

"I can only imagine that hothead Gerardo has been really upset by her reigning her own kingdom," Juan chuckled as he wiped his mouth with a linen cloth.

"You know, I think that was a very wise decision by King Celestino. Between us, I never really cared for Gerardo; and, you take my word for it, he will be a menace to be reckoned with one day," George took a bite off a turkey leg he'd been working on.

"Do you really think Gerardo is that bad?" Juan asked, surprised.

"Oh yes," George answered between bites. "Do you not remember when we were young, he always got what he wanted, and if it wasn't given freely, he would take it by force with one command to his escort?"

"Well, at least we can rest assured that Camila will play nicely with us. Thankfully, her territory stands between ours and Gerardo's," Juan held his chalice aloft and then took another big gulp. George raised his chalice and returned the toast.

"Well, what are you worried about, anyway? Your little kingdom is not worth fighting for," George needled his friend, laughing aloud.

"Ha! For your information, my kingdom was *earned* unlike yours, inherited from a rich papi," Juan answered smugly and was only half kidding around.

"Okay, okay, we both have some pretty good kingdoms. Salud," George raised his chalice to compliment Juan, who responded by raising his own chalice and clanking it with his friend's. Lifelong comrades.

King George had experienced some combat in his earlier adulthood and learned many crucial lessons on battlefield tactics. In his role as king, he had yet to be tested or challenged. It could be due to the fact that his land was surrounded by other peaceful kingdoms and territories that had thus far intercepted any oncoming attacks before they got to him.

He had sent support to assist his allies whenever they needed them. It was easy to justify these proxy battles that kept his own country uncontested. He had expressed a firm alliance with Camila and pledged to be there should she ever need his help.

King Juan was not quite as close to Camila as George was, but he also knew all the same acquaintances and attended some of the same gatherings that they did. Juan's battlefield experience was brief but substantial enough to have territory awarded to him.

John II acknowledged him for his actions in service in the first phase of the Hundred Years' War between France and England and asked his father King Phillip VI to grant him his lands. For the most part both George and Juan were peaceful lords that loved a good inter-kingdom gathering. Such festivals allowed them to meet new people, catch up with old acquaintances and, in general, enjoy themselves; one of those acquaintances, however, was Lord Mullah.

⸎

The New Moon Royal Gathering

On the day of the grand ball, nobilities from every land arrived to the "New Moon Royal Gathering," where games and jousting made for a fun day of celebration and showmanship. These games allowed rulers to show off their champions in action even during times of peace. Kings George and Juan had combined forces to send out a mass invitation to all the nobility of the surrounding kingdoms.

Lord Mullah also received the invitation, and he was debating on whether to attend, since he felt the added pressure to be present in Galicia to watch over his interests there. However, when he received news that Camila was attending the festivities, he immediately announced he would be present as well. This grand ball promised to be a major success since the royalty from all over Europe were to be in attendance.

Mullah was one of the first to arrive. He wanted to make sure his presence was fully known and, of course, he wanted to be there as everyone else arrived. Noble guests filtered into the main ballroom, and as they entered, they were being announced.

"Presenting Queen Camila of Asturias who is accompanied by Her Majesty Queen Mother Joanna." Upon Queen Camila's arrival, everyone in attendance cheered as she made her way towards the center of the court where the usher seated them. The other royal attendees gushed over her.

"It is great to see you here, Your Majesty."

"I'm glad you made it, Your Majesty."

"What an honor to have you, Your Majesty."

She smiled pleasantly and thanked each one. Shortly thereafter, Camila heard a commotion among the guests who were abuzz about the next arrival. She turned towards the entrance of the castle to see what the fuss was about.

"Presenting King François du Basque of the Basque kingdoms," the announcer proclaimed in his loud baritone voice. The guests flocked to him like pigeons to a pastry.

"Your Majesty."

"Welcome, sire."

"Good evening, Your Majesty."

Everyone revered this man who immediately held the whole room's attention upon his entrance. The usher escorted him to the center of the court and seated across the table from Camila. She noted that he did not have a female escort, just his royal courtiers.

François locked eyes with Camila and gestured a dramatic flourish with his right hand. "My lady," he greeted her with a slight bow but never breaking eye contact.

Camila sat there radiantly, soaking it all in. "My lord," she also gave a little nod.

Her elegance and beauty enraptured him. François noticed her soft, glowing skin and her highborn mannerisms but noted that she didn't carry herself with the uptight demeanor of the typical blue bloods. Her royal gown was astonishing. As captivating as she was.

Camila also shared admiration for François as he sat down across from her. She would discreetly look over at him from time to time and notice him looking at her. Each time she became a bit flushed, and over time began to suspect that François was equally as smitten with her.

They were not the only ones looking at each other, though. Queen Joanna noticed, as well, and did not hesitate to whisper a reminder, "You see? I told you that you would meet someone here."

"Mother," Camila blushed again. She grabbed her mother's arm, silently pleading for her discretion and not to say anything further.

All the other lords and ladies carried on with their rousing conversations, simply enjoying the evening.

"It is made of the finest silk," Lord Mullah said to a group of people, referring to the shirt he was wearing. "As smooth as a lamb's ear."

Queen Joanna harrumphed into her goblet that she'd been drinking from, "Same old peacock, always trying to impress the ladies."

"Of course," Mullah continued to an admirer, "I know who Lord Farquhar is. He and I have known each other for quite some time now."

Joanna leaned closer to Camila, "Now that he is a Duke and acting as monarch of Asturias and Galicia, he feels like a king among kings."

"Let him be, Mama. Don't let him ruin the night for you," Camila responded. "Maybe less wine, if it will temper an overly honest tongue. Hm?" She slid the cup farther from her mother and turned her attention back to François.

Mullah, of course, noticed the flirty looks and the laughs between Queen Camila and King François and did not like them. He saw it as a potential obstacle to his well-laid plans. Worse than that, the king and queen were ignoring him, which rubbed him the wrong way.

Mullah turned towards Jibril, who, as always, was nearby and complained to him, "King François seems to have an interest in our good Queen Camila."

"My lord, do you wish me to take care of him? Allah wills it," Jibril suggested.

"No, Jibril. King François is not an easy target. Do not underestimate him. Let us simply keep an eye on them and after tonight assure that he shall see her no more," Mullah seethed.

"As you will, my lord," Jibril returned to his nearby perch, where he could remain available but securely out of the way. He was trying to remain incognito in the background, but he saw Marquess Albert of François's court was watching him very closely.

Mullah decided to simply focus on his own favorite party game of attracting naive young ladies.

New ladies unspoiled by the rumors of his sordid reputation. And there were plenty here. He dallied and strung them along as if he had the whole moon and stars in his grasp to offer the right maiden.

Meanwhile, after greeting everyone around the table among the nobles, François looked for an opportunity to start a conversation with Camila. "My lady, it is such an honor to see you once again."

"My lord, have we met before?" Camila answered back, a little surprised.

"We have," François said. "Back when we were young. As you'll recall I used to come out to King Celestino's gatherings. I played with George and Juan, and sometimes you showed up to spar with us. You were quite good, too. As a matter of fact, I started playing as part of the group, thanks to you welcoming me in. For that reason, I have been forever grateful."

"Wow, why can't I place you, my lord? It is true that I used to come out and play with George and Juan. I feel terrible that I do not recall you," Camila answered, apologetically.

"Do not feel bad, my lady. I was a boy of few words," he chuckled. "Few words and fewer fencing skills. The important thing to remember is that I remember every lesson you ever taught me, and I am grateful to see your beautiful face once again."

"My lord speaks too highly of me," she studied him closely trying to remember. "But perhaps this is the line you use to charm all of the ladies," she challenged him. "Using the shadow of our own memories against us."

"I am a man of my word and a man who leans always upon the truth. I have no reason to beguile you, nor anyone else, with flattery," François replied looking her in the eye and continued with his soft-spoken tone. "Your beauty and your honorable kindnesses to me of old speak for themselves. But even so, the reputation of your good heart among your people precedes you always, my lady."

"I thank you for your kind words, sire," she was humbled and flattered at the same time by his keen observations. And now she grew more nervous from the palpable chemistry and attraction she felt towards him.

Queen Joanna, who doted on every word, pressed Camila's hand in her own, signaling her approval of François. Others simply smiled at them and nodded their heads with joy and respect, not wanting to detract from the moment or break the spell.

At her prompting, François went on to tell Camila the story of how they'd met for the first time. When George and Juan roughed him up good. "So, that is how we met. You were and will always be," François paused to search for the right words. He smiled at her and shrugged, "my hero."

Camila laughed, finally having remembered the awkward French lad that had suffered a tough hazing from her friends. "That was you? You do not look anything like you did back then."

"I know, I was an ugly duckling back then," François chuckled along with her. "But no longer. Now, I am an ugly swan."

"No," she laughed, "that is not what I meant François. You were a handsome lad, but you just look different now. Maybe with more lumps and bruises on your face," she joked with him. "But back then, you were always my François," she said holding her chalice up to toast the memory.

He smiled back, picked up his own goblet and returned the toast before taking a sip. Then he added, "Well, thank you, my lady, and as ever, the whole room dims in comparison to the light from your smile. And by the way, please continue to call me that: my François."

Camila nodded a 'touché' and turned to Joanna who had been watching their whole sparring match.

"And to think," François continued after a swallow of wine, "That I almost didn't come...I usually skip these festivals."

"Same here," Camila responded with a sly wink. "I'm only here to find my poor mother a suitor."

Joanna almost spit out her own wine. François laughed aloud and raised his goblet in a toast, "To a smart match... for your mother."

"Here, here," Camila said lifting her own glass high.

After dinner Camila and François took a walk to a more quiet and private area where they could talk.

"I thank you for thinking so highly of me, King Francois," Camila blushed nervously.

"Just François, my lady," he gently corrected her with a friendly smile. "You do not have to address me as king. After all, we have known each other since we were young, have we not?"

"Very well, then, François," she smiled at him. "You, sire, are right. Again. And you—you can call me Camila. Do we have an accord?"

"Yes, of course, my lady."

"What was that?" It was her turn to chasten him.

"Pardon moi," he recovered quickly. "What I meant to say is, yes, of course, Camila."

"There you go," she replied with a soft laugh. Camila was happy to finally confide in François about her current situation with her kingdom and the nefarious plot between Gerardo and Mullah.

"I do not know why I tell you this, François, you simply have a nice presence about you that makes me feel like I can tell you anything. Forgive me, if this sound like a full, gushing confessional, for that is not my intention," Camila said a little embarrassed.

"Please, don't ever think like that. It would be my honor if you were to consider me as your greatest ally, my lady," He answered resolutely. "As you have always been mine. Anything that you need, you can count on me."

"Thank you, François. This magical night marks the beginning of a new friendship and alliance." They continued to talk and laugh deep into the night.

Afterwards, when the celebration was coming to an end, and people began to stagger back to their quarters, François walked her and the queen mother to the hall where the footman showed them to their rooms.

The next morning, François was waiting in the courtyard to see them off. "I shall see you soon, My Lady," François said with a kiss upon her hand.

"Yes, I look forward to it, my lord," Camila replied. The carriage door closed between them, and the driver clucked his tongue twice. They were on their way. Camila and François watched each other until the courtyard gates finally came between them.

Once they were on the road back home, Camila spoke to her mother. "Mother, I feel like… like I finally found a new ally. Someone that I can feel at ease to talk to about anything. Comfortable. Too comfortable. Isn't that a red flag, Mama? Remember the last time."

"On the contrary, I am glad, Mija. Last time you had a snake masquerading as a lion. This time you have the lion," Joanna responded with a knowing gleam in her eye.

"One step at a time, Mama. We need to work as allies before we can even dream of working as man and wife. Let's keep the lion in the cage for now. The eyes of all the kingdoms are upon us."

"Well, I do not think the lion was too concerned about who was watching him tonight. He only had eyes for you, Mija," Joanna nudged her arm.

Camila knew this to be very true. She could hardly believe that this well-spoken gentleman had been the awkward little boy she had once defended. It made her laugh again. "Wow, that brought back so many memories of our carefree days together, back when we were young," Camila sighed.

"Memories? You mean to say feelings," Joanna corrected her.

And for the first time, Camila conceded. "I'll say. Aye yi yi, Mama. Feelings that I did not expect to have ever again," she confessed.

King François du Basque

Camila's trip back to Asturias seemed like it was taking much longer than the trip to the gathering had taken. In her mind she kept revisiting thoughts of Lord François du Basque and the moments and conversations they had had together.

"Still thinking about him?" Joanna cackled as they rode along inside their carriage.

There was a small delay before Camila answered, "Pardon, Mama? Did you say something?"

"I said, still thinking about him," Joanna repeated.

"Is it that obvious?" asked Camila with a blush.

"How can it not be? It is only you and me in here, and, usually on our journeys, your words and ideas are flowing like a river from door to door," Joanna said. "We've passed six villages without a single observation from you."

"My mind is going and going, Mama. I am just curious to know more about François. I have decided to meet with Pablo, who can give me more information about him, when we return."

Joanna simply looked at her and patted her hand lovingly. She turned her attention back outside the window to take in village number seven which they were passing by. All in all, she was happy to see her daughter's blossoming love.

Upon their arrival at the castle, Camila proceeded to the living room. The room was cold, and she drew closer to the fireplace, which had only recently been stoked with a few logs, freshly burning and crackling. She rubbed her hands and arms to warm up faster. Pablo entered the room, and Camila turned to welcome him in, "Pablo, please have a seat," she motioned towards a chair.

"Thank you, Your Majesty," replied Pablo. "I hear the trip was very successful."

"It was, indeed. And the reason why I want to talk to you is, well, I wonder if you are familiar with Lord François du Basque?" she asked.

"But of course, ma'am. King François has been a loyal supporter and valuable ally of your kingdom going back to your father's reign. He was a young lad when he began visiting the castle, I think you may remember him," Pablo prompted her.

"I am embarrassed to say that it took me some time to recall who he was." The corner of her lips turned up in amusement. "It has been a couple of decades since I saw him last. He does not quite look like the same ruddy kid he was back then."

"I should say not, my lady. Not since he went on to become a true warrior and loyal protector of the lands to the north. Lord François was referred to as 'The Knight of the Light' by the people throughout the kingdoms."

Camila listened raptly as she digested this new and interesting information. "The Knight of the Light?" she prompted him finally.

"Yes, ma'am, Lord François became known by this name due to his honorable disposition and his brilliant, shining armor." Pablo continued. "He gave hope to those who needed it when they found themselves under siege from enemy attacks."

"I see," she mused. Camila was impressed by this description. She stood up and went back to the fireplace and threw another log on top before returning to her seat.

"Is there anything else?" she wondered.

"Let's see, well, ma'am, François later became the heir to the kingdom of the Labourd Pays Basque. Specifically, the Pyrenees-Atlantiques," Pablo added.

"Oh yes, I do remember him being from the northern region. I knew he was king but I didn't know about all his accomplishments!" Camila exclaimed.

"Some say that his ancestors came from Scandinavian lands, while others believe him to be of an old royal blood line from the northwest era European kingdoms," Pablo continued his litany, adding this notable fact: "One thing that they all agree upon is that Lord François has never been defeated in battle, ma'am."

"What battles did he fight?" Camila probed.

"During the troubled days when our lands were under regular attacks from the Moors, most of the kingdoms were under siege and on the verge of losing everything to their enemies. Right before their defeat, Sir François du Basque showed up with an army of his own and defended his allies against the attacking enemies. François won decisive battles that helped defend these territories. All the while, obtaining peace throughout the lands," Pablo explained to his eager audience. An audience that was trying not to seem as eager as she was.

"That's all very fascinating, indeed," Camila said thoughtfully. "But something doesn't make sense. It is my understanding that he has been out of sight for some time. If he fought in the region, and he was recognized as protector of the lands, why did he disappear, and where did he go?"

Pablo was finally stumped with her inquiry and shrugged apologetically, "That is a question that you may have to ask him yourself, ma'am. Lord François is a private man who does not say much when it comes to his accomplishments. However, there are many different stories—rumors, really—that have surfaced regarding his whereabouts."

"What stories?" the queen leaned in quite expectantly.

Pablo scratched his chin to recall the most recent account, "Well, some say that François questioned the loyalty of his own allies. That perhaps they didn't fully appreciate his protections and took him for granted, which discouraged him. So, he decided to head back to the highlands of his own kingdom to focus on his own affairs. Others said that he joined a new order of crusades and was sent to fight another holy war. And others claimed that he returned to his ancestor's lands to train and become the fierce warrior that he is today. Perhaps it is a combination of things," Pablo speculated.

"Before Father died, I heard him talk about a great ally that everyone was grateful for. Could he have been talking about François?"

"The one and the same, ma'am. The truth is that François fought fiercely to discourage any enemies from advancing. He defended in such a devastating way that even the lords, allied to the lands, prayed to never have him as an enemy. Furthermore, he met with the kings of the alliance and returned their lands to them. This action was a noble gesture, since Lord François could have easily taken claim of all the lands and kept them for himself," Pablo said.

"He wouldn't have," Camila replied. "As someone of high integrity and honor, taking possession of those kingdoms was never an option for him." She stared a moment longer into the fire and then turned back to her friend. "Pablo, I thank you so much for taking the time to share this information with me. I have learned a lot and have a better notion of who Lord François is."

"You would be hard-pressed to find a finer man in all of Europe, Your Majesty," Pablo excused himself, and they both retired to their chambers.

After attending the gathering and seeing Camila again, François had a good reason to return to the lands where he often spent time during his youth. Per his agreement with Camila, he would now head to Asturias to offer his assistance to her and her kingdom.

"Is my order of chivalry ready to travel, Albert?" François asked his marquess.

"It is, my lord," Albert said, settling a chain mail gauntlet onto his belt.

"Very well, then. Begin the march to Asturias, and be on high alert for a possible ambush, possibly from Lord Mullah. We are heading towards treacherous territories," François commanded. "The queen, at the center, may be our ally, but the vast moat around her is crawling with gargoyles and ogres."

"Of course, my lord. Pertaining to Lord Mullah, I saw that he did not like you talking to Queen Camila." Albert recalled the observation to François. "It was so much to his disliking that Jibril, his baron, was called over and volunteered to take care of you. Mullah did not authorize it, of course; but gave the order to make sure you would not be seeing her again, my lord."

"Were they aware of your presence?" asked the king, pensively.

"Absolutely not, my lord," responded Albert with a sly smile.

"Good, Albert. You have been my eyes and ears out there, and will continue to be so. We cannot drop our guard right now; we will travel through unwelcoming territories with ambiguous allegiances, and our objective is to restore peace in the lands by helping Queen Camila."

"Oui, my lord, I am, as always, at your service," Albert bowed with a hand over his heart.

A group of knights rode towards François. These were the scouts returning from their foray ahead. "My lord, we are heading towards hostile territory. It looks like Lord Mullah's men are awaiting our arrival," Count David Ascough reported.

And it was true. Further down the road, Captain Khalid of Mullah's frontline division had ordered his archers into position, following instructions from Jibril to treat every oncoming army as enemies.

"My lord," David reported to Lord François, "they are only defending with a small force, perhaps about twenty-five percent of their usual numbers."

"Albert, go make contact with their commanders, and let them know we do not need to have this fight. Take David with you," François ordered.

"Yes, sire," Albert and David responded. They proceeded to move on ahead to make contact, as instructed. Khalid saw them coming and moved a squad down to meet with them in the middle of the road.

"As-salamu alaykum," Khalid waved formally as he rode up opposite them. David sat by, warily minding Khalid's guard.

"Et que la paix soit avec vous," Albert replied.

"I am Marshal Khalid, Captain to Duke Mullah's army and protector to King Gerardo's territory. You are attempting to enter a land without a welcome. Go back or you shall suffer the full attention of my skilled warriors."

Albert was unmoved. He spoke calmly, "I am Marquess Albert, Commander to Lord and King François du Basque. I request that you reserve such treatment for a true foe. We are allies and are not here to fight you. In fact, Queen Camila has welcomed us and we are here on her behalf. Stand back and allow us to join her, as this is her kingdom. If you comply with our demands, I can guarantee your men will survive the day."

"I will do no such thing. If I am to die here today, it will be because Allah wills it, not because you speak with haughty words," Khalid practically spat back at him.

"Marshal Khalid, Captain, you are outnumbered four-to-one. This is a losing battle, which you do not need to add as a stain on your glorious war record. I urge you to reconsider your options," Albert asked again nicely.

"I will not yield to an infidel. Allah is with us, and he will not stand down for anyone," Khalid said harshly. He yanked his horse around and dug in his heels and galloped away.

"That went well," David smirked.

"Their haste to meet their maker is an inspiration to us all," Albert smiled back at him.

They returned to the army to report. "My lord, many alternatives were presented, but their captain refused to stand down. He seemed eager to shuffle off this mortal coil in Allah's name. Cet idiot," Albert said.

"Very well, then. Albert, maintain the position here. David and I will each take a division and split behind them, to surround them," François outlined the plan. "And if they object, they can take it up with Allah soon enough."

"Yes, Your Majesty," they both affirmed and proceeded as assigned.

"Les archers préparez-vous. Préparez les catapultes," Albert commanded.

Just upon the next rise, Khalid watched the movement down below. "What is this?" He angrily asked. "How dare he leave only a division behind and leave. Those infidels, I will make them pay for their insolence and destroy them. Archers prepare to fire," Khalid yelled. "In the name of Allah and our Lord, fire!" Khalid commanded, and his archers opened their first volley at Albert's knights.

Albert's men protected themselves with their shields to defend against the attack. "Catapultes, archers, feu!" Albert commanded, and his men began to return fire in waves. The first unit released their shots, then the second unit followed as the third and fourth units followed in cadence to initiate a continuous wave of counterattacking arrows. This was followed by the catapults, which pounded the enemy position.

"Take cover. Fire at will, and take cover as needed," Khalid notified his men after seeing the overwhelming counterassault on them.

Meanwhile, François and David's divisions were coming around behind Khalid's back, approaching them at a fast pace with their cavalry. Khalid saw the riders too late.

"Look to your sides! Look to your sides! The enemy is surrounding us," Khalid yelled in desperation as the attack from behind closed in upon them. He and his men found themselves surrounded by François and his knights, who blocked any retreat.

François shifted forward to close in behind David's advancing unit. "Cavalries, move on forward. Archers, catapults, stop your attack. Prepare to protect the king," Albert commanded.

Khalid's men turned to protect their flanks by shooting their arrows and engaging in hand-to-hand battle in vain. François' skilled men-at-arms began to cut through them at a feverish rate.

King François yelled as he approached Khalid, "Stand down, and you shall live. Stand down for you will not get another proposition to live."

"Stand down, stand down," Khalid surrendered immediately. Having lost more than two-thirds of their small unit so quickly, the remaining men dropped their weapons to save themselves from imminent annihilation.

François's knights quickly had the last of them surrounded and closely guarded them to make sure they did not try anything now.

"Come forward to the center of this area and have a seat," David commanded Khalid and his men. They proceeded forward.

François rode up, and his warhorse pawed the ground ferociously. "May the Lord be with you Marshal Khalid. I am King François du Basque. I praise you for your good judgement and for sparing the lives of your knights."

"Wa-alaykum-salam. And unto you, peace, Lord François. I thank you for showing mercy to us. That action speaks very highly of you. We shall all remember you for that, and may Allah keep you in his will," Khalid answered.

"I am most grateful for your kind thoughts, Marshal. I will grant you and your men access to the south lands. I must warn you though. If you or any of your men rejoin Mullah, your lives will be taken on sight. Do we have an accord?"

"We have an accord, Your Majesty," Khalid responded and bowed his head to show his respect and gratitude towards François.

This action was important for several reasons, primarily because Mullah would not receive news that his army was no longer in control of Asturias, as expected. In addition, Mullah had just lost twenty-five percent of his total army, and those men—what was left of the army—now had an opportunity to start a new life.

François replaced Mullah's men with his own to secure the Asturian border. That would assure the kingdom would be secure from any other invaders. Now, Camila would soon be able to reclaim her lands with his military support.

⁂

"Good evening, Your Majesty, I bring news to you from our borders," Count Gregorio approached Camila, who was seated reading a book.

"Good evening, Sir Gregorio. What message do you have for me?"

"King François enters our lands, ma'am, after having defeated Mullah's division that was preventing access. Lord François now heads to the castle as we speak,"

Camila stood up triumphantly and clapped her hands, "Gregorio, we must make the necessary preparations to welcome the king. We need to muster all the assistance we can for the men that may have been injured in battle." Her voice rose with delight, "And then we need to celebrate, tonight."

Queen Joanna caught the last of this as she entered the room, "I beg your pardon?" Joanna inquired.

"Mama, François just defeated Mullah's division that was left behind, and he is now on his way here," she explained excitedly.

"Dios bendito," Joanna exclaimed, as Camila pulled her into a victory hug.

Gregorio excused himself, "As you wish, right away, Your Majesty."

King François du Basque's arrival to the queen's castle was epic. The bells rang and rang to announce the coming of the kingdom's new hero. People came out to receive and welcome them as they cheered and jumped with joy.

Camila's Green Dragoons made two ceremonial rows, facing each other with their swords drawn out to honor him and his knights who passed in between. The trumpets echoed from the high towers. Camila was waiting to receive François at the castle's entrance, together with her mother and Archbishop Nicholas.

This was a great day for the Kingdom of Asturias with the acknowledgement of their new allies. François arrived at the entrance of the castle and climbed off his horse to meet Camila, who eagerly awaited him.

"François, I received the news of your victory over Mullah's men," Camila said, as she hurried towards him as quickly as her royal bustle would allow.

"My lady, you have heard correctly," François replied and kindly leaned forward to bow to her.

"My lord, please come inside. We have prepared accommodations for you and your men.. And, if any of your knights are in need of medical attention, Archbishop Nicholas will escort them to the healing room to be looked after," she said.

"You are very kind, my lady. Do not mind if I take you up on your kind gesture. Please allow me to introduce the commander of my court, Lord Albert Collins, and my captain and count David Ascough," François pointed at them, respectively.

"We are at your service, Your Majesty," They both bowed in unison.

"Why, thank you both," Camila responded with delight.

"And this is my beloved mother, Queen Joanna," Camila drew her mother forward on her arm.

"Our pleasure, Your Majesty," All three of them bowed.

François turned to his men, "Albert, please coordinate between the two of you for the men that need healing to follow the archbishop. The others go get cleaned up and see to the horses," François ordered.

"Yes, my lord," Albert saluted.

François turned towards Camila and Joanna, who were waiting to go inside the castle. And further down the courtyard, as the men were entering, they could hear the archbishop blessing them as they passed by.

———————◆———————

After they were all settled into their living quarters, they were invited to a celebration dinner. Once seated at the table, the queen addressed everyone in attendance. "I would like to thank King François du Basque for his heroic action to come to our kingdom's assistance and provide us with much needed aid," Camila said and raised a chalice in his honor. Everyone lifted theirs as well to follow her lead as they cheered, "Long live the King and Queen!"

François stood alongside her and raised his own chalice with these words. "My lady thinks too highly of me. I thank you for this dinner and for allowing my men and me to partake of this celebration. We are forever in your debt for such a grand welcoming. As I have served your father, may he rest in peace, I am happy to serve you, as well."

Once again all in attendance stomped their feet and banged the tables with their fists in support of their great new alliance forged in strength and honor. The night went on, and the people of Asturias had not felt this good since King Celestino's bygone days of peace.

Chapter 10
The King's Karma

Gerardo and his war party continued to advance deep into Jacob's territory. It had taken him much longer than he planned. He now had to worry about all the heavy equipment and items such as the catapults, food, and supplies. All while seventy-five percent of his army was on foot. He was now approaching the final valley before reaching Jacob's castle.

The passage was very treacherous, as the road led into a valley. They would have to go in between mountains which left them with no easy escape routes. Gerardo and his army took this path and committed to entering the valley.

The army would need to take their time going down into the valley so they would not break any of the heavy equipment they carried with them. The road was long and narrow, and, for an army the size of Gerardo's, it would take time to cross through. The downhill climb was bumpy, hot, and humid.

During their descent, once they had crossed the midway point, the sky suddenly darkened, and the day became as night. Buzzing sounds overhead caused them to look around just in time to see their comrades suddenly drop to the ground dead. Wrecked with arrows.

"Sire, we are under attack, my lord. Protect the king," Gerardo's army realized all too late that they were being ambushed from above the lip of valley.

"Take cover! Retreat," Gerardo commanded immediately, and this was echoed by his men, who were tired from pulling their bulky weapons and were completely caught by surprise.

"Sire! Sire," the knights called for him. "Protect the King! Protect the King!" they echoed in desperation. Many of them surrounded him and raised their shields. Gerardo looked towards the hilltop and saw Jacob looking down at him.

"Retreat, retreat," Gerardo called out in a panic to his men. Gerardo and a very small group of his court began to ascend the long way back to the top where they had started, as Jacob looked smugly down at his impending victory.

"Make sure to kill them all," Jacob sneered at his knights.

"Yes, my lord," they replied dutifully.

Jacob contemplated with delight the annihilation of King Gerardo's army. He returned to his tent and sat down to rest on his portable throne they had brought with them. As his hand dipped into a bowl of plump grapes nearby, he recalled the moment he'd heard of the king's audacious plans.

It had been a couple of weeks prior to this moment when one of Jacob's barons, Bernard Perez, approached him. "Requesting permission, my lord. An emissary to Lord Mullah is here with a message for you."

They made their way into Jacob's conference room within his castle.

"Lord Mullah? What would Mullah want to contact me for? Allow him to enter," Jacob allowed.

"Yes, my lord," the baron brought the emissary forward as instructed.

"What brings an emissary of Lord Mullah to me?" Jacob asked impatiently.

The emissary moved towards Jacob and took a knee in sign of respect. "I bring a letter from Duke Mullah, my lord." He rose and handed it to him.

Jacob took the letter and proceeded to open it and read it.

Count Jacob,

I am giving you the opportunity to obliterate the one that cost you the kingdom that rightfully belonged to you. King Gerardo did not only take pleasure in stealing the Kingdom of Asturias from you, leaving you deserted and fending for life, but now wants to completely take over all your remaining territories.

His plan is to attack you by surprise by entering your lands undetected. I want you to know that he is taking the road that leads through the valley. This will give you the perfect opportunity to have the upper hand to finish him once and for all.

He plans to bring heavy equipment, and most of his knights will be on foot. Once you have killed him and laid siege to his army, I will order my knights, that are guarding the Kingdom of Asturias, to join you and your knights to lead you into his castle, here in Asturias, where you will encounter little to no resistance.

You will once again be able to take your claim as King. In return, I ask for your pledge of loyalty and unconditional alliance and your formal recognition of me as the new King of Galicia.

I hope that this letter gives you the opportunity that you have longed for. Between you and me, we will have defeated Gerardo, and we will be set as the rightful kings of Galicia and Asturias without contest, thereby ending King Celestino's abominable lineage. I suggest you then align yourself with Camila via arranged marriage, since she will have nowhere else to go, and thereby secure your dominion and claim.

Furthermore, by the time of your receiving this letter, you will also have established yourself as the rightful King of Toledo, since I have recently received news that its king has died in his campaign to aid the Kingdom of Aragon, having suffered from what they are calling the bubonic plague, known as the Black Death.

Cheers to the start of your reign over your new lands. I look forward to our future reigns in the region.

Mullah el Hassan, King of Galicia

Mullah had signed as the King of Galicia in anticipation of King Gerardo's death. Jacob smiled to himself at the thought. "Yes, Gerardo, your time to pay has come." Jacob threw some grapes at the back of the closest guard by the door to the tent. "Hey! Are they done killing everyone? If so, we need to get our people ready to go back to my kingdom of Asturias," Jacob called out. "And back to my beloved bride-to-be."

"Yes, my lord," his men responded.

Gerardo's men had been struck down by the masses. Most of them had several arrows in their bodies, faces and limbs. Their blood was starting to flood the pit they found themselves in, and their cries of pain echoed along the valley walls.

Jacob's knights chased after Gerardo, having killed most of his knights along the way. The Galician flag lay shredded and bloodied on the ground.

Jacob's pledge to ally himself with Mullah would be the perfect ending to a masterplan in the making. Gerardo's quest for expansion and his own greed had kept him blind to any betrayal from within. Mullah's twenty-year plan had finally paid off, and Jacob marveled at his patience all these years.

Gerardo's overconfidence in a supposedly weaker foe would lead him to a fitting end. Mullah's timing and their collective advantage here was too good to pass up. Entire kingdoms would be laid at Jacob's feet, and all it cost was the lives of some men in a ditch? That was the easiest two-second decision he had ever made.

Long live the King.

Restoring Asturias

Queen Camila had now hosted King François as Asturias' guest of honor in the welcome celebration. She was ever grateful for his genuine interest in her kingdom and its ultimate protection.

The queen mother was delighted by the idea of having someone like François around and was delighted to see how well he got along with her daughter. What sensible mother wouldn't be? They were a smart match.

As the spring time began, François and Camila began to take outings on horseback together, traveling throughout the kingdom and visiting the villages. They interacted with the people of the land and listened to their needs.

"Your Majesties, we are grateful for having you look after us. We are your loyal servants," the people reminded them everywhere they went. "We are grateful for your loyalty and your hard work," Camila and François expressed in return.

Camila enjoyed the time with François. She enjoyed getting to know him better, to see him when he was playful, when he was sullen, when he was cautious or even when he was cranky because he hadn't eaten in so long. She was learning to read him like a book.

Her people loved him, her mother loved him, but Camila maintained her conservative posture to not rush into things. She wanted to focus on governing the best she could. There would be time for love if it came to that, she reasoned. And in the meanwhile, she would keep a sharp eye out for any tricks and subterfuge. Everyone was capable of it, regardless of what good intentions they claimed to have. But hadn't he passed all her silly little tests? Was he not in the clear? Was it time to maybe, she wondered, let the lion out of his cage?

This particular morning, Camila was by herself in the privacy of her bedroom. She overlooked the land from her high balcony, pondering all-things François. The queen mother entered the room and noticed her pining.

"What's wrong, Mija? I know something is bothering you. You cannot hide it from me," she pressed.

Camila looked over at her mother and sat down on a nearby sofa. She patted the space beside her, and her mother sat and lovingly took her hand in her own. "I am okay, Mother. I just keep making the same mistakes repeatedly, and... here I am being selfish and thinking of myself, instead of what is required of a queen," she explained. "I know I should be thinking of the well-being of the kingdom and the planting season right around the corner. But it is just that François is so—so—. Agh. Never mind... please, Mother, it is nothing, forget about it," she laughed it off.

"My daughter. François is and has always been a trustworthy gentleman. We have known him since you two were young," Camila leaned back and pulled up an ornate throw pillow to hold in her arms. Joanna continued in a very stern demeanor, "Now think about it, if he wanted to take this land by force or wanted to take advantage of the situation, he would have taken it already. Just like Jacob and your brother did. His army owns our borders. Don't you realize that?"

"Yes, I know, Mother. I understand on one level that this time it is different. I know that all the actions prove exactly to what you just said, but—."

"But? But now you have feelings for him, correct?" she asked. "Well, to that I say, it's about bloody time."

This made Camila smile, "I don't know, Mother. When I am with him, I feel great. I feel protected and heard. I feel that he really cares for me. But I have a responsibility to the kingdom. To move cautiously."

"Cautiously? Fine, but you're moving like a long-tailed cat in a room full of rocking chairs."

Camila snorted at this mental image her mother created.

Joanna continued, "Remember the advice that your father told you when he gave you and Gerardo the kingdoms?"

"A lemon a day keeps the scurvy away," she joked.

Joanna leaned in close and whispered, "Una mano lava la otra."

"One hand washes the other," Camila nodded. "But what does that—."

"You have a responsibility to yourself. You have the responsibility to be happy. To choose a husband that cares for you, and that you take care for in return," Joanna said firmly.

"Well, not to beat a dead horse, Mama, but the last mano stole mi reino," Camila said. "Some see fear, but I think I am very, very, very wise. Like my mother."

Joanna narrowed her eyes at her feisty daughter, "Do not flatter me, young lady. And do not let your mind overthink the obvious. Especially when it comes to true love, my daughter. True love. For us it is a luxury if you find it. And when you do, you hold on to it like a secret treasure. And do not let it go," Joanna instructed.

Camila paused momentarily to consider it. "Thank you, Mother, I hear you. I get it. We make our decisions with the best information we have available, and I guess only time will tell what our future will bring."

———————— ❖ ————————

The next morning, François and Camila mounted their horses at the stable, after a hearty breakfast. It had now become a part of their daily routine to ride through the kingdom.

Today Camila seemed a bit shy. Quieter than usual. François noticed the difference right away. She was not her usual, outgoing, and outspoken self, so he carefully dipped his big toe into the troubled waters, "Is something bothering you, my lady?"

"No, my lord," she replied with a blush. "I apologize, it is just that, I worry about—people. My people. Please do not pay attention to me."

"As you should, my lady. I don't have to tell you; this is a monarch's number one job. Their people. Don't apologize for that. It's a true—and sadly a rare—virtue that you have. If every kingdom had a monarch that felt the same way that you do, the kingdoms would be living in peace. With no malice."

"You know, François? You seem so different from everyone I have ever known. There is something about you. I feel comfortable with you. I do not know what it is, but I feel that I can be myself with you."

"Thank you, Camila, I think it is the magic love potion I have the cook stir into your porridge each morning," he joked.

"I'm serious," she said, flashing him a smile. "I feel like you understand me, and I think that you and I are very similar in our way of thinking. I find you very caring. Thoughtful. I just—," she paused searching for the right words.

"You just...?" François prompted.

"I just do not want to be wrong about you. It's too important for me to get this one right. Because there have been others that have come into my life and given me a brilliant masquerade of themselves. Suddenly, their shape shifted into a viper and destroyed my trust. And that has cost me dearly, it has cost my land dearly. My actions have hurt my people, and frankly I cannot bear the thought of making another mistake like that," she explained softly.

François nudged his horse closer to hers. He reached out a hand to touch her arm, "Camila, I withhold nothing from you intentionally. I think that by now you have gotten to know enough about me to know that I have the best intentions towards you and towards your kingdom. Would it not be true that, if I had any malice, that I would have shown my hand at some opportune time? Yes, I think that Evil François would have probably started by taking claim of your land, correct?" he reasoned.

"Yes, I know. For that I will forever be indebted to you. However, do not think that I owe you any special favors," Camila pulled away from him.

"Of course not. I am not like that, Camila. I am not sure who you are used to dealing with or who has done you wrong. If they are still alive, I would like to have words with them on your behalf. But rest assured that you know me. And you know I would never do that to you," François responded emphatically.

"I know, François, I apologize if it came out too harsh, but I have experienced—well, very harmful situations," Camila explained.

"Worry not, my lady. Please, I would be greatly honored if you were to allow me to continue helping you protect your kingdom. At least until your own army becomes strong enough to be self-sufficient." François stopped his horse and both horses paused on their journey. "I will have my knights provide the proper training that your army needs and give them council, as needed, should you grant me permission," François raised his eyebrows expectantly.

Camila considered the request and could see no flaws in the logic. She exhaled a deep breath and then told him, "Thank you, François. Yes, I trust you. And it is a good plan."

François relaxed, "I want them to be ready to fight against anyone. For now, if I may be frank with you, you are vulnerable and therefore prone to be attacked. Don't you agree?"

"Is it that obvious? Yes, I am aware of our vulnerabilities. That is the reason why it would just kill me if you were to betray me," Camila answered with a slight chuckle. "I mean, I would have your head for it, obviously, but it would gut me."

"That would never happen. You have my word," François swore, "On my life and on my honor, you shall never meet Evil François."

"Ah ha. So, he *does* exist!" She laughed at her own entrapment.

"Only in the shadows of your imagination, my lady," he put a hand over his heart and bowed slightly. "Of this I assure you."

"Hm," she nudged her horse, and they continued riding along in silence. They could both feel their deep connection. François snuck a peek over at Camila, and she was caught looking at him. They both laughed nervously and looked away shyly. They did this back and forth as if they were a couple of awkward, infatuated teenagers. Only it was deeper than that. Much deeper. In fact, Camila felt like she had run out of excuses not to fall headlong in love with this man.

A New Threat

King Gerardo barely survived Jacob's initial ambush. He now travelled with the small group of elite knights that remained by his side. Together, they were trying to make their way back across the border to Galicia. They were a ragtag group for sure. Low on supplies and hadn't eaten in hours.

"I cannot wait to return here for a full forward attack when I bring Mullah's army with me the next time," Gerardo growled. His eyes glazed over as he imagined all the vengeance he would personally enact upon Lord Jacob.

⁕

Back at Galicia's castle, Jibril approached Mullah with news, "Lord Mullah."

"Speak," Mullah said, looking up from a table of charts and maps.

"We have word of a small group of men approaching your kingdom, my lord. It is believed to be King Gerardo. His banner colors are led by his guardian knights."

Mullah was surprised to hear such news. He took a moment to think it over with a heavy sigh. "I handed Jacob the opportunity of a lifetime, and he failed, that fool. If Gerardo enters the kingdom, it will surely make things very complicated for me. I will finish what Jacob could not do," he decided. "Send the division of the area to intercept and kill these imposters. They should *not* be able to enter our lands. This is my kingdom, and I command it."

"Yes, my lord," Jibril withdrew to follow up on Mullah's request.

━━━━━━━❖━━━━━━━

Meanwhile back in Asturias, Duke Pablo approached Queen Camila and took a knee, "My Queen, we have received word that Lord Jacob is approaching the kingdom. His army does not have large numbers. Nevertheless he has broken the pledge to not return. We believe he's planning to attack us."

François, who was presently seated across from Camila, looked at her and postulated, "He must be joining forces with Mullah's army, thinking they are still here. Otherwise, it is not a logical plan to attack with such small numbers."

"I worry that perhaps my brother is now dead, François," Camila said, sadly. "I received word that Gerardo went to siege Jacob's lands. So, how is it that Jacob is now coming towards Asturias?" she wondered aloud. "Unless he is running away, but is he lost? He knows that these lands are protected by Gerardo's men," reasoned the queen.

"Gerardo is on his own. Whatever the case may be, we must see to the best interest of Asturias for now. If that is the case, Jacob will be surprised when he realizes that there are no more of Mullah's knights for him to join forces with."

Camila looked to the side and wiped a tear off her face. She couldn't help but think of her poor brother. No matter what he'd done, he was family after all.

François stood, "My lady, if I may have the honor to lead this defense for you, I will take care of things once and for all," François promised.

"I thank you greatly, François," she stood and paced around the table before them. "Please allow me to bring this idea to the table and see what you think."

"Of course, my lady," he said, intrigued.

"Mullah is definitively not someone to be trusted, do you agree?" She paused to let François and Pablo heartily agree. She continued, "If Gerardo put him in command of Galicia and Asturias, Mullah has a lot to gain if Gerardo were to be killed, whether in battle or not. He acquires both kingdoms," Camila explained.

"Of course, that's true," François answered without hesitation.

"Well, if Jacob is alive then it stands to reason that there is a good chance that he was given prior notice in order to escape Gerardo's attack. A power-hungry Mullah would have just such information. Without Gerardo, Mullah gets to keep Galicia. And since Mullah and Jacob are apparently best friends now, what is stopping Jacob from returning to claim Asturias once again?" Camila asked the room.

François's eyes opened wide. "I think that you are absolutely right, my lady," he said, and Pablo was nodding his agreement, too.

François frowned, "Jacob claims Asturias and Mullah would then have the responsibility to attack Jacob in Gerardo's defense. You are very wise, my lady. If only Gerardo had half your intellect, he would have never put himself and everyone else in this predicament."

"Thank you, François," Camila replied.

François continued, "If Jacob's plans are to join Mullah's knights as allies, we should not deprive him of such. We could pretend to be that army he is looking for, and besides, he does not know that I am even here," François proposed.

"Yes, that is a good plan. I will join you in our defense. It is after all my kingdom to defend," said Camila. "Pablo, please get the knights ready, and brief them of our plan."

"Yes, of course, My Queen," Pablo left quickly.

———◆———

Back along the Galician southern borders, Mullah's knights were waiting to ambush the King Gerardo upon his arrival.

"Sire," Count Daniel addressed the bedraggled king after halting the advancement.

"What is it now?" Gerardo whined.

"Sire, there should have been contact with the patrolling unit or division by now, my lord. It is too quiet. Something seems wrong," Daniel said.

Gerardo lowered his voice, "What are you saying? Has Mullah betrayed me?"

"That would make sense, My King. Jacob knew where exactly to attack you, sire," Daniel suggested.

"That also means that Mullah is likely waiting around here to ambush the survivors, as well."

"Let us wait here," Gerardo ordered. "Send a couple of scouts to survey the land."

"Yes, sire," Edward and Miguel were sent to investigate. They were fast and experienced in battle. They rode back from the main road. As they approached the area into the defensive points, they saw Mullah's men waiting for the king's arrival. An ambush indeed. They took note of their findings and returned to notify the king.

"Sire," reported Edward. "The enemy awaits your arrival, my lord. They are entrenched upon the other side of the hill, lying in ambush, My King."

"So, Mullah, that ungrateful bastard, has indeed betrayed me," Gerardo seethed. "We need to deviate for now."

"Where should we go, sire?" Daniel asked. "If we go back south, Lord Jacob's army are sure to catch up to us and finish us. If we continue moving north, of course Mullah's men are waiting for us. The same goes if we go east, we will run into Mullah's men from the Asturias patrols. Should we head west, my lord?"

"It seems we have no choice, do we? Very well, then, west it is," Gerardo called the final decision.

"Yes, sire," they proceed as commanded. And the whole company turned off the main road and towards the western corridor.

Jibril reported to Mullah with his update. "Our border vigil has waited all day for Gerardo's arrival, My King, and he never made it. Scouts have returned with no sign of them anymore."

"So, he did not show up? Something must have tipped them off. Continue covering the area to make sure he does not enter my kingdom. I shall wait for Jacob to overtake Asturias," he blurted out arrogantly, "After that I can focus on hunting down both Gerardo and Jacob."

"Yes, sire. It shall be done," Jibril responded and left the room.

❖

Entrapment

Queen Camila and King François arrived at the hillside on the northern side of the Asturian border to meet Jacob's attack. Along the way they saw Mullah's flags and shields that were left scattered around from the previous battle with them four days ago. This gave Camila an idea.

"I propose," Camila told François, "that some of our men take Mullah's shields and flags and post themselves at the frontline, to give Jacob the illusion that we are Mullah's division. This should bring them in nice and close. How do you feel about that, my lord?"

"I couldn't have said it better myself," François replied.

François and Camila took up a strategic point where they could see all the battalions already in position.

"We should be making contact with Mullah's knights soon," Jacob said to Bernard. "When we meet them, we will allow them to lead us to the castle. Let them do all of the charging and the fighting. We will preserve our own knights and simply walk into the castle once it gets taken over by them," he commanded, deeply satisfied with his master plan.

"Yes, my lord," Bernard responded. "We have a visual of Mullah's knights, my lord. They wait for us at the hillside."

"Very well, then. Up the hillside it is. Quite an army Mullah has left behind," Jacob observed, "These knights should be a great addition to my kingdom."

Upon Jacob's arrival to the hilltop, they were immediately surrounded by knights whose archers pointed their arrows at them.

"Stop, stop, you imbeciles! Do you not know who I am?" Jacob yelled, red-faced in anger. "I am your new king and ruler of this land. Surely, King Mullah told you about our alliance, and you are here to serve me."

At that cue, François and Camila stepped out from the ranks to reveal themselves and their thorough trap, which had caught the biggest rat of them all.

"Count," Camila smiled icily at him, "you asked me once whose approval you needed to enter my land? I will answer that question for you, again. My approval. Which you do not have," she enlightened him.

"Ah, I see," he stood his ground. Some rats, it seemed, were too dumb to know when they'd been defeated. "So, do you think that by choosing Mullah over me you will get your kingdom back? How silly can you be, Camila? These men you see before you are under *my* command, you silly woman. King Mullah has presented these knights as my own," Jacob laughed maliciously.

"The only silly one here is you, Lord Jacob. Downright idiotic, in fact," she paused to let that sink in. It worked. Jacob got red around the gills. "These knights before you are *not* yours, nor will they ever be. In fact, these are the knights that easily defeated Mullah's weak little army just before you arrived. And they are under my sole command," she added.

"Silence, woman," Jacob answered so angrily he squeaked.

At this outburst, François rode forward towards Jacob, who was still on his horse, and met him face to face. "You, sir, will never say another word to her ever again. For today you and your knights will die."

"And who might you be?" Jacob shrank back a little at his imposing size and close proximity.

"I am the last person that you shall ever see in the remainder of your short and miserable life. I am François du Basque."

Jacob recognized the name, and immediately his face drained of color.

With but a hand signal from François, his awaiting garrison immediately released their arrows, killing what was left of Jacob's army. They fell from atop their horses and lay scattered upon the road, dead. All but one.

Jacob reacted immediately and yanked his horse trying to turn it around to escape. It reared up defiantly and threw him from the saddle. Once on the ground, Jacob curled up like a child. "Please, please. Mercy," Jacob begged.

"You are nothing but a coward, Jacob," Camila spat. "You were warned by Gerardo what would happen if you ever returned. Now, I shall kill you myself," she slid off her horse and pulled her sword from its sheath and began to move towards him, she raised it high overhead and paused.

Just then, François, who had also dismounted, put a hand upon her shoulder gently. "My lady, as the queen you should not have to dirty your sword, nor your soul, with the blood of a filthy rat."

Camila's chin jutted out defiantly, "No, François. I will stand my ground. A queen must defend her own honor as well.

François nodded, understanding completely. Camila turned back towards Jacob who was still lying on the ground. "Get up, Jacob. You ask for mercy? I am a just woman. The just thing for me to do is to allow you to stand and take up your sword. I will allow you to fight for your life," she commanded him.

Jacob was trembling but decided to take the opportunity to crawl towards his sword and grabbed it. He was facing away from Camila who stepped forward, closing the distance between them.

Jacob slowly began to stand, first by taking a knee to gain support. When he felt that Camila was close enough, he whipped around towards her and swung his sword to strike her in the midsection.

François saw the underhanded move first and tried to call out a warning, "Look—."

But in the same moment, Camila reacted by deflecting the blade and using that same momentum to counterstrike Jacob; she slashed her sword across and lopped Jacob's head off neatly.

She then stepped away, leaving Jacob's body listing shakily for a moment before it collapsed to the ground. The head simply rolled away down the hillside.

François moved back to her side, much relieved that the entire ordeal was over. They looked at each other and embraced happily.

"In all my days, I have never borne witness to a finer kill shot, my lady. My Queen. My Love." He paused to look into her eyes, and she smiled back at him. And then she kissed him. It surprised him at first, but he pulled her in closer and kissed her back.

The knights cheered and applauded as they were happy to finally see them both together. Camila and François pulled apart. Both trying to catch their breath. François was the first to recover, "As long as I live, no one will ever yell at you or talk to you in such derogatory manner," he told her, as he pushed a lock of hair back behind her ear.

"The lion is out of the cage now," she practically purred back at him, deeper in love than ever before. "Thank you, my lord. My King. My Love!"

Chapter 11
The New Monarch of Galicia

Back in Galicia, Mullah was living a carefree and opulent lifestyle without restraint—financial or moral. He laid upon Gerardo's bed with multiple women attendants at any one time. Many of them were being forced to be with him and had no other choice but to please their new king or face death.

This morning, Mullah rose from the gigantic featherbed and pulled on a robe to cover himself before summoning his guards. "Give me more wine," he commanded.

"Yes, my lord," the guards answered, rushing to obey.

"Ladies," Mullah addressed his love slaves, "you are looking at the king with the biggest territory in this part of Europe. I now reign over Galicia. Tomorrow, I shall pay a visit to my dear friend Jacob in Asturias, which he will gift back to me after some, uh, *convincing*," Mullah chuckled to himself.

He weaved back and forth unsteadily, intoxicated. "Once I reign over Asturias, I look forward to expanding over Jacob's lands in León." He yelled back over his shoulder, "Guards!"

"Yes, my lord," two guards entered quickly.

"Who am I to you?" Mullah questioned them

"You are our Lord and King, sire," both guards answered him without hesitation.

"Yes, that is correct. Now tell me this, why is it that I have not yet heard whether Gerardo has been found?" Mullah questioned them again.

"They are still searching for him, My King."

"Have them search faster," Mullah waved them away, "Now get out of my chambers, can't you see we're busy," he bellowed and staggered back to the bed to finish what they had started.

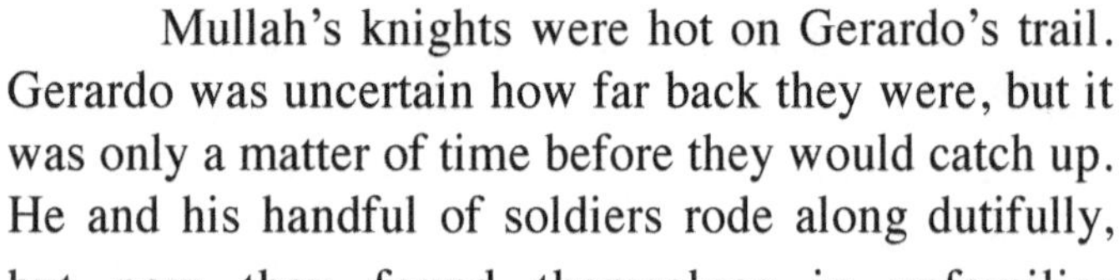

Mullah's knights were hot on Gerardo's trail. Gerardo was uncertain how far back they were, but it was only a matter of time before they would catch up. He and his handful of soldiers rode along dutifully, but now they found themselves in unfamiliar territory.

"We need to rest," Daniel observed. He raised a hand to halt their advancement. They all listened for any signs of pursuit. But, the area seemed quiet and tranquil.

"Sire," Daniel called to the king.

"What is it?" Gerardo grumbled.

"We need to stop, sire. The horses are tired and cannot continue. We need water and a place to camp and get some rest, my lord. Or we are not going to make, not it at this pace."

Gerardo was beyond exhausted himself, "Very well, then. Set up camp off the road and provide some cover," the king commanded.

"Yes, sire," they began to set up camp so they could get some rest. There was chatter among the remaining men.

"Quiet," the count hushed his men. The men stopped their chattering and looked at the count.

"Did you hear that?" Daniel asked, searching the treeline around them.

"Hear what?" Marshal Miguel answered.

"I do not know. I thought I heard something," Daniel said. "Cuidado!" Daniel yelled, pointing at arrows being shot towards them. They all ducked for cover as the attacking army came at them from all directions on horseback. They found themselves once again having little chance of defending themselves against the superior numbers.

"Carajo vamos maje," Gerardo shouted when he heard the commotion taking place outside his tent. He quickly escaped from underneath it and ran away.

The king looked for a horse to commandeer or even a place to hide before being spotted. He recognized the attackers to be Mullah's men. They spotted him and gave him a chase. *Thwack!* An arrow pegged into a tree beside him.

Gerardo ran for his life, but he was quickly exhausted and dizzy, he was not physically fit enough to run. "If only I could make it to the hill, I could have a better defensive position," he gasped, as he pushed himself onward.

Daniel headed for Gerardo's tent, thinking to protect him. Arrows flew past him, barely missing their target. He dove to the ground to dodge them and then rolled over for coverage. As he began to look for the king, he saw Miguel take three arrows to the back, killing him instantly.

Enemy knights thundered into the camp on horseback looking for survivors. Daniel managed to thrust his sword up and deflect a sword strike from a man passing by him.

He looked behind him and another knight rushed him, swinging his sword at him; Daniel jumped out of the way of the strike. He rose fast to take an en garde position, once again; a third knight charged him on horseback. Daniel immediately threw his sword at the attacker, spearing him with a blow through his solar plexus.

Daniel turned to look for a fallen weapon and saw Jibril leading the attack. Jibril lined up his longbow with a pair of arrows and fired them towards Daniel, striking him twice in the chest. He was dead before he hit the ground.

Gerardo continued to make his getaway and heard horses gaining ground behind him. He continued to climb onto the hilltop, managing to make it only out of pure adrenaline and desperation. Once there, he lost his footing and tripped down onto the other side of the hill.

Out of control, Gerardo rolled down towards the edge of a fast-approaching drop-off. Every bump and stumble created a new injury for him, but there was no fighting it anymore. He gave himself over to the fall, and he realized that this very well could be the end of his life.

Horsemen fired arrows at him, but he was too wild of a moving target, and they each missed. His body continued to gain speed, rolling out of control. The men on horseback rode parallel to him down a gentler grade before they all pulled up short.

Gerardo wondered why they had stopped and then suddenly felt his body floating in mid-air without any more ground contact. He craned his neck and saw that he had gone off a cliff and down a long waterfall drop. He plunged down into the turbulent pool below and crashed onto a rock at the pool's deep bottom, where he lost consciousness.

Jibril's knights watched as his crumpled body, whisked away face down in the brisk current.

"King Mullah will be happy to receive the news about King Gerardo's death."

"Yes, he will. Maybe now he can relax, and we can sleep in our own beds for two nights in a row for once."

"Not a chance," another one countered. Mullah's men argued amongst themselves. They laughed and chuckled with sarcasm. Their mission to kill Gerardo and all his cohorts was now over. As they reported everything to Jibril, he immediately ordered everyone to return to Galicia to notify Mullah.

❖

In the castle of Asturias there were many festivities. The people celebrated throughout the kingdom as word spread of their victory over Jacob's army.

Not only was the land defended against invasion, but their beloved Queen Camila now had King François by her side as a protector and companion to her and her lands.

"The queen has a king by her side," the people shouted.

Inside the castle's ballroom, the king and queen sat happily, enjoying the celebration as they drank and feasted.

Baron Diego approached to inquire of King François, "Your Majesty, now that you have acquired Jacob's kingdom of León and have rightful claim to it, how will you expand, my lord?"

Everyone in the room paused their celebration, awaiting his answer.

"That is not for me to decide," François calmly responded. His answer confused most of the nobles who were listening. "Was Lord Jacob not defeated in the Kingdom of Asturias?" François reminded them.

"He was, my lord," the marshal answered.

"Under the defense of Asturias and in the name of Asturias?" François added.

"He was, my lord," Diego answered again.

"Was the reigning Queen of Asturias not present, leading the defense and commanding the army?"

"Yes, my lord," Diego agreed, as did most in attendance.

"Very well, hence my answer," François brushed his hands together as if the matter were settled. "This question is not for me to answer, for it is not in my rightful place to do so."

The nobles looked at each other with certain disbelief at the king's answer. Some chatter spread throughout the room. Any other monarch would have claimed Jacob's land without hesitation. The queen saw their reactions and put her hand up, calmly waiting for everyone to quiet down.

"King François is a gentleman. A man with integrity who has once again proven his courage, chivalry, strength, and honor. The protection and victory that he has brought to us have always been meant to advance the well-being of our kingdom. I believe in him and his good intentions. He has proven to all of us that he has no ill will. No ulterior motives. For that reason and many more, we now celebrate together as one." With that she took his hand and held it high.

"Long live the King and Queen. Long live the King and Queen," everyone cheered her response joyfully.

As the celebration continued, François and Camila stepped out to a courtyard overlooking the castle, where they could have a more private conversation.

"Camila, you have once again honored me with your kind words," François told her. "I cannot in any way take claim to any of your lands, and I thank you for acknowledging the best of interests that I have towards you, your family, and your reign."

"François, without you my people and I would not be here celebrating like this," Camila admitted. "Please allow me to share with you claim to the Kingdom of León, at least. It will be a token of my appreciation, thus giving credit where credit is due. The people of the kingdom love you. I love you."

"And I love you," François said, running a finger along her chin. "I will accept under the condition that we share that land under a co-regency, as it will afford Asturias greater security from the south. But it is certainly a time for caution. I needn't remind you that if what we hear is true, Mullah has taken position as the reigning king of Galicia now that your brother is absent. It will be only a matter of time before he realizes that his knights no longer Asturias and that Jacob did not take over the kingdom as they planned."

"I do not need to be reminded. That is something that I wish I did not have to deal with, but I know we must. If I'm not mistaken, it sounds like you may have a plan for how this needs to be handled, my love," Camila smiled. "Am I right?"

"As always, my lady. We need to take advantage of our unique situation. Mullah thinks that everything is going his way, as he planned. We need to get him out and away from his stronghold. Might I suggest, perhaps an invitation from our dear, departed Jacob?" François explained. "He will already begin to hear news of celebrations in Asturias. Let him imagine that Jacob celebrates his own victory. That will draw Mullah here faster than anything else. And that will give us the best chance to face him."

"And take him by surprise, too," added Camila. "I like that idea. We need to move on it quickly, because he will be sending his men to investigate if he does not hear anything from Jacob immediately" As the conversation carried on, they both headed back into the castle.

The queen called for her scribe, and they formulated a letter of invitation to Mullah. They wrote it as coming from Jacob on the heels of his glorious victory. The last step was to bind it up and send it out with their fasted courier.

The next morning Camila met with François.

"Good morning, my lady," François greeted her happily.

"Good morning, my lord," she replied, planting a sweet kiss upon his lips. When he pulled back to gaze into her face, he saw that she wore a troubled expression.

"What is it, My Queen?"

She finally said, "François, I need you to do something for me."

"Of course. Anything. Name it."

"François, if anything should happen to me…"

"Nothing will happen to you," François interrupted her. "I will not allow it."

"Please, François," Camila looked at him and placed her hands on his shoulders. "If anything, should happen to me, please take care of the people of the kingdom. I do not want them to suffer because of me. That is the reason why I made public that you are to share the lands with me."

"I love you as well as this land. Everyone in your kingdom will be okay," François promised. He pulled her closer as she searched his face.

"Thank you, my love," Camila turned to take in the beautiful morning view of their castle and their kingdom while being embraced.

———————◆———————

A short time later at Galicia's castle, Jibril returned to inform Mullah of his news. "Allah is with us, My King," he entered, giving Mullah a courteous bow.

"Tell me that you have good news, Jibril," said Mullah.

"I do, my lord. King Gerardo fell down a cliff while trying to run away like a coward. His fat body crashed down onto a rocky riverbed. I saw this with my own eyes," Jibril lied.

"Excellent," exclaimed Mullah. "What of the rest of his men?"

"All dead, My King. I personally took care of both Daniel and Miguel. The other few never stood a chance," he bragged.

"My Lord Mullah," stated Marshal Khalid. "You have a messenger here to see you."

"A messenger? Send him in."

"Yes, my lord," replied the marshal.

"Greetings, my Lord Mullah," the messenger approached Mullah and took a knee before him.

Mullah was seated on the throne and spat out impatiently, "Speak."

"Sire, I bring a message from King Jacob of Asturias. I am to bring back a response, my lord." The letter was sealed, and the messenger gave it to

Jibril, who in return handed it over to Mullah. He proceeded to rip off the seal and tear into the envelope to find a letter reading:

King Mullah of Galicia,

It is with great pleasure that I announce to you that I have taken possession of the Kingdom of Asturias. Your gallant assistance and tactical planning have helped me annihilate King Gerardo's forces at my Kingdom of León and subdue Queen Camila at the reconquest of my Kingdom of Asturias.

Your knights were instrumental and efficient in the overtaking of the castle, enabling my return as their king. For that I am indebted to you. Our alliance is strong, and together we can accomplish anything that we want.

For now, I would like to invite you to Asturias to celebrate our alliance. I feel that this is only the beginning of our expansions throughout out the lands. We shall discuss further plans once we are together.

Cheers to our friendship and our victory,
King Jacob of Asturias and León.

Mullah folded back the letter and smiled contentedly. "My plan is working to perfection," he said.

"Tell King Jacob that I will accept his invitation," Mullah ordered. "I will be there one week from today to leave the king enough time to prepare for our arrival."

"Will do, my lord," the messenger stood up and was escorted back out by the marshal.

Mullah opened the letter again and began to reread it. It made him so happy. For starters, it addressed him as a king in a formal, written document and that made him feel nearly invincible.

"Ha," Mullah chuckled to himself. "Jacob is an idiot. He could not finish anything without my help and assistance. My taking over Asturias will be easier than I ever imagined."

***

The Will to Survive

Somewhere south of León, there was an isolated countryside, where a riverbed gently directed the water downstream. At the edges there were rocks and fallen logs. The river of this remote forest was far away from any signs of civilization.

Gerardo's body lay at an edge of the river. Battered and bruised from the rough fall, he was just barely alive. Fortunately for him, his armor had taken most of the impact, protecting his ribs from being shattered. All the way down the river, he continued to have flashes of pain, but that was good; it kept him lucid enough to understand his armor was weighing him down.

Although he had been tossed around by the strong current of the river, he had somehow managed to unstrap himself from his armor and push himself fully to the surface, where he took a much-needed gulp of fresh air.

He was then dragged, tossed, and submerged again and again by the strong currents which he had no control over. His strength began to leave him again, and he finally fainted. His body floated there on the surface and was carried downstream until he was washed up at the river's edge.

As he regained consciousness, his eyes fluttered open. Pain stabbed at him all over. "Aghhhh," Gerardo tried to sit up, now in full panic. He imagined his pursuers were close by. However, his legs did not respond. They were too bruised and damaged from having crashed onto the rocks along the way.

He calmed down enough to realize that he was alone and safe from immediate danger. Gerardo rolled his body to be face up, feeling every knick and scratch and injury.

As he laid down on the sandy bank exhausted, he wondered aloud, "How is it that I am still alive?"

After a short period of resting, he was finally able to pull his torso upright and pushed himself up off from the bank of the river and further up onto the land. He kept pushing until he found cover under the trees. Afterwards he tried to assess his wounds and knew that he must find a resting place before nightfall.

"Where in God's name am I?" he said to no one.

After a half hour, he managed to stand up, unsteadily, and work his way slowly along the river in search of any signs of civilization.

After a few hours of walking, he saw a traveller who was walking through the forest. He called out to him. The young vagrant saw him and approached him with excitement.

"Cavaleiro oco," the vagrant exclaimed.

"Vamos vale. What makes you think I am a knight?" Gerardo responded.

"Ha. It's not like you have to say it," the vagrant surmised. "Where are you headed? It looks like you need shelter, knight."

"Do you know the direction to such a place?"

"I do indeed," the vagrant said.

"Agh. Very well, then. Do speak. Where is this place?" Gerardo demanded impatiently due to the stabbing pain he was in.

The vagrant frowned at Gerardo. "I do not appreciate your demeaning tone, knight. How much is this place worth to you?"

"I have nothing to give you," Gerardo lied. "But if you help me, I will make sure that you get well compensated once I return."

The vagrant laughed in response, "that's not the way it works around here, knight." He then moved closer to Gerardo and reached out to put his hand on Gerardo's shoulder.

The king immediately deflected the hand away from his body. The vagrant looked Gerardo up and down. "I tell you what," said the vagrant. "Give me one of those rings on your fingers, and it shall suffice as payment for my services."

"I will do no such thing," Gerardo said brashly. "Get away from me, and let me be. I do not need you."

"Very well, then. Have it your way," the vagrant responded, as he stepped aside to let Gerardo pass before him.

The king disregarded him, after seeing him as no threat, and proceeded forward. As soon as Gerardo had walked by him, the vagrant hit him over the head with a small billy club that he had pulled out of his satchel, rendering him unconscious. He then took Gerardo's rings and searched him for any other valuables, finding a sack of gold coins and a gold necklace. And Gerardo, with his cracked skull, was left for dead

———————❖———————

When Gerardo finally awoke, he found himself lying on a bed in an unknown house. The room was a small, darkly lit area. Most of the light was coming from a nearby fireplace. In one corner of the room, he saw a shimmering surface reflecting the fire's light. The king couldn't make sense of what it was, but it appeared to be reminiscent of a sword handle. He tried to get up, but he felt severe pain across his body, in particular his head, which was wrapped with a cloth.

"Ay, ay, ay," Gerardo whimpered.

"Permanecer calmo e tentar descansar," said an old man's voice. He looked quickly to his side and noticed the man leaning over a pot of stew, stirring it slowly as it hung atop of cozy fire. It was not the vagrant from before, so he relaxed. This man had clearly been keeping watch over him. He was an elderly man with a full, white beard. His hands were wrinkled but strong. He displayed good posture and a gentle poise.

"Where…where am I? Who…are you?" Gerardo managed to ask.

"Well now, my friend, have no fear for you are here." The man grabbed a bowl and dished some broth into it before handing it to Gerardo for him to eat.

"My name is Riccardo Santos. I own this land. I found you unconscious and beat nearly to death in my field. I could not just let you be, so I dragged you here and cared for your wounds. That is a big hit you took behind your head. It must have been some fight," Riccardo speculated.

Gerardo carefully sat up and grabbed the bowl. "Thank… you. I appreciate you not… leaving me to the vultures. Tell me… good man, where is this land?" asked the king.

"Estamos em Porto. The Douro River runs alongside this land," Riccardo poured some stew in another bowl for himself to eat and sip while they talked.

"Porto?" Gerardo repeated.

"Porto is in the Kingdom of Portugal," Riccardo explained. "If I had to make a guess, I'd say you must come from the Spanish kingdoms, young man."

Gerardo remained silent. His country had had a connection with this kingdom before Portugal had become independent in 1128. Now he did not know the current reigning monarch personally.

"I must get back to where I come from. You must help me," Gerardo managed to say softly.

"Was I correct? Where do you come from, young man?" Riccardo probed again.

"I come from the kingdom beyond these lands, the Kingdom of Galicia," Gerardo confessed.

"I know your kingdom. I knew your beloved King Celestino. I have heard that his son is now the new king and that he is not a decent man. Unlike the king's daughter. Why would you want to go to Galicia and not Asturias," Riccardo said.

"Actually, agh..." Gerardo fumbled. "I am indeed going to Asturias. I only said Galicia to make a reference of the general direction I am headed."

"Good for you. Queen Camila has established herself well." Riccardo said. "Especially now that, as a traveling band of minstrels recently told me, she now has King François du Basque by her side as an ally. Her kingdom will be most prosperous."

"Mm," Gerardo grunted. He was very surprised to hear the news about François and knew that his plans to overtake Asturias would need to change. His bigger problem now was that he could not tell anyone who he was, especially because of the horrible reputation he had in these lands.

"Which road will you wish to take to start your journey back, young fella?" Riccardo asked.

"I need to go east, towards León," Gerardo replied.

"Very well, I will provide a horse, a few coins for your trip and a fresh set of clothes, when the time comes." Riccardo offered. "That way you will blend in better with the villagers."

"Thank you, abuelo," Gerardo answered him.

A few days passed by, and Gerardo's wounds got better, he was finally ready to make headway on his own again. "I thank you, old man." Gerardo said. "I shall keep you in mind when I make it back home."

"You take care, young man. I never did get your name."

"You can call me Gabriel," the king replied.

"Thank you, Gabriel. Is there a surname to go along with your given name?"

"Gomez," Gerardo lied.

"Ah. Gomez means 'man.' Farewell Gabriel Man. Go out there, and make your family name proud," Riccardo beamed at him.

Gerardo hopped aboard the old horse and headed down the road. Riccardo watched him until he was no longer able to see him.

Gerardo arrived at a small village where he came upon a tavern. It was a busy place. He heard music and laughter from men and women. He decided to stop and have a meal and a drink before heading back out to the open road.

Gerardo entered the tavern, and the music and dancing immediately stopped. Everyone turned to look towards him, sizing him up for trouble. He simply walked in very calmly and found a place to sit down.

Once the villagers noticed that he was alone and did not pose a threat, the music continued to play, and everyone returned to dancing and having fun.

The bar tender approached him. "What will it be, señor?"

"I need something to eat and drink," Gerardo replied.

"Very well, then you came to the right place for that. If you do not mind my asking, who are you? What brings you down to this village, my good man?" the worker asked.

"Just give me what I ordered, and let me be," Gerardo said in a rather foul manner.

The bar tender frowned upon the rude response and walked away into the kitchen area to get his order. A group of four men inside the tavern overheard the response that Gerardo gave the bar tender, and they did not like it. After all, Gerardo was a stranger in their town, and they did not appreciate an outsider who came into their town to be rude.

They approached Gerardo, surrounding the area where he was seating. "Ei... ei," they called for his attention.

"What do you want?" Gerardo asked. "Not in the mood."

"What do you want, he asks?" The leader answered with an amused look. He had a good size to him, one that would intimidate the average person. He also had a scar across the face.

"What we want is for you to show some respect. That is what we want," he answered him.

"Look, I'm not here to cause trouble," Gerardo responded remaining seated. He then looked away, trying to ignore them.

"Actions speak louder than words, you stupid bastard," the leader of the group replied, as he struck him on his back, knocking him to the floor. Gerardo tried to stand, to protect himself, but the men continued to beat him down.

"Let him be," a man, dressed in a hooded cloak, stepped in to defend Gerardo. He was tall in stature and, for what they could see, had a fit physique.

The men looked at the mystery man, and two of them decided to attack him at once. One swung his right fist towards his head, while the other grabbed a bottle to throw at him. The other two continued to beat on Gerardo.

The cloaked man slipped aside to miss the first strike and countered it with an upper cut of his own, giving the first attacker a bloody nose as he dropped to the ground in pain.

He then saw the second man with the bottle in hand and moved in towards him, quickly striking him across the jawline, rendering him unconscious.

The other two men saw their friends go down and turned to square up to him as well. The third ran to tackle him. The cloaked man stepped to the side and kicked him in the stomach, causing him to immediately drop.

"Aaaah," the fourth man, the leader, charged him in a rage with his right hand up to strike him, but the cloaked man kicked a chair into his path and caused him to trip on it. He then followed behind the chair with a leaping cross strike to the side of his face, which caused the attacker to immediately drop to the ground.

The cloaked man stood over Gerardo's body. Everyone in the tavern had moved aside creating space for them. No one dared to make a sudden move in fear of getting knocked out by this mysterious and ferocious man.

A couple of the fallen men tried to recover and stand. They wanted to see who this man was, but they could not see his face nor his eyes due to the cloak's hood covering his head.

"Who is this man? Where did he come from? How did he beat all those men at once?" Everyone chattered speculatively throughout the tavern.

"Who the bloody hell are you?" the bartender finally asked straight out.

His voice was as strong as his hammer fist. "I am simply the one that is asking for you to let me leave with this man. He is no longer a threat to you," the cloaked warrior responded.

"Suit yourself. But you will regret taking up a sojourn with this useless, rude excuse of a man," the tavern regulars replied angrily.

"Thank you, I shall take my chances," he bowed his head slightly as a sign of respect and placed a few coins on a table, "For your trouble." He then proceeded to help Gerardo stand and took him away, while everyone else moved aside.

Later that night, Gerardo woke up and found himself inside another unfamiliar room. He was bruised and in pain, but his injuries were looked after. He heard people talking and celebrating in another room. He looked around and noticed the fierce man that helped him at the tavern seated by his side. He had a full goatee and shoulder length hair. His cloak was opened from a side, and Gerardo could see he had a sword hanging from his belt. Behind him there was a shield leaning against a wall; the shield had a coat of arms at the center. So, he was a knight.

Gerardo looked around before sitting up and rubbing the back of his head. "What happened?" Gerardo asked him, "Who the devil are you?"

"Who I am is not as important as who you are, my lord," the cloaked man replied earnestly.

Gerardo glanced up, surprised. "Y-you know who I am?"

"I do, sire. You are King Gerardo of Galicia, son of King Celestino Garcia," he replied.

"Are you here to kill me, too?" Gerardo ventured, bracing himself for the hard truth.

"There would hardly be any sport in that," the man replied cryptically. "Besides, if I wanted to kill you, you'd be dead by now."

"A loyal servant of mine, perhaps?" Gerardo ventured.

"I am, sire. At your service." He stood up and gave him a slight bow. "My name is Albert Collins. I am a loyal servant to the Kingdoms of Asturias, Galicia, León, and to the lands of the north, the Basque kingdoms. I am a marquess and commander of the royal knights of His Majesty King François du Basque. It was he who sent me to find you. I have searched for you throughout the territory of León and tracked you across the Portuguese lands, my lord. You were not an easy man to find."

"Lord Albert? King François? Why would he send you to look for me?" Gerardo wondered.

"My lord, King François is the one that assisted Queen Camila in regaining her kingdom and in bringing peace back into the lands of your father," explained the marquess.

"I see," Gerardo asked very carefully, "and what is to become of me?"

"I am to take you before Queen Camila, sire. There you shall await your destiny," Albert said matter-of-factly.

"What if I refuse to go with you?"

"Wouldn't advise that, sire. My orders are to take you back. If I must accomplish my task by force, I will do so, my lord. Please know that in your current situation, away from anything familiar, you could not be any safer than with me by your side." Albert leaned in conspiratorially. "There are people that would do anything to find you. There is even a fair price put on your head by other lords, my lord."

Gerardo swallowed hard. Once again, he was between a rock and a hard place. "Very well, my lord. Do as you were commanded to do, but make sure that I stay alive."

"Goes without saying, my lord," Albert answered with an almost amused grin and placed his right hand across his chest.

The next day, Albert and Gerardo prepared to leave the room where they had stayed without incident. Upon their departure, Albert went to produce their horses, and Gerardo waited for him. A group of men from the tavern noticed and recognized Gerardo standing there alone, and they proceeded to approach him again.

"Small town, stranger. You shall pay for the beating that you meted out unfairly upon us," the man said.

"I do not know what you are talking about," Gerardo replied.

"Well, we do, and we'll explain it to you!"

Albert returned, riding hard upon his massive stallion, and charged straight at the men who dove to the side when they saw the cloaked man approaching.

Gerardo took the opportunity to climb upon his own horse and rode away while Albert was busy distracting the attackers. Once he saw that Gerardo was clear, he turned his horse in the same direction.

"La esta ele, pegue-o," an angry villager pointed at Albert. The other men he had chased off were returning with a larger group of villagers that were the opposite of a welcoming committee.

"Oh merde," Albert swore. "If I fight these men, I will have to hurt them." Albert sized up his challengers but decided it was best for him and everyone to just move along. He dug his heels into his horse and yelled, "Hyaah!" The horse scampered off, leaving the villagers in a cloud of dust while they launched some arrows at him.

Albert headed in the direction in which he had seen Gerardo leave. He was a true tracker and didn't take long for him to pick up his trail. It led him off the road into the forest and across a riverbed. Then a storm broke upon the area, and it began raining hard, making it impossible for him to track the path.

There was no sign of civilization nearby, but he did find a house amid the storm, and he headed towards it, hoping for shelter.

An elderly gentleman came out to greet him, "Olá, bom cavaleiro. What are you doing outside in this terrible storm?"

Albert directed his horse to approach him. "Hola, buen hombre. It was not my intention to be out, but as you can see, I can't control nature's capricious behavior. A friend one moment and a mortal enemy the next."

The elderly man nodded his head in agreement, "Well now, my friend, have no fear, for you are here."

Albert nodded to the man. "Tell me, good man, have you seen another rider come by your property in the last hour or so?"

"No one comes my way except for a bunch of lost, stray animals," the elderly man shook his head sadly. "I'm afraid I live too far out for anyone to come visit a'purpose."

Albert looked around for any signs of movement and any possible signs that may lead him to Gerardo.

"Would you like to come in and dry up?" the elderly man offered, waving his hand in invitation to enter. "This storm won't let up for a while. Might as well sit it out with some beef stock and ale."

The storm didn't bother Albert. He was on a mission to find Gerardo and kept surveying the area. However, he thought it might be useful to look around. "Thank you, good man, you are very kind. Do you mind if I look around your property in case the convict has latched on to you like a worthless tick without your knowing?"

"Vá verificar," the elderly man replied, waving his hand to go ahead.

Albert gave him a nod and pulled his horse around to slowly circle the house. When he came around to the stables, he was met by the elderly man, again.

"Come off your horse, young man, let me take a look at that wound of yours."

Albert looked at him with surprise, before glancing down at his right mid-ribs and right forearm area, which were both bloodied.

"I appreciate the good gesture, sir, but this wound isn't mortal and is, in fact, fairly agreeable."

"Well, come on down anyway, I know you want to check the stables. I'll walk with you."

Albert dismounted his horse and led it along with him while walking. They entered the stables, and Albert saw that the owner had many fine horses, each in their own stable.

"Well, young man, let me give you the tour," he said as he grabbed a lantern. "I miss riding these stallions; at my age I don't get to ride much anymore. Not like they want to be ridden."

As they walked down the aisle looking at the horses in the stalls, one detail caught Albert's attention. "These horses are destriers," Albert whistled appreciatively. "Best warhorses a knight can buy." And they were. Similar to his own horse and identical to the one that Gerardo had been riding. These were high-priced thoroughbreds and not very common.

"A little hobby of mine, from a previous life. Keeps food on the table, as it were," the old man smiled.

As they approached the end of the stables, the elderly man's brow furrowed briefly when he saw the last horse. It was the one that he had given away to Gerardo when he had left his care not too long ago.

He stifled a yawn and looked up at Albert wearily, "Well, there you have it. Once you've seen one warhorse, you have seen them all. Now, how about we go take a look at that scratch?"

Albert also glanced at the last stall and saw Gerardo's horse but made nothing of it. He had seen enough to know that this man had to be in service to the Portuguese kingdom. A knight of some high rank. And he knew did not want to cause any political missteps for François. It was time to leave.

"I thank you for the tour, good sir. The rain has abated, so I shall not be a burden any longer. May you find peace along your journey."

The elderly man held the lantern aloft for Albert to step up into the stirrups. "May you also find peace and what you are looking for along your own path."

With that, Albert rode out of the stables and off in the direction of Asturias.

Chapter 12
The Rise and Fall of a Nemesis

Mullah swayed back and forth rhythmically as he rode inside his royal carriage en route to Asturias. Baron Jibril was by his side. This elaborate carriage drawn by a team of six horses had once belonged to King Celestino and Queen Joanna. Mullah, of course, had taken possession of it, along with everything and everyone else in the kingdom that he fancied.

"Perhaps, you will be receiving a hero's welcome in Asturias, my lord," Jibril mused.

Mullah grunted back, "I practically handed Asturias over to Jacob. That's the least they can do for me."

"I am certain that he will, My King. If I may say so, King Jacob desperately needs this alliance. It would be a shame if he did not recognize that."

"Jacob is making things easier than I planned," Mullah chuckled to himself. "Once we are inside the castle celebrating, make sure everyone is ready. We will take him by surprise."

"Allah is definitely with you, my lord. Your knowledge and experience are without equal, My King," Jibril bowed towards him in respect.

"Soon, I will be the most powerful king among the kingdoms. Let me ask you, how long has it taken me to arrive at such a place?"

"Twenty long years," replied the baron "For twenty years you've been planning this final ascension."

"Twenty long bloody years," Mullah agreed.

❖

"Albert, I see you have returned to us empty handed," François addressed his friend. "My curiosity is piqued."

Albert approached François, riding at a moderate pace. "Votre Altesse Royale," Albert happily paid his respects to the king before turning towards Queen Camila with a small bow, "Your Majesty."

She nodded to him as well. Albert returned his attention to the briefing at hand. "I had Lord Gerardo in my grasp and was about to ensnare him, when I realized where we were, Your Majesty," Albert explained rather dramatically. "Marialva."

François laughed, "But those are fairy tales, my friend! You don't believe for a second that—."

"I saw him," Albert said, stone serious.

"You saw him?" François stopped laughing, but he was still not convinced.

"Oui, le Boucher," Albert let that information sink in. "In the flesh. Still alive and well."

"It could not have been the Butcher," François shook his head incredulously. "Or you would not be alive."

"I swear by it, sire," Albert insisted. "I don't know why he let me live, perhaps he has grown soft in his old age. But it was him. And Gerardo was under his protection."

"Did he cause this?" François pointed to Albert's side caked with dried blood.

"No, sire, while Gerardo was escaping I had to fend off an entire village to keep him from harm. Then he escaped, and I tracked him as far as Marialva. I apologize, sire, but he is deep within Portuguese custody now."

"You did the right thing, Albert; we will deal with them later. For now, go take care of that wound, refresh yourself and your horse, and then meet your division and fall-in for the battle against Lord Mullah."

"Oui, Votre Altesse," Albert complied.

Duke Pablo arrived to report, "We are ready to defend your Majesties."

"Very well, then. To the horses!" François ordered. "Make sure everyone is in position. Nobody moves until we give the signal. Please send Marshal Diego back with a division to protect the castle in case anyone gets past us."

"Yes, my lord," Pablo nodded and left. François and Camila climbed upon their horses.

"Who is the Butcher of Marialva," Camila wondered aloud as they mounted.

"Hm," François shuddered at some dark memory. "That is a story for another time. Suffice to say, he is the devil in the flesh. Every time we think him dead, he pops up again."

"Sounds made up," Camila needled him.

"Every song from every minstrel I have ever heard that tells of any knight's story has been deeply embellished. My own, included," François checked the sky thoughtfully. "But the Butcher of Marialva works in the shadows. If anything, his feats of terror are underreported by the score."

"Lovely," Camila clucked her tongue and sent her stallion into a canter, François following close behind.

Upon arrival at the main road that led to Galicia, their knights were ready in position waiting for Mullah's imminent arrival. Camila's loyal and trustworthy clansmen arrived alongside them.

"If it is okay with you, my lady, I suggest Pablo break off from the main force and lead an attack from the enemy's flank." François outlined his plan. "I will have Count David Ascough join him in his line, and they will be able to surprise them."

"Of course, my lord," Camila considered it a solid plan.

"Did your clansmen bring their warrior women as advised, Pablo?" François asked him.

"They did indeed, Your Majesty," Pablo said.

"Very well, then. Have the clansmen position themselves at the entrance of the road," François said. "Again, giving Mullah a hero's welcome. It will feed his ego and give him the false sense of power and pride. He'll be excited to be within our kingdom and not suspicious."

"Everyone, take your places," the queen announced.

Mullah's caravan approached the Asturian border. "Lord Mullah," his carriage driver called to him. "It looks like your arrival is well-received, my lord. The people of Asturias are gathered in celebration of your holy presence, my lord."

"You see, my lord," Jibril said. "I knew you were getting the hero's welcome, as you deserve."

"Good," Mullah's chest swelled with pride. "Let them honor me as they should. I am to be their king and master after all."

Camila and François watched Mullah's army from a hilltop, out of sight. "Mullah has a large army, François," Camila observed, nervously. "I am worried that we will not be able to take them all by surprise and that now our forces have been splintered off into too many groups. We may not be able to withstand their defense once they realize they are under attack."

"All part of the plan, My Queen. First, we need to focus on Mullah," François assured her. "He rides in the royal carriage, so as soon as it is within striking distance, we can focus on him. Cut the head off of the snake and the rest of them will crumble to the ground."

"François, I apologize," Camila touched her hand to his arm. "I do not mean to question your battle tactics. Despite your humility, I think the minstrels have underreported *your* skill and victories. But, I am concerned for the innocent people of the kingdom we have drawn out today."

"My Queen, you do not have to apologize to anyone, least of all me," François encouraged her. "You have valid points and every reason to care for the people's welfare. There is risk. But this risk we have mitigated, as much as possible."

"Thank you, for your understanding, François. That is one of the reasons why, for the first time in my life, I feel protected. Hopeful. Even as a massive army bears down upon us. Thank you for standing by my side, my love."

He squeezed her hand as they gazed upon each other lovingly. Then they turned their focus back towards the imminent battle.

"Albert, are we set?" François asked.

"We are, my lord," the marquess confirmed.

"Now that they are set in position, we wait for Mullah to enter the target area," François said.

"Cheers to the King. Cheers to the King," Camila's clansmen and women were cheering to Mullah. His army passed slowly through rows and rows of villagers, as if they were on parade.

Mullah's army could only fit through this stretch of the narrow road in a small, double-file line . The warriors enjoyed the shower of attention.

"Waqef," Mullah commanded to halt the carriage. "Bring my horse. I will ride, myself."

"Yes, My King," Jibril acknowledged. "Allah wills that you be seen by one and all, my lord."

Once Mullah and Jibril had mounted their horses, the column resumed their advancement.

"Whew," Camila let out a sigh of relief. They had been unsure why the formation had stopped, and she thought for a second that the enemy had seen through their ruse. But, no. That pompous jackass had just made himself an even easier target.

"Raise the flag to attack," commanded Camila. This was a signal for the army, as well as the clansmen and villagers, to know it was time for them to take cover during the oncoming attack.

"Archers, fire!" François chopped his hand into the air and the archers, led by Baron Edward and his division, fired the first round arrows.

The villagers withdrew just in time as a rain of deadly arrows swarmed down upon Mullah, taking out a lot of his leading knights.

"My King, we are under attack!" Jibril yelled, wheeling his horse around. "Protect our Lord!"

Mullah immediately positioned himself behind some of his men for protection. Everyone else scrambled to take cover and looked for a defensive position.

The clansmen were now entrenched to intercept any of Mullah's knights that were escaping towards the sides of the road. Flags and banners were ripped away to show deadly pikes, and they also lifted bows and arrows from under their robes to fire at their targets riding close by.

Mullah was in shock, like a lost little boy amidst the bedlam around him. He looked to find Jacob but, to his bigger surprise, he saw King François du Basque. His heart beat faster as confusion and denial were replaced by clarity and fear.

"Retreat! Retreat, immediately," Mullah yelled.

His men began to turn around as commanded. Many of them continued to die within the clogged corridor. Others stood their ground and fought back. Mullah saw an opportunity to escape towards the outer roads, where Camila's clansmen were successfully defending.

"Hold the line," Commander Juan Carlos yelled. "This is for our queen and the kingdom!"

"My King, follow me," Jibril took his shield and put it behind his back as a couple of arrows struck him but did not penetrate.

Jibril charged towards the clansmen defenders and stood up the stirrups. He took out a couple of his own arrows and fired them into villagers that were trying to run away, striking them in their backs.

Jibril took his longbow and swung it at another clansman, hitting him in his head. The blow killed the villager but dislodged the bow from Jibril's hands and clattered to the ground.

Juan Carlos, who was on foot, saw Jibril causing mayhem and ran to confront him. Jibril took out his sword and swung left and right to hack his way through more villagers.

"Ivan, make way so that the women can get out of here," commanded Juan Carlos. Ivan acknowledged his order and saw him heading towards Jibril. He took out his own longbow and an arrow and aimed it at Jibril.

Ivan fired the arrow, but Jibril saw it coming at him and stopped his horse and swung his body aside, narrowly dodging the deadly projectile.

Jibril turned 360 degrees and swung his sword at will, killing those around him. Juan Carlos arrived to confront him and lowered his body to strike the front legs of Jibril's horse, causing it to fall and Jibril to be thrown violently off of it.

Jibril was quick to get back to his feet and immediately looked for Juan Carlos, who was approaching him in a charge. Juan Carlos swung his sword with a left, right, left combination, and Jibril deflected them accordingly, before pushing forward to interlock their swords.

Juan Carlos adjusted his footing to gain leverage and begun to push Jibril back in the struggle for balance. Jibril quickly brought his right arm down and pulled out a dagger that he swung across Juan Carlo's face, slicing it and causing Juan Carlos to fall to the ground.

Jibril heard fast footsteps approaching him and noticed Ivan was charging him. Jibril threw his dagger at Ivan and struck him between his eyes, killing him.

Jibril turned towards Juan Carlos, who was on the ground wiping blood from his face. He was about to attack Juan Carlos again but heard more enemy knights approaching and decided to keep moving and return to be closer to Mullah.

"Albert, reinforce the flanks," François advised.

"I will take that position, my lord," Marquess Albert responded. François immediately saw Mullah's intentions to escape and proceeded to maneuver his horse down the hill to reinforce the area and give the clansmen some much needed assistance.

Camila followed behind, while her Green Dragoons held a perimeter around her at every turn.

Mullah and his knights began to overwhelm the clansmen who fought bravely. The clansmen were taking heavy casualties in the fight, but a brigade of François's knights immediately engaged to assist them.

"Charge!" A battle cry was heard as Duke Pablo and his brigade arrived from the backfield and began their attack taking the enemy by surprise. Mullah's men began to literally lose their heads, as Pablo and David's swords went to work dispatching the enemy.

Mullah and his knights were now surrounded in all directions.

"Reinforce the front," shrieked Mullah in desperation. "Keep King François's attack from breaking through! Hold the line!"

"Charge!" François yelled, heading straight towards Mullah. "Keep moving forward. We must clear a path."

François and his knights engaged in battle with Mullah's guard. The fighting intensified, as arms and limbs were hacked away. Bodies fell from their horses and writhed upon the ground, some without heads.

"Third division, reinforce the frontal attack," Jibril commanded, sending more knights to intercept François's fast approach.

"Another division is being sent, my lord," Albert told François. "I will handle this; perhaps you should look for a way around, Your Majesty."

"Xavier, look for an alternate road to get down to Mullah, quickly," François ordered his baron.

"Oui, Votre Majesté," the baron complied.

François was locked in battle with too many men at once. Camila, however, was able to circumvent the main pile up and came around to directly confront Mullah.

"Ah, Camila," Mullah sneered triumphantly. "Finally, I meet you in the battlefield."

"Xavier, the queen!" François directed the baron's attention to Camila's new suicidal route. "Protect the queen!"

"On my way, my lord," Xavier replied. The baron drove his heels into his horse's flanks to launch him forward to intercept Mullah. "Your Majesty!" Xavier yelled to Camila, "I will fight Lord Mullah, please stay back."

Xavier approached Mullah, charging him full-force to intercept, his sword level-steady in strike position. Just then, an arrow pierced his throat ending his charge. His body slid from atop his horse slowly as the blood spewed like a geyser. There was no way to contain the arterial bleed, and he lay writhing on the battlefield as his life drained out.

"Oh no!" Camila watched the baron fall. She turned to see that Jibril had fired the arrow, before resuming the fight with those around him. The queen was enraged at the death of her chamberlain and dug her boots into her horse's side, urging him to close on Mullah.

Count Gregorio joined her side, finally. "Your Majesty, it is not wise for you to engage Lord Mullah alone. Please allow me to fight him." He quickly moved to the front of her escort and began to clear the path, striking foes along the way and making his way towards Mullah.

Suddenly his horse was struck, too, by another of Jibril's fearsome arrows, which caused it to immediately collapse. Gregorio flew off his horse but managed to hold on to his sword. He quickly turned around, in time to see an enemy throwing a lance at him, which he dodged, throwing himself to the side. The lance barely missed its nimble target.

A knight ran up to finish off Gregorio, who was still on his back. Gregorio kicked his shin, causing him to lean forward and collapse downwards.

Then Gregorio thrusted his sword onto the enemy's mid-section to halt the attack. The enemy dropped dead. This gave Gregorio a moment to stand up, recover his sword, and continue the fight.

Camila saw that he had survived the fall and continued riding past, taking advantage of the opening that he'd created. When she turned to look for Mullah, she realized that Mullah stood high on his horse looking at her and laughing. The queen's men continued to fight all those around them, attempting to stop their advance by killing them in their tracks.

"Your Majesty, take cover," Gregorio pleaded once again, while fighting a large group of enemies on foot.

"As-salamu alaykum, Your Majesty. I see you have survived," Mullah taunted her. "I did not know you had enlisted King François as your errand boy. Perhaps I should have killed you like I did your father and your brother when I had the chance," he laughed, evilly. "However, that is a mistake that I will fix right now by sending you to join them."

Camila was stunned by Mullah's confession, "You call yourself a man? You are nothing but a coward. Face me now like you should have done with my brother and my father!" She pulled out her sword and charged her horse towards him.

Mullah also charged his horse at her, and they met in the middle.

"Aaaagh!" François screamed when he saw that Camila and Mullah were engaged in battle. With renewed vigor he burst forth in an explosive charge to reach her defense before Mullah had the chance to injure her.

Camila swung her sword at Mullah first. She threw a right-hand strike which Mullah intercepted and countered with a right strike of his own.

Camila blocked his strike which caused her to lose her balance and nearly fall off her horse. Mullah turned his horse around and struck her again with a downward strike. Camila regained control and pulled her sword upward to intercept the strike.

Mullah's next strikes were powerful and almost caused Camila to fall from her horse again, but she recovered. Mullah charged his horse towards the side of her's, ramming her, but again she managed to hold on.

Camila immediately pulled her horse to maneuver around and regained her balance while striking Mullah with an outside strike towards his mid-section. Mullah backed his horse in time to miss the strike. In return, Mullah struck Camila's horse on the side of its neck.

Camila's horse immediately jolted back and dropped to the ground, trapping Camila's leg beneath it. "Agh," she struggled to get out, being pinned to the ground. Mullah saw the opportunity to easily finish her off by running her over with his horse.

As he charged towards her, François managed to clear a path to get to them. "Fight me!" François yelled at Mullah.

François intercepted Mullah's charge and kept him from getting to Camila and, with his own charge, rammed Mullah off of his horse.

Mullah slammed onto the battlefield, and the impact caused him to lose his sword. He was able to recover quickly and retrieved his sword as well.

François was instantly attacked by several of Mullah's men, keeping him from finishing him off. Mullah saw his chance and immediately looked for Camila, who was still trapped under her writhing horse.

Then Duke Pablo arrived at the scene and confronted Mullah in the queen's defense. Both of them afoot, Mullah ran towards Pablo and engaged in battle.

Mullah used his momentum and pushed his sword at Pablo's mid-section. But Pablo defended the strike by swatting it away from his body. Mullah then used the same momentum to strike downward towards the left side of Pablo's head. Pablo backed away, and gained distance from the strike.

Mullah immediately charged forward and executed a low strike towards Pablo's legs and followed up by turning around 360 degrees, striking his sword into Pablo's solar plexus.

Pablo was able to block the first strike towards his legs. But, since Mullah was charging forward and he was backing away, Pablo tripped on a boulder that made him lose his footing and was not able to react in time to deflect Mullah's combination strike.

Mullah did not hesitate to strike his sword across Pablo's body to finish him off. By this point Camila was being helped by Gregorio and David, while her knights were struggling to defend them and keep them safe.

"Pablo!" Camila cried out when she saw Pablo struck down by Mullah. The surge of anger gave her the burst of energy she needed to finally pull out from beneath her horse.

A few more men rushed to attack. Count David stood up to face them in an en garde position, wielding two swords. He stood in front of them, and the first attacker moved in, swinging his sword.

David deflected the strike with his left sword and, using the momentum, he immediately struck with a right-left combination strike, raising both swords towards his opponent's neck, and scissoring the man's head from his body. The twitching body fell on its knees. He met the next attacker and again deflected a forward-thrusting sword strike and followed up by turning 180 degrees and thrusting the other sword onto the attacker's body.

He noticed a third attacker who swung his sword with a downward strike, and he immediately brought up both swords to intercept the strike and circled them around to strike the man's leg, slicing it off.

Mullah looked in Camila's direction and saw that her escort was busy fighting. So he began to pursue her again.

François was surrounded by five additional men that were preparing to attack. He charged his horse into them, swinging his sword right and left, cutting two of their heads off.

He continued towards the remaining three. One of them prepared to thrust his sword onto his horse, but François pulled back on the reins and his horse stood back on his hind legs, kicking in defense. The attacker raised his arms up to protect himself from the savage hooves, but the horse bore down on him, crushing him instantly.

François looked towards the remaining two, who had taken up positions on opposite sides, waiting for François to pass their way. François picked up a lance that was plunged through a body and jousted the left side attacker, spearing him in the chest.

The remaining attacker on the right turned around to run away, and François threw his sword, striking him in his back. He used the same momentum to ride towards the fallen body and retrieved his sword. And then he proceeded on to look for Mullah.

Camila looked all around the battlefield, momentarily disoriented by the clamor and fog of war. All of her knights were fighting, and some were dying in very close proximity. All to protect her and her kingdom.

She heard both the battle cries and screeches of pain and agony from men getting injured. Some were missing limbs, and others were overwhelmed by the number of attackers, not able to defend themselves and dying valiantly but hopelessly.

François managed to get to Mullah and finally took his position between him and the queen.

"Mullah, I have always known you to be a slippery snake, but today you made the biggest mistake in attacking Queen Camila. For that, you will not live to see another day." François dismounted his horse to fight him one-on-one.

"My fight is *not* with you, François," Mullah replied.

"I beg to differ. If your fight is with Asturias, then the fight is with me," François responded.

"I have heard of you, 'Knight of the Light,' and I am not afraid of you," Mullah grinned at him wickedly. "You'll find you're not in Basque anymore, where you won all your little skirmishes."

"And I have heard of you, Saracen Knight. All bloated talk and no action," François taunted him back. "Come, show me that famed cowardice of yours!"

"Argh," Mullah became irate and charged François, swinging his sword above his head.

François took a step back and elevated his sword to protect himself. Mullah missed François and momentarily exposed his right flank.

François stepped forward and shoved Mullah back, causing Mullah to lose his balance momentarily before scrambling to regain his footing.

François took advantage of the situation and charged Mullah with a series of strikes from different directions, but Mullah's curved blade was quick and managed to block the strikes successfully.

François sent Mullah a second series of attacks and followed with a front kick into his midsection.

Mullah was literally fighting for his life. And, although he managed to defend against the strikes, he was not able to protect against the kick. It caused him to step back, and he dropped to one knee, gasping for air.

"Get up, Mullah. It's too late to ask for forgiveness. You will not be getting a warrior's death today, you bastard," François swore at him.

Mullah got back up and took a step back to keep his distance while holding his sword in the guard position. He quickly realized that he was being outclassed by François.

François moved in for another series of attacks when he suddenly groaned and fell to the ground. An arrow shimmied in his back. It had cut through the arm and into his torso.

"Nooo! Dios mío," Camila cried as she saw him fall to his knees.

Albert, who was rigorously fighting others, saw that Jibril was the one that struck François with his arrow and immediately headed over to confront him.

"Jibril. Fight me man to man, filthy jihadi," Albert said as he charged him.

Jibril looked towards Albert, surprised to be singled out. He pulled another arrow, pointed at Albert and released it when he had him in his sights.

Albert continued his focused charge yet stepped aside to get out of the line of fire as the arrow whistled past.

Jibril tossed his longbow to the ground and reached for his shield. He held it tight and, with his sword in his other hand, waited for Albert's approach.

Albert grabbed his two-handed sword and launched himself up, with a swinging downward strike, onto Jibril's head.

Jibril placed his shield high to block the attack, but the strike was too strong for the shield to protect it. Albert's sword went through the shield and cracked it in half, hitting Jibril's helmet and making him fall backwards.

Jibril tried to recover quickly and rolled over to stand. Albert kept his sight on him, and, as soon as Jibril stood up, Albert repeated another power downward strike.

Jibril made the attempt to block the strike. But his one-handed sword was not able to stop the power of Albert's two-handed strike, which then went on to slice his head through his helmet, sending him, finally, to the ground.

Albert stuck his sword into Jibril's chest, stabbing it clean through to his back. He put his leg on Jibril's chest plate to pull out the sword and recover it.

"Mullah! Here I am, come and get me," Camila yelled at him to pull him away from François. As she walked forward, she limped on one leg.

Mullah, who had just watched Jibril's climactic end, spun around enraged and immediately moved towards the queen to finish her off.

As he arrived her within a few feet, Camila moved swiftly towards her left and swung her sword at Mullah's midsection.

Mullah got hit, but his armor took most of the damage. Camila turned towards him and began to swing her sword from left to right back and forth in an overwhelming combination attack.

Mullah blocked her attacks in a panic before stepping forward towards her to lock swords. They were momentarily locked in a sheer battle of the wills. Two kingdoms hung in the balance.

Mullah suddenly struck his fist across her face. Camila got hit so hard that she spun halfway around and dropped to the ground, almost getting knocked unconscious.

Mullah stayed behind looking down on the fallen queen. Camila slowly started to crawl to get back up. Her face was bleeding from a cut above her eyebrow.

Mullah extended his arms wide open, showcasing his power and imminent victory. "Behold, Asturias. Bow to your new king," he scoffed at them.

The surrounding knights looked to see what was happening. They looked on in despair, seeing both the queen and king on the ground in rough shape. Mullah moved in closer to Camila, holding his sword over her to stab her body.

Camila managed to roll over quickly and stood up to face him. Mullah ran towards her and executed a downward strike intended for her head, the same way that Albert had done with Jibril when he finished him off.

But Camila took a step forward and brought up her sword to intercept the strike. She then followed up by taking a step in and turning away towards the opposite side, as if she were to run away.

Mullah saw her turn and believed that she was trying to get away in fear for her life. He moved in quickly to impede her from running.

That's when Camila suddenly dropped to one knee while thrusting her sword into a back strike.

Mullah, who was upon her, was stabbed in the lower abdomen under his armor which caused him to immediately fall onto his knees, dropping his sword. He grabbed her blade with his bloody hand, holding the sword that was now inside his body. Camila recovered and stood in front of Mullah, who was not able to talk.

"You took the lives of three beautiful kings that meant the world to me. My Father, my brother and now my love, François. Twenty years you've climbed to the top of the mountain," Camila said evenly to Mullah, who simply looked at her defenselessly. "Unable to finish what you started. As Allah wills it!"

Mullah began to bleed from his mouth and choked in his own blood before falling face forward to the ground.

"Victory! We have victory! The queen gave us victory. Long live the Queen," her army reacted euphorically, while Mullah's army began to retreat or throw down their weapons in surrender.

Camila looked around in search of François, but she was not able to find him in all the commotion.

She saw her warriors, her friends, all over the field. She noticed that a lot of them had fallen, others were wounded. Commander Juan Carlos amongst them, whom she saw pulling Ivan's body out of a pile of dead bodies. Other warriors, however, stood tall. She delegated men to assist their fellow soldiers. Others were assigned to contain the enemy.

The queen ran towards the direction where François had fallen, but was not able to find his body.

Panic and sorrow came over her and tears began to blur her vision.

"Your Majesty, over here," Albert called for her, pointing towards the ground where she finally saw François being attended to by Gregorio, David, and others. She saw that he was still was alive, conscious, and alert and she ran to his side as fast as she could.

"The impact of the arrow was mostly absorbed by his backplate, Your Majesty. Although it did penetrate his body, it did not puncture any of his organs," explained Gregorio much to her relief.

"François. Are you okay? I thought I lost you." Tears streamed down her face as she embraced and kissed him.

"I am now, my lady. I am so proud of you, my love. You did it. You defeated your enemy and saved three kingdoms," François said, wincing with pain. "As you can see, it was not yet my time. Now do me a favor."

"Anything, my love," Camila said anxiously. "But first you must promise me that you will not die."

"I will survive this, My Queen. Now turn and address your subjects, old and new, in victory," François advised her.

Albert cupped his hands to his mouth and bellowed, "Kneel before your queen!" And everyone including himself put their swords onto the ground and took a knee.

Camila looked behind her and saw all of her people gathered around, waiting for her to direct them. She rose and looked around to acknowledge everyone. Her subjects looked at her and nodded their heads in respect as she made eye contact with one after the other.

"Hermosa victoria!" She raised her sword up triumphantly to claim, indeed, this beautiful victory. And all of her remaining knights and clansmen joined in the celebration.

"Long live the Queen! Long live the Queen! Long live the Queen," their cheers echoed across the mountains throughout the kingdom.

Epilogue
A Kingdom United

The Kingdom of Asturias was finally safe under Queen Camila's reign, which had preserved the legacy of her ancestors. François was recovering from his battle wounds and was enjoying the pleasant times with Camila attending to him with love and affection.

"My King and Queen, we have an emissary from León, your Majesties," Albert informed them.

"Please allow him in," Camila replied.

The emissary entered and knelt to pay his respects before he was asked to rise. "Your Majesties, my name is Baron Jack Courtois. I come to surrender the Kingdom of León to you as its rightful king and queen. We are overjoyed to have you lead and be our monarchs."

"Thank you, Baron Jack. We, too, are thrilled to incorporate León as our kingdom. Please, make yourself at home. Eat and rest before your return. We will be visiting shortly," Camila nodded, respectfully.

François added, "I knew your former King Alfonso XI. He was a great king, and we are most honored to be part of his respectable legacy."

"Thank you, Your Majesties. With your permission, I shall depart to bring this great news to everyone," Jack bowed low and departed.

⁂

Meanwhile, in Galicia, Marshal Saul Torres reported to Baron Christopher Varney who had been left in charge of the Galician castle until Mullah's return. "My lord," the marshal said, "we have word from Asturias."

"What is the report, Marshal?" Christopher asked.

"King Mullah is dead, my lord. There was a devastating battle that took place while traveling to Asturias, which annihilated the army," Saul informed him. "The Asturian monarchs want to know where we stand, Lord Christopher."

The baron was stunned to hear the news. "H-how can this be? Is there someone from Asturias waiting now?"

"Yes, my lord. Count Gregorio Gutierrez himself is waiting a reply," replied the marshal.

Christopher walked over to grab a chalice and pour himself some wine. As he stood there thinking, his hand had a slight shake to it. He took a big swig of the wine and went to sit down.

"Is there any news of King Gerardo?" the baron asked.

"No, my lord," Marshal Saul answered. "There has been no report of him since King Mullah sent men to search for him. He was never found."

"What of King Mullah or Baron Jibril?" Christopher winced, not wanting to hear this answer, either.

"Killed in action. You are now the highest ranking leader, the one in command, my lord," answered the marshal.

The baron was quiet, thinking it all over.

"My lord, will you be stepping in as the new king and defender of Galicia?" Saul asked.

"Marshal, please allow the count to enter. We have kept him outside too long," Christopher said, ignoring his question altogether.

The marshal returned with the count, who took his place in front of the baron.

"Greetings, Sir Christopher," Gregorio said amiably. "It is good to see you, again."

"Hello, Sir Gregorio. Yes, it is good to see you again. Please join me, have a seat," replied Christopher.

Gregorio removed his sword, still in its sheath, from his belt and laid it on the table between them with a resounding *clang*. Then he settled into the chair facing the baron. "Christopher, Their Majesties King François du Basque and Queen Camila Garcia are eager to know your position," Gregorio prompted, cutting straight to business. "Will you be taking claim to the crown, or will you forfeit to the rightful sovereign?"

Christopher glanced nervously from the sword back to Gregorio. Then he stood up to grab another drink and filled one for Gregorio, also. He returned and handed over the chalice to him before sitting again.

"How long have we known each other, my friend?" asked Christopher. "We have come a long way, you and I. During all this time I stopped to think who has claim to Galicia. Kings Mullah and Gerardo are presumably no longer alive. Apparently, fighting for this kingdom is a bad omen," Christopher paused while Gregorio listened, growing impatient. Christopher held up a calming hand and continued, "This is a fight in which we need not partake, my friend. We will vacate the land and let those entitled to it take their places as such."

"Wise decision, my lord. What is to become of you? Why don't you join us," Gregorio offered. "I would place you under my command, or you can lead your own division."

"Yes, thank you for your most kind offer," Christopher responded. "My loyalty runs deep within my veins. I have an unfinished responsibility to take care of. So, for now I must decline your offer. I will take the division assigned to me, and we will vacate the castle. Please send my regards and best wishes to the king and queen."

"Very well, should you ever be in need, I will be here for you, my friend," replied the count. "I will notify Their Majesties. Farewell."

Gregorio rose and took his sword in hand again. Then he left without another word and headed back to Asturias.

Baron Christopher sighed with relief after Gregorio had gone. "Get the men ready to leave," he ordered.

"Yes, my lord," the marshal answered and paused briefly before adding, "You would be a great king should you ever have the right opportunity."

Christopher simply looked at Saul and added thoughtfully, "Another time, perhaps."

———————❖———————

Upon Christopher's departure from Galicia with his entire division of soldiers, Camila was able to claim Galicia, unifying the lands of her father once again. Childhood friends, Kings George and Juan were elated to know that François and Camila had prevailed against Mullah and his army. They bragged to everyone that they had known the monarchs since their teenage years while pledging their loyal alliance towards them.

The future of the kingdoms would always remain uncertain, of course. Perhaps there would be other battles to fight. No one could know for sure. But nevertheless, the outlook was very promising.

As for François and Camila, they loved every moment of being together: traveling, horseback riding and most of all spending time together.

So, in essence, the kingdom had finally found its King and Queen.

The End

Bravo Bay is the fictional top-secret test facility for fighter jocks and experimental aircraft in David Acuff's soon-to-be-released sci-fi epic *Battle Tides*.

BravoBay Books, on the other hand, is a top-secret test facility for word jocks and experimental *ideas*.

Those who have read our books *Historians Proper* and *Slay Bells Ring*, and now *A Kingdom without a King*, know all too well the high quality of our authors, our work, and our commitment to first-rate storytelling.

Stay frosty and bleed the edge, my friends.

www.bravobaybooks.com

ABOUT THE AUTHOR

Frank J. Marquez is an Angeleno with 34 years as a security protection specialist, and a Martial Artist with 46 years of experience in self-defense. Frank is both a dreamer and a fighter.

He has received many awards for his time and dedication to the martial arts including being inducted into the Martial Arts History Museum and the Golden Gate's Hall of Honors, and the 56th Book Edition of the World's Greatest Martial Artists. He lives by the warrior code of Loyalty—Courage—Strength —Honor.

Frank is a spiritual person who is proud of his Hispanic heritage, which he explores deeply in the historical fiction novel *A Kingdom without a King*.

When he is not spending time with his family, Frank enjoys watching road-racing competitions, sports, listening to music and watching movies—his favorites being those with medieval and chivalrous content.

Keep tabs on him via Instagram: @OfficialFrankMarquez

APPENDIX

Albert Collins: *Marquess of Labourd Pays Basque. Commander in chief to King François du Basque's army.*

Alfonso XI: *"El Justiciero," King of the Kingdom of León. Assigned Count Jacob Cedillo as his steward in his absence.*

Bernard Perez: *Baron of the Kingdom of León. Captain of Lord Jacob Cedillo's army.*

Camila Garcia: *Queen of Asturias. Daughter of King Celestino Garcia and Queen Joanna Garcia. Sister to King Gerardo Garcia. Descendant of King Garcia I of León.*

Carlos Montes: *Count of the Kingdom of Salamanca. Commander of King Juan Velasquez's army.*

Casimiro Garcia: *King of Navarre and Aragon. Duke of Castile and Léon. Father of King Celestino Garcia. Descendant of King Garcia I of León.*

Castillo del Eliseo: *The Asturian castle.*

Castillo de la Galantería: *The Galician castle.*

Celestino Garcia: *Known as 'The Just.' King of Galicia and Asturias. Son of Casimiro Garcia. Duke of Castile, and León. Descendant of King Garcia I of León.*

Christian Balian: *Under-marshal of the Kingdom of Asturias. Captain of the South Squad.*

Christopher Varney: *Baron of the Kingdom of Galicia. Division captain assigned to foot soldiers. Warden of the Galician castle.*

Danny Gutierrez: *Son of Count Gregorio Gutierrez.*

Daniel Lemus: *Count of the Kingdom of Galicia. Captain in King Celestino's army, assigned to the cavalry division. Commander of King Gerardo's army.*

David Ascough: *Count of Labourd Pays Basque. Second-in-command in King François du Basque's army.*

Diego Skaggs: *Marshal of the Kingdom of Asturias. Green Dragoons captain. Awarded the title of baron by Queen Camila.*

Edward Preston: *Baron of the Kingdom of Galicia. Captain in the Galician army assigned to the archers' division.*

Faris: *Arabic masculine name, meaning "knight," "horseman," or "cavalier."*

François du Basque: *King of Labourd Pays Basque. Known as "The Knight of the Light." The true heir to the kingdoms of the Basque countries, north of Spain and south of France. Protector and companion of Queen Camila.*

Gabriel Gomez: *King Gerardo Garcia's fictitious name. He was told that the name "Gomez" means "Man."*

George Sanchez: *King of Segovia. Ally and childhood friend of Queen Camila. Host of the New Moon Royal Gathering.*

Gerardo Garcia: *King of Galicia. Son of King Celestino Garcia and Queen Joanna Garcia. Brother to Queen Camila Garcia. Descendant of King Garcia I of León.*

Green Dragoons: *The elite royal forces dedicated to the protection of King Celestino in Asturias and Galicia. After Celestino's passing, they stayed on in service to Queen Camila in Asturias.*

Gregorio Gutierrez: *Baron of Galicia. Awarded the title of Count of Asturias by Queen Camila. Second-in-command of the Asturian army during the queen's reign.*

Henry Johnson: *Baron of the Kingdom of León. Awarded the title of Count by King Jacob Cedillo. Commander in chief of Lord Jacob Cedillo's army.*

Holy Cave of Covadonga: *Alternative safe haven for the Asturian clansmen. An ancestral refuge.*

Ivan Escobar: *Clanmen's leader awarded the rank of Captain to the Kingdom of Asturias.*

Jack Courtois: *Baron of the Kingdom of León. Steward of the Kingdom of León under King Jacob Cedillo.*

James Wise: *Under-marshal of the Kingdom of Asturias. Captain of the North Squad.*

Jibril Asbat: *Baron of the Moorish kingdom of Malaga. Commander in chief of Lord Mullah's army.*

Joanna Garcia: *Queen of Asturias and Galicia during King Celestino's reign. Wife of King Celestino Garcia. Mother to King Gerardo and Queen Camila. Queen Mother of Asturias during Queen Camila's reign.*

Jacob Cedillo: *Count and steward of León during King Alfonso XI's reign. Went on to betray Queen Camila and became King of Asturias.*

Juan Carlos Herrera: *Clan's leader awarded the rank of commander of the Asturian army.*

Juan Velasquez: *King of Salamanca. Ally and childhood friend of Queen Camila. Co-host of the New Moon Royal Gathering.*

Karina Gutierrez: *Daughter of Count Gregorio Gutierrez.*

Khalid Siraj: *Marshal of the Moorish Kingdom of Malaga. Captain of Lord Mullah's army.*

King Garcia I: *King of León in 910 AD. The meaning of the name Garcia is "Brave in Battle."*

Matthew Boyd: *Under-marshal of the Kingdom of Asturias. Captain of the West Squad.*

Miguel Valente: *Marshal of Galicia. Captain of King Gerardo's cavalry division.*

Mildred Miller: *Wise woman of El Castillo del Eliseo* in Asturias.

Mullah el Hassan: *Count of the Moorish Kingdom of Granada. Saracen knight and emissary of peace throughout the kingdoms. Awarded the title of Duke by King Gerardo Garcia and became his army's commander in chief. Later on became King of Galicia.*

Nicholas Loftus: *Archbishop during King Celestino's reign. Became part of Queen Camila's court in the Kingdom of Asturias. Liaison between the kingdom and Rome.*

Pablo Cervantes: *Duke of Asturias. Commander in chief of the Green Dragoons. Loyal royal adviser and commander of Queen Camila's army.*

Riccardo Santos: *Elder good Samaritan that healed King Gerardo Garcia. Noble of the Kingdom of Portugal at Porto.*

Robert Alvarez: *Marshal of the Kingdom of León under the reign of King Alfonso XL. Later, awarded the title of Viscount by King Jacob Cedillo under his service becoming a Captain of his army.*

Saul Torres: *Marshal of Galicia. Assigned to foot soldiers division. Captain in King Gerardo's army.*

The cloaked man at the tavern: *Marquess Albert Collins disguised as a ranger while tracking deposed King Gerardo Garcia.*

The Sidron cave: *Clansmen refuge area, protected by clansman Captain Ivan Escobar.*

Thomas Diaz: *Under-marshal of the Kingdom of León. Captain of Lord Jacob Cedillo's army.*

Timothy McCarthy: *Under-marshal of the Kingdom of Asturias. Captain of the East Squad.*

Tito Bustillo Cave: *Clansmen refuge area, protected by clansman Commander Juan Carlos Herrera.*

Walter Gallegos: *Count of the Kingdom of Segovia. Commander of King George Sanchez's army.*

Xavier Aguirre: *Baron of Labourd Pays Basque. Captain of King François du Basque's army.*

*Queen Camila and King François will return
in their next adventure…*

"A Kingdom to Reign"

www.ingramcontent.com/pod-product-compliance
Lightning Source LLC
Chambersburg PA
CBHW020056310726
48970CB00002B/341